Tuurh

BOOK 1

Demun Warriurs

ELISHA BUGG

First edition. January 1st 2021

Copyright © 2021 Elisha Bugg

ASIN: B08NK9DD27

Cover design by: Ink Wolf Cover Designs
https://www.facebook.com/groups/271911274197974

@ElishaBWrites
www.Elishabugg.com

CHAPTER 1

"Last few checks and you're free to go," Oliver called over his shoulder, that usual smile curving his lips as Rosalyn followed him into yet another ward.

Her feet throbbed in her otherwise comfortable shoes, eyes burning with each fluorescent light they passed under. Her fifteen hour shift finally took its toll on her, and yet, she couldn't be happier to be here. Just one more step to achieving her dream and becoming a real doctor.

Luckily for her, she got the young, friendly and kind Oliver to shadow during her studies, unlike her roommate Sara, stuck with the old, cranky matron. A woman so strict she put any headmistress to shame.

"Good evening, Ms. Graham," Oliver chirped, pulling up a small stool by the elderly woman's side before he took her arm in his hands and wrapped the cuff around it, taking her blood pressure for the final time that evening.

"You look much perkier than you did this morning."

"Those painkillers you gave me are doing just the trick," she replied with a quick nod, aiming a little smile in Rosalyn's direction.

Though it had been Rosalyn to notice the woman was still in a lot of pain, and not in the area where the bruising from her fall was, she never expected that Oliver would give her the credit for the catch.

When she pulled him aside and told him about the grimaces she noticed when the nurses had lifted her to the gurney for her x-ray yesterday, she thought he would shrug it off and think she was making a fuss, but he hadn't, he'd believed her, something she wasn't used to. He looked deeper into the woman's records and found that she had been going back and forth with her general practitioner for months, and sent her for some further tests confirming Rosalyn's suspicions.

The elderly woman hadn't broken a bone in her fall like all the other doctors and nurses seemed so certain of, she had kidney stones. Large ones. The pain from those likely to have caused her to stumble whilst she climbed her stairs.

Oliver hadn't only believed her words, he'd praised her for the find, and told all the other staff members that it was her who had discovered the truth, allowing her to be the one to book Ms. Graham in for her Extracorporeal shock wave lithotripsy to help break the stones into smaller pieces.

"We'll come back to check on you again in the morning once you're back on the ward to see how it goes. You'll be home in no time," Oliver announced, patting her arm as he stood and headed for the door, Rosalyn racing to catch up to him.

"Good job, Rose," he remarked when she joined him on the other side of the swinging doors. "You don't mind me calling you Rose, do you?"

"Yes. I mean no. Thank you," Rosalyn spluttered, unsure how to answer him, her heart beating frantically as she returned his smile.

She wasn't used to people believing in her words, or being particularly friendly for that matter.

Sara was the only person she really spoke to for any length of time, unable not to when they lived in the same apartment.

She'd certainly never had a nickname before, at least

nothing normal or non derogatory like, *Rose*.

"Oliver!" a loud voice shouted, forcing both of their heads to turn to see one of the female nurses jog in their direction, giving Rosalyn the side eye before she turned to him with a sweet smile. "We've got an unusual emergency incoming. Five minutes tops."

Oliver moved instantly, Rosalyn following along behind in silence as he made his way toward the front desk.

Part of her was excited. A real emergency to watch and learn from, and an unusual one at that. The other more exhausted and rational part was a little apprehensive.

Not only did she long to go home and rest before her next shift tomorrow, she was inexperienced and would likely just get in the way whilst the others all worked on the patient.

"Something wrong?" Oliver asked, pausing in front of her with his arms crossed, the action so sudden that Rosalyn almost bumped into him.

"I'm fine," she blurted, taking a step back from their close proximity, her cheeks aglow.

"You don't need to worry. It wasn't all that long ago that I was a student. You won't be in the way if that's what you're thinking. Just stand back and observe," he told her, giving her shoulder a gentle squeeze, his hand lingering a little longer than she would have expected.

"If your observation skills prove as helpful as they were yesterday, we'd benefit from you being in there with us."

Rosalyn opened her mouth to respond, ready to argue with his confidence in her, when the double doors at the end of the corridor flew open and a hospital gurney pushed by several paramedics, battling with a large, muscular man passed them by. His shouts and growls vibrated through her body making her tremble. A look of pure fury and agony contorting his face.

Demon.

Rosalyn froze, that word bouncing around in her head while she watched on in horror.

Impossible.

She was supposed to be cured, wasn't she? So why now all of a sudden was she thinking such abnormal things?

There were no such things as demons, everybody had told her so. No vampires or shifters, or any other creatures from myth or fairy tales walking among them like she used to believe.

"Rosalyn? Are you coming?" Oliver called, already walking in step with the paramedics.

She jogged to keep up with them, her earlier fatigue forgotten as she focused her eyes on the patient who continued to fight against them.

Open your eyes, Rosalyn willed him, needing to prove to herself that she was just imagining things. That he wasn't like those people she used to see when she was younger. That his eyes would not change black like she thought theirs had.

For almost ten years she hadn't thought of demons or other creatures, not seeing them everywhere like she once had, so where had that crazy thought come from?

If such creatures existed, she would have seen them before now, wouldn't she?

"Stab wound to the chest. Unsure of the extent of the injury, he won't keep still long enough to examine it thoroughly," one paramedic commented through clenched teeth, doing his best to hold the patient's shoulders down as

CHAPTER 2

The rhythmic sound of beeping roused Rayner from his drug induced sleep. An overwhelming odour of antibacterial spray and disinfectant stinging his nose as he looked around the bleached white room.

"Where am I?" he groaned aloud, eyes heavy and blurry under the fluorescent lights above him. That beeping much louder; faster.

He attempted to sit, only to be held in place. Thick straps tied around his wrists and ankles.

Pulling against them, he tried to gain leverage and break free, but they wouldn't budge.

"Damn medication," he grumbled, some of what had happened coming back to him.

He was in a hospital; a human hospital. The Soulless he'd been fighting had overpowered him, shoving a needle like blade dangerously close to his heart.

Some human must have found him bleeding out and called for an ambulance.

All those hands on his body agony, burning away at him, until she had stopped them.

That female had noticed the marks on his skin when none of the others had bothered to look. Their hands peeling away from him quickly before that damn doctor had injected him again, knocking him out cold, and turning his stomach.

Human medicines always did play havoc on their bodies, reacting in a way they weren't designed to.

13

But that wasn't all.

The voices in his head; the ones that never left him around anybody but his brothers, and those *Other* strong enough to shield their minds were muffled, almost silent. So much so, he could hear muttered voices and footsteps coming from outside the room, followed by the squeal of the door as someone approached his bedside.

The female.

Heck, he could even hear her breathing when she paused by his feet, her intoxicating fragrance filling the air.

He followed her movements with his eyes, watching her shadowy figure pull something from the foot of his bed. His vision slowly coming back into focus, doing nothing to ease his still churning stomach.

Long, raven black hair tied behind her head in a loose braid, small wisps escaping and hanging down around her face. The thick braid tumbling over her shoulder when she leant forward to write on the thing he could now see was a clipboard. Her sapphire eyes scanned across the pages she flicked through, the paper rustling.

Rayner closed his eyes again and breathed in deeply through his nose, filling his lungs with her wild berry scent, taking peace in the silence that surrounded him.

No voices. No thoughts or feelings of another to fill his brain. Not even a murmur.

Pure bliss.

At first he'd been unsure who was responsible for the silence, unable to concentrate with the hands all over his skin, but there was no confusion now. It was her.

He wasn't sure how she did it, or why, but there had to be a reason for it.

No doubt some cruel trick on him by the Council, filling him with hope before it was taken away, but for now, he would enjoy it.

Heavy stomps in the hallway outside however soon chased the peace away, reminding him of the dire situation he was currently in.

He couldn't stay here with her, even if he was intrigued. Who knew what sorts of tests these doctors could have performed on him whilst he was unconscious? What information they could have found out about him, his brothers and the rest of the Other?

He needed to get out of here. Now.

If the Council found out he had been in a human hospital, potentially revealing their secrets, giving them knowledge of their kind, they would have his head, and hers.

But, perhaps the female could be of some assistance.

Rayner tugged on the restraints once more, testing their hold now some of his strength had returned, making her gasp and drop the clipboard to the ground with a clatter before she took several steps back, her chest rising and falling rapidly while she eye'd the door.

"S-stop. You'll hurt yourself," she said in an attempted command, but her voice lacked conviction.

She was afraid of him. No surprise there. "Do you need a doctor?" she asked, the purity and sweet lull of her voice like a caress against his sore skin, making him forget momentarily what he was doing, and what he needed from her.

Studying her briefly, in awe of the impact her voice alone had over him, he shook his head and reminded himself she had asked him a question.

"No," he finally ground out when she took another step toward the door, halting in her tracks at his word.

He continued to watch her while she did the same,

transferring her weight from one foot to the other, nibbling on her lip, drawing his attention to her mouth, making him stifle a groan.

Was she not a doctor?

His eyes drifted lower, to her scrubs, almost matching the colour of her eyes, where he spotted the name tag that hung around her neck; *Green Oaks Hospital. Rosalyn Manar. Student nurse.*

"No doctors."

"But, you're–"

"No. Doctors," he repeated through clenched teeth when she reached a hand for the doorknob.

"I-is there anything I can do for you?"

He could think of a few things he would like her to do for him. Coming over here and kissing him with those shapely lips for starters. Untying his hands so he could bury them into her thick locks, allowing him to run his fingers through it as he pulled her closer and onto his lap, allowing his hands and mouth to explore her further.

What am I saying? he growled to himself with a shake of his head, his eyes still glued to her, unsurprised by her trembling hands and wide open eyes, but in awe of her courage and determination when she stepped closer and paused by the bedside.

It had to be the restraints. He doubted she would come so close to him otherwise, not after the rage she had witnessed him in when he arrived.

"Morphine? Or a drink perhaps? Your throat must be sore from last night."

Last night?

Damn it. He'd been here that long already. All the more reason he needed to make this quick and get the hell out of this place.

Rayner tried to sit, straining against the straps, groaning when they bit into his wrists.

"Untie me," he demanded, turning back to the female who now hurried back several steps.

Just great, he groaned internally. He couldn't afford to scare her off.

"Please," he added, trying his best to sound sincere and a little less threatening.

"I can't. Only a doctor can–"

"Sure you can. You just pull on that little strap there and hey presto I'm free."

She just looked at him, her lips pursed at his joke, her arms crossed in front of her when the door suddenly flew open, followed by the heavy footfalls of someone familiar.

"Niko."

"Sorry I took so long," he smirked, blocking the door before he turned toward the female and paused, the smile vanishing from his face. An expression that Rayner knew all too well.

He'd had a vision about her. Interesting. Niko rarely had visions that involved humans.

"You dropped your phone so I couldn't track it. Lorkan had to hack into the CCTV."

"Y-you can't just burst in here," the female, Rosalyn insisted, attempting to step around him. "This ward doesn't allow visitors, even if this is a private room."

"I'm not visiting, Darlin'," Niko muttered, taking several menacing steps toward her, "and he is coming with me."

The female's face paled, her heart rate accelerating through the roof as she backed away, crashing into the table behind her, causing the metal tray to fall and crash to the ground. The loud, foreing sound making Rayner's ears ring.

"We need to go. Now," Niko demanded, flicking the strap on the restraints that kept Rayner in place as the female continued to fight for her breath, clinging to the table behind her in order to remain standing. Her fear of Niko far more severe than Rayner would have expected. He was the most placid of them all.

"Go. I'll take care of the female."

Rayner paused, rubbing at his wrists, watching Niko approach her.

He knew Niko wasn't going to hurt the female. None of them particularly liked humans much, some of them more so than others, but they didn't go out of their way to hurt them either. Part of their job was to protect them after all. Niko meant to merely wipe her memories of all she had witnessed since his arrival last night, like he most likely had already with all those he had passed on his way up here. Lorkan hacking into their system to erase all traces of him from their records, any tests they might have performed and any video surveillance in the place.

Still, his hands clenched tightly, fighting the urge to shove his brother away from her, unhappy with the thought of him touching her, wishing he could do it himself even though he knew the idea was foolish. The contact he would need to make would cause him agony, drawing attention to them when he roared out in pain, unable to concentrate and keep his hold on her head long enough to rewire her brain and plant new memories in their place.

"Let's go."

CHAPTER 3

"You're late, Warrior," Henry spat the moment Rayner stepped into the Great Hall, drumming his long, bony fingers against the desk in front of him, earning a few snickers from those closest to him. "I even hear you were taken into a *human* hospital," he sneered, his nose scrunched in disgust, and though normally Rayner would agree, he had found his time in this particular hospital quite interesting because of her; *Rosalyn*. The dark haired nurse who had been at the front and centre of his mind since he first laid eyes upon her.

He'd been around plenty of beautiful women before, the vast majority sat around him now were stunning to look at, and not one of them human either, but there had been something different about her. Something impossible to ignore. He was drawn to her. His long ago dormant desires sparked to life within him while he watched her do the most mundane tasks. Longing to touch her even knowing the pain it would cause him if he ever should.

But it wasn't his desire alone that he found odd. No, it was her unusual ability to silence the noise inside his head. A feat that he never would have believed possible if he hadn't noticed it for himself.

"I take it everything was wrapped up neatly?" Kael, another of the lead members of the Council asked, drawing Rayner's attention back to the room, and away from the nurse he longed to see again.

"Of course."

"And how was it, such a strong, muscular Warrior

like yourself ended up in the care of some meagre humans?" a female Rayner didn't recognise asked, licking her lips when he turned his gaze to her. No stirring within him when her eyes raked over his body like there had been with that nurse. A reaction he was much more accustomed to.

"The Soulless are adapting."

"How so?" Kael asked, leaning his chin on his hands as he edged forward on his seat. His blue eyes bright whilst he stared in Rayner's direction.

"The ones we've fought recently have been different from those we are used to seeing and fighting. They don't feast with the horde, they separate into smaller groups and hunt with weapons, using strategy and tactics we've not seen from them before."

"That is concerning, indeed."

"Whatever for?" Henry scoffed, sitting up higher in his seat with his arms crossed in front of him. "It's reasons like this that the Warriors came to be in the first place."

"That may be true, Henry, but you appear to be overlooking the threat which the Soulless present to those living among the human populus."

Rayner couldn't agree more.

The Soulless had always posed a problem if left unchecked. Their numbers could quickly grow out of control if allowed, their horde-like mentality keeping them safe from the majority of threats. Only now they weren't just a problem due to numbers alone, but in their ability to fight back.

In all his years as a Warrior, Rayner had never seen a Soulless carry a weapon, let alone know how to use it, but over the last month or so, he'd seen more and more of them with those odd blades, reminding him of a large needle.

They may not have much skill when it came to using those blades just yet, but already he had seen improvement from those first few they had encountered. Add their numbers and resilience into the battle and they would soon become far too much to handle, even for them, as Rayner had already discovered, taking his own skill and strength for granted.

The Other that hid among the humans would be susceptible to attack, unable to protect themselves for long against this new breed.

"I trust the four of you will be able to handle it?" Kael asked with a raised brow.

"For now."

"You don't sound very certain?"

"The way things are currently, we're able to manage, but that could change quite quickly. If the horde decides to join this new more intelligent breed, or if they grow even smarter as we have already seen in a short time, they may become too much even for us," Rayner sighed.

He hated to sound weak in front of anybody, especially the Council, but they all needed to be prepared for a war just like the four of them had already predicted.

These Soulless were not like those they were used to. They could just be hungry and evolving to better keep their population going; or they could have a common goal which they had yet to discover.

Either way, things didn't bode well for anyone.

Many humans had believed that vampires were a plague on the earth for their need to drink blood from living creatures. Many feared them and the shifters for their speed and strength. Afraid of the demons' psychic powers, claiming them to possess others minds whenever somebody did something bad, but the humans didn't know the horrors the Soulless possessed. A creature so relentless and hungry that even the Other feared them.

"We may need to contact other Warrior groups and see how far this Soulless threat has spread."

Rayner and his three brothers were not the only Warriors under the Council. Each continent had their own group who were expected to do the same job.

It had been a long time since they had been in contact with any of the others, but then something this big hadn't happened in a very long time either.

"Then speak with them to make sure none of those things happen," Henry growled, slamming his palms flat against the desk as he stood and looked down at him from his higher vantage point. His seat positioned a good foot higher than the rest of the Council leaders to prove he was in charge, despite them all knowing he only got his position through corruption and bloodshed. Problem was, none of them could prove it.

"We don't plan on letting it get out of control," Rayner replied, biting down hard on the inside of his cheeks. The tang of blood hitting the back of his throat when he turned, ready to leave.

"Oh, and Warrior."

Rayner paused, his fists clenched when he glanced back over his shoulder.

"I believe it goes without saying that you need to keep away from that hospital."

"So– Why are we here when the Council and Niko said to stay away?" Lorkan groaned, spinning one of his daggers between his fingers whilst he paced back and forth across the hilltop. "Shouldn't we, you know, be searching the outskirts of town for any more Soulless rather than standing outside some human hospital."

Lorkan was right of course, not that Rayner planned to tell him so. He would never hear the end of it.

They should be out hunting for the Soulless rather than being here, but it was precisely because the Council, specifically Henry, had told him to steer clear of the place why his intrigue grew. That and the fact that he couldn't keep away any longer. The female nurse plagued his thoughts day and night.

He'd tried to forget her, really he had, but it was proving to be an impossible task, and with Niko's vision that he refused to talk about, telling them that the hospital was off limits, and Henry saying the same, he couldn't help but wonder why.

Ever since his punishment he'd steered clear of busy places like this, soon learning he was overcome with thoughts and emotions from others. An ability he had once controlled. Yet, he still came, his curiosity getting the better of him, and he was glad he had.

Usually a building of this size, with so many people coming and going would be havoc on his mind. The magnitude of voices overwhelming him, making it impossible to concentrate, but not here. Not today.

All was quiet.

Those thousands of voices that would normally fill his mind, hushed. A steady murmur of sound he could bear. The few times he'd spied her come outside, those voices had grown quieter still.

Usually it was only his brothers, and some powerful Other strong enough to shield their minds whose thoughts and desires didn't reach him, unless he chose to make skin contact with them; and why would he do that, knowing what it would do to him? He'd learnt that the hard way. His skin blistering and burning from their touch.

Yet, when he ventured out with them, all those other people's voices would be back. Not theirs, but all those around them. A constant reminder of his disobedience to the Council all those years ago.

With her, it was different.

Not only were her thoughts and emotions hidden from him behind some impressive shields which he'd never seen the likes of before, the emotions and body language the only ones which he could discern. She seemed to nullify those around her as well. Almost like a vacuum; which sounded ridiculous even to him, but he couldn't deny what was happening to him either.

"I'm not buying Niko's excuses, and if Henry said to stay away you can bet he's hiding something," Rayner answered at last, his eyes still glued to the entrance down the hill from where they stood.

"I guess, but still, I don't get it," Lorkan sighed, slumping down against the wall behind him. His dagger finally back in its holster at his hip. "What would he hide in a human hospital?"

Rayner remained silent, unsure how to answer.

He hadn't been in a fit state to roam around the hospital to find the answer to that question, but he knew Henry was up to something. He usually was.

Either he thought they would be put off searching for whatever he'd hidden with so many humans around, or he was bluffing. There wasn't anything hidden at all, it was just to trick them in some way. Possibly luring them into a trap. His demand for Rayner and the others to stay away only fueling their desire to return and discover the secret.

Rayner wouldn't put it past the bastard. They all suspected he had killed their brother, Helmer. Why not lure them to their deaths too for speaking against him so frequently?

Still, if he was honest with himself, he wanted to come back even without the warnings not to.

He wanted to see her again, unable to keep away.

The desires he'd had back in the hospital room were just as strong whenever he caught a glimpse of her, no longer believing that his reaction was just a side effect of the drugs they had injected him with.

"Look," Lorkan snarled beside him, already back on his feet, pointing down toward the emergency entrance below. The department in which he had met her.

Two Soulless carrying their blades emerged from the darkness behind one of the ambulances parked out front. No doubt the one he'd been in previously.

He couldn't forget his journey trapped in that cramped space with the smell of pungent bleach and disinfectant burning his nostrils. The piercing sound of the sirens that made his eardrums bleed, drowning out some of the voices that bombarded him. Agony all over as they continued to place their hands upon his flesh in an attempt to keep him still, unaware they only made it worse. The rich, metallic taste of blood filling his mouth when he'd bit down hard on his tongue to stop himself from screaming out in pain. The whole experience havoc on his senses; something he would really rather not endure again.

"Rayner?"

"I see them," he groaned, watching their bodies flicker in and out of focus as they moved. There one moment and gone the next. Their presence here far too much of a coincidence after his warnings to stay away.

"Are we going in after them?"

Rayner wanted to follow just to be sure what they

were doing here, but Niko had already wiped the doctors and nurses memories once. Doing so again could cause some major problems for everyone involved.

Brains were difficult to rewire. The process took a high level of concentration, something Rayner doubted they would have time for in such a busy hospital. Add in the extra complication of the previous invasion, and the pain he would have to endure to maintain contact, and it would be near impossible.

If he made a mistake, tripped up in any way, their brains would be turned to mush, leaving them an empty husk. Unable to move or even think for themselves. And with the Soulless nearby, he'd be defenceless and prone to attack.

In a normal situation, Rayner would have left them to it knowing that the Soulless tended not to hunt humans unless they were truly struggling to find their next meal, but not knowing how this new breed of Soulless worked, their aim, or why they had been warned away, as well as how Rosalyn's unusual abilities works, he wasn't prepared to take the risk.

If they found her and sensed the unusual energy coming from her like he did, she could be in danger.

"I'm going," Rayner snarled, already headed down the hill toward the entrance as the Soulless slipped inside.

To hell with those that might witness him and trigger some of their memories to return, and to hell with the Council if they found out he interfered with their plans and a human life. He couldn't let those Soulless find her. He needed her. Craved her even.

"In and out, Lorkan. Try to blend in," he groaned, sliding a pair of sunglasses over his eyes so not to draw more attention to himself, Lorkan lifting his hood over his multicoloured hair in order to do the same.

Each step they advanced, the chatter inside Rayner's head grew in volume, more and more people surrounding them. Their murmur of voices turning into a mad crash of shouts and screams, forcing Rayner to hold his head.

This many people so close to him was too much, even for her remarkable gift.

If only she were closer.

"I can go in alone?"

Without a reply, Rayner gritted his teeth and entered through the automatic doors.

This curse had ruled him for too long. He wasn't going to let it control him now.

He would protect this female from whatever threat, no matter who or what it came from. She may just be the key to breaking him free of his punishment.

CHAPTER 4

Heading back to the department Rosalyn spent the majority of her time, she noticed two men wander casually through the double doors opposite her.

Visiting hours at the hospital had finished hours ago, and they certainly shouldn't be roaming through the area freely, but that wasn't the worst of it. There was something unusual about them, and not just because of their demeanour or the fact they were here when they shouldn't have been.

There seemed to be a strange haze surrounding them, making them appear to flicker in and out of focus while she watched on, reminding her of ghosts in a horror movie.

Rosalyn stared at them, unsure what she was seeing, unable to make out whether they were really there, or if she were hallucinating.

She hadn't slept much over the last few days, what with all the nightmares and vivid dreams she'd been having again, so it was possible that her mind was simply playing tricks on her, like it had when she thought that man was a demon a few weeks ago.

Rubbing at her eyes, Rosalyn turned back relieved to see that the men were no longer there, until she noticed they had moved toward the front desk, unnoticed by the rest of the staff around them.

One foot slowly put in front of the other, she made her way across the corridor toward them, curious what they were looking for. So engrossed in what they were doing she didn't notice Oliver approach, until he spoke, making her jump.

"What do you say?"

"P-pardon?"

"A coffee? You've been working hard and you've still got a few hours left until the end of your shift. I thought a coffee together might be a nice break."

Rosalyn glanced back in the direction of the front desk but saw no sign of those men anywhere.

Perhaps she had imagined them after all.

"Sure. A coffee sounds great."

The cafeteria was as lively as ever. Crowded with staff, patients and visitors speaking loudly and clattering trays as they made their way to tables. The rich aroma of coffee, bacon and fresh cakes filling the air, making her stomach grumble.

Oliver took the seat opposite her, sliding a coffee mug in her direction whilst he sipped his own. His chocolate coloured eyes watched her above the rim of his mug.

Lifting her own drink, Rosalyn leant forward onto her elbows and stared off into space, too lost in her own thoughts to really drink or speak with him.

She couldn't forget about those men.

Had they really been there and everybody else was just too busy to notice them? What could they have been searching for in those files?

She knew she'd been working a lot of hours and that she hadn't had much chance to sleep in between shifts and her nightmares, but she didn't think she could have imagined something like them, even with her past. There were too many details. Like the pungent floral scent that overpowered the bleach. Their bloodshot eyes, and the way they spoke, making all the hairs on her arms stand on end.

Surely not even her imagination was capable of fabricating something so complex.

As if on cue, the two men walked by the large cafeteria windows. That same odd, blackish mist surrounding them.

Slowly one of them turned as if sensing her stare. His mouth curved up at the sides into a cruel smile that showed far too many sharp, yellowish teeth.

"Rosalyn?" Oliver called, gaining her attention when he took her hand in his, making her flinch. The sudden heat of his skin fighting away the chill that coursed through her body at witnessing such a frightful smile.

"You've not touched your coffee. Is everything alright?"

"Sorry, I guess I'm not feeling myself."

"Come with me," he sighed, pulling her to her feet with a firm grip on her hand, guiding her toward the doors, his warm hand somewhat comforting, but a little too tight.

"We'll grab your things."

"But, I haven't finished my shift."

"You have for today," he commented with a half smile over his shoulder. "You need rest. You've been here nearly the same amount of hours as me over the past few weeks, and you're just a student."

Just a student, Rosalyn repeated to herself, hurt by his words.

Hadn't she already proved how useful she could be, on more than one occasion? Yet still he classed her as just another student, like the rest of them.

Her heart sank.

It wasn't like she expected him, or anyone else for

that matter to think she was incredible, or that she would become a doctor before she had finished her training. She knew she had a long and tough road ahead of her, but she had hoped that she'd proven to all of them that she wasn't just like everyone else. That she was meant to be here, and that she was good at what she did.

She'd been working so hard to try and prove to them, and herself that she belonged.

"I'm sorry," Oliver muttered, breaking the silence that fell between them before he paused and pulled her a step closer. "I think you're very talented. A real asset to us. Ah, heck. I'm no good with words, Rose," he grumbled, pinching the bridge of his nose before he shook his head and moved in even closer, sealing her lips with a kiss. His hands captured her cheeks to hold her still.

At first she was too shocked to react, standing completely frozen as he edged her back against the wall. Her mind black, searching for an appropriate response.

She might have thought Oliver was handsome and friendly, but she never thought she would kiss him, and now that she was, she felt, nothing. No lust. No desire sparking to life inside of her. Just, someone's eyes on them.

Rosalyn pushed him back and turned away. Her heart pounded painfully in her chest as it tightened. Tears gathered in the corners of her eyes when she slowly turned, expecting to see the matron with a scowl on her face, and hatred in her eyes.

"Forgive me. I shouldn't have done that," Oliver whispered, lowering his gaze to the floor.

All she wanted was to become a doctor. It was all she had left, and she might have just ruined her chances. The maton wouldn't overlook something like this. Only, it wasn't her at all. Instead she saw a tall, well built man headed toward them. The same man she couldn't stop thinking about.

Almost two weeks had passed since he'd been bought in as an emergency. A deep, circular hole pierced through his left pectoral, barely missing his heart; a wound that didn't appear to be affecting him at all now as he strolled down the corridor with ease.

Each night since, she'd lay awake thinking of him. This man her head insisted was a demon, unable to push the thought away.

Those times she had managed to sleep, she'd dreamt of him too.

His skin may have blistered when the doctors and nurses touched him, but in her dreams, he'd reached for her and held her to him, protecting her even. His skin unaffected by her contact, even when she had stroked her hands across his solid chest, covered in more of those unusual colour tattoos she had seen on his arms. Or when her lips had met his, exploring and tasting him all over. His hard body supple beneath her roaming hands.

Her cheeks reddened as she tried in vain not to remember the lingering taste of him now. A rich, spicy tang that made her lick her lips, desire flooding through her, even though she knew it was wrong to think of a patient that way.

Kissing a member of staff, especially one who was supposed to be her mentor was bad enough.

Having fantasies about a patient was far worse and would certainly get her kicked off the course if anybody found out.

Rosalyn held her breath and hung her head in shame, awaiting a comment, but the man remained silent while he strolled past them, his hauntingly beautiful eyes concealed behind dark sunglasses when he turned his face ever so slightly toward her.

Demon.

Her heart pounded even faster as she leaned back against the cool wall behind her in need of the support.

After he'd left with the other man, she'd asked the doctors and nurses on the ward to help her find him before he caused himself more damage, and none of them had known who she spoke of, not even Oliver.

She'd hunted for every person who had been in the room, fighting to hold him still while Oliver examined him, even attempting to search the system for his files and admission notes, only to find nothing there like he never existed, but that wasn't possible. She could remember it all so clearly. The tortured sounds of his pain. The blood and the reaction of his skin. Even Oliver's still bruised eye where he had taken a hit to the face.

There had to be a logical explanation. She couldn't be having visions again, or seeing things that weren't there like before. She couldn't end up in *Greenbryer residential* again. That thought terrifying her more than anything else.

CHAPTER 5

Forcing his feet in the opposite direction, Rayner battled with himself to turn back and pull the female behind him, even if it caused him agony; it would be worth it to wipe the arrogant grin off that doctor's face. Except, he didn't have time for that. There were Soulless in the hospital somewhere. He couldn't risk being slowed down by pain. Nor could he allow himself to stand around in their view any longer, unless he wanted their memories of him to return.

She may not remember him thanks to Niko, but he certainly hadn't forgotten her, and though part of him was curious about her, he knew it was dangerous.

Up to this point he had been lucky, managing to avoid those who had been there that night. In fact, he'd barely seen anybody whilst he made his way through the corridors. Not even a trace of the Soulless he hunted. Until now.

Foot hovered in midair above the next step, Rayner paused, debating whether he should head up or continue his path down. He inhaled deeply, attempting to focus on the direction the scent came from and cursed under his breath.

He'd led them right to her.

Two steps taken at a time, heart thumping quickly, he rushed through the halls, headed back to where he'd seen her and that doctor.

He may not know why the Soulless had come here tonight, but he couldn't shake the feeling that she was in danger, that they might have come here for her no matter how impossible that sounded.

Surely even Henry wouldn't keep a human a secret. He'd have imprisoned her if he suspected anything, not left her alone to roam in a hospital where she could spread rumours of the Other. Nor could he picture the old vampire working with the Soulless. The fool was terrified of them, despite his attempts to shrug off any news they had about them.

All Rayner did know was that he had to protect her from them all. His need to see her likely only putting her in greater danger, but how could he leave her to fight alone?

"Where is she?" he growled loudly, striking his fist into the wall beside him, cracking several of the tiles in the process, drawing a lot of unwanted attention to himself when nearby staff stepped into the hallway.

Rayner scowled, ignoring them as he looked up and down the long corridor, searching for any sign of her, all the while that floral scent grew weaker. The Soulless moving further away from him.

Those muffled voices in his head, the ones that had been deadly silent when he'd passed her now increasing in volume the further she moved away, and the more onlookers joined him in the hall, gawking.

He needed to get out of here, quickly.

From behind, he heard the *ding* of the lift. The unmistakable fragrance of wild berries coaxing him forward, turning his body to stone.

"U-up, or down?" the male nurse asked when he stepped inside, his finger visibly shaking next to the buttons.

"Down."

Rayner knew he should stay and help Lorkan with the Soulless, but right now his main priority was to check on Rosalyn and make sure those monsters weren't on her trail for whatever reason. Lorkan would be able to deal with the clean up far better than he could.

Several floors later, Rayner burst from the lift, grabbing hold of the metal doors before they had a chance to close after he caught a glimpse of her across the room.

There, by the stairs. Her long black hair swayed from side to side with each step as she pulled a black jacket over her shoulders, before descending down another flight of stairs. Her sweet scent luring him closer, struggling to keep his distance.

"Are you sure you're alright, Rose?" he heard the doctor ask, rubbing his hand up and down her arm in a far too friendly manner making Rayner see red, especially when he saw her flinch away from his touch. Flashes of her pushing the doctor back causing Rayner to grit his teeth. It took all his might just to remain still and not rush forward, shoving the doctor away from her. Perhaps even giving him a second black eye to match the one that had yet to fade completely.

The only thing that held him back was the knowledge that if he did approach them, he risked her sanity even more than he had already.

"I'm fine, really. I just need some sleep."

That voice. So lovely and pure, coaxing him even closer. His feet already headed in her direction before he managed to control himself.

"I'd still prefer to check you over properly."

Biting down on his tongue to stop the growl he could feel building in his chest, Rayner circled around them, his eyes flicking between them and the shadows, searching for any sign of Soulless in an attempt to distract himself from the far too handsy doctor.

"I told you, it's nothing, just lack of sleep playing with my mind and perhaps a little too much caffeine," she argued, her laugh sounding hollow, and her expression guarded as she continued to watch the doctor.

"Hallucinations aren't anything to be taken lightly, Rose, even if caffeine related. And you were adamant you'd seen that man upstairs before. I remember you asking about it weeks ago."

Impossible.

She shouldn't have been able to fight Niko's memory alteration that quickly. He'd only passed them by briefly. That had never happened before. Niko was the most powerful one of them when it came to the psychic stuff.

It appeared that nothing worked on her.

Interesting.

He didn't get a chance to figure out what this could mean for any of them, or how it was even possible; the Soulless were close.

His eyes darted to the darkness of the closed shops further down the hall. A pair of bright blue eyes shimmered despite the lack of light around it. It's long, narrow blade gleaming when it stepped forward and disappeared from sight again.

Bastard.

"You need to move, now," Rayner commanded the female, finally approaching her now he knew she could be in danger, and that she seemed to already remember him.

He needed to get her away from here before that monster got too bold and made its move.

"Who the hell are you?"

"I don't have time for you," Rayner growled, snarling at the doctor before he turned back to her.

"They're coming," he muttered under his breath,

pinching the bridge of his nose when a chill ran down his spine.

The Soulless was moving closer.

"She's not going anywhere with you," the doctor snapped back, stepping forward to put himself in the middle. A surprisingly bold move.

Very few people, or Other got in the way of a Warrior.

He might have been impressed, if he wasn't so irritated.

Damn it.

There was no other choice. The Soulless was already too close. The doctor would have to come too.

"Move. Now," Rayner grumbled, pushing the male out of the doors, clenching his teeth the longer the contact remained.

The layers between their skin insulated the worst of the pain, but not for long. His hands were sore and throbbing by the time they got outside. Luckily for him, the female chose to follow close behind him, smart enough not to waste more time with pointless questions, unlike this fool in front of him.

A few more steps forward, and a faint snicker echoed throughout the carpark making Rayner freeze, both humans doing the same. Their faces pale while they searched the space around them, even though they wouldn't be able to see the creature until it was right in front of them, too late to run.

Sensing the danger, the female stepped closer to Rayner causing him to smile despite the situation they were in, especially when he saw the frown on the doctor's face before he looked away from her.

Fighting the overwhelming urge to pull her close to

his side, Rayner turned his attention back to the shadows, unaccustomed to the sounds he could hear around him, without all those voices in his head. Noises that others took for granted. Each of them just as disorientating as the voices.

"Protecting humans? How admirable, demon," the Soulless scoffed, continuing to circle around them, sending a shiver down Rayner's spine.

He'd never heard a Soulless speak before, and he hoped he never had to again. It's oddly distorted voice sounded more like a shriek, just like the wail they let out when they died.

"What are we–"

"Shh," the female scolded, her attention focused in the same direction Rayner looked making him curious whether she heard it too.

"Sweet, little, *Rose.*"

She flinched, the timing too perfect to just be a coincidence, moving another step closer to him, leaving him torn between the pleasure of having her close and lean into him for protection, and the pain it would cause him should she actually attempt to grab him, beads of sweat trickling down his face as he clenched his fists and jaw.

"So pure. So, *delicious.*"

"Enough," Rayner barked, stepping between the female and the space in front of them where he could sense the Soulless.

"Clever, demon," it snickered, its face appearing slowly out of the darkness. It's bloodshot eyes opened wide, the feral grin on its face revealing all those pointed teeth before it tipped its head to the side and licked its lips. Eyes moved between her and the doctor behind, making her gasp and lurch forward, clinging to the back of his t-shirt.

Rayner's body tensed, Frozen and unsure whether to jump away quickly, or keep completely still so she didn't accidentally brush against his skin, despite his crazed longing for her to do so.

He wasn't used to anybody being this close to him, and yet she didn't cause him pain through the thin layer of cotton as she kept her hand at a small distance from his skin, the material bundled in her grasp.

Either she didn't fully trust him and therefore was hesitant to touch and rely on him fully, or she had truly remembered what happened here almost two weeks ago.

"Get her out of here," Rayner ordered the doctor through clenched teeth.

Though he detested the thought of sending her away, especially with him, he didn't want her in danger or seeing what he was about to do, even if he did crave her next to him, the gentle tug on his t-shirt the closest thing he had felt to physical contact in years.

"Come, Rosalyn." The doctor grabbed her arm a little roughly, but she pointed with her free hand toward the Soulless and the blade it held.

"No. He'll be stabbed again. Look," she pleaded.

"Stab wound?" the doctor groaned, his face pale as he pressed his fingers into his temples, some of his memories trying to break through the alteration.

"Move. Now!"

This time the doctor didn't hesitate, pulling her arm in the opposite direction to the creature, even while she fought against him.

The Soulless attempted to reach around Rayner, stretching its claws toward her, but Rayner was faster, grabbing hold of its arm, forcing it back, biting down hard on his lip to fight his own body's reflex to shove the source of his pain away.

"Go!"

"Stop!" she screamed, eyes fixated on him while she was dragged further away. "He's hurting himself."

CHAPTER 6

Rosalyn's eyes stung with tears watching the agony cloud that man's face as he held the other one back. His skin red and blistering while she watched and attempted to break free from Oliver's tight grip around her arm.

He may have a strong physique, possibly even used to fighting, the way he held himself reminding her of a soldier, but that other man had a weapon. A weapon that looked like it could have been the cause for his hospital admittance previously.

None of the other doctors or nurses could remember him, but Rosalyn knew differently.

He had definitely been to the hospital before. It was either that, or she had a vision of him coming in and this was the incident responsible.

She wasn't sure which was worse. Everybody believing her crazy because she remembered him when nobody else could, or having visions like she used to. That combined with the constant thought that he was a demon, no matter how hard she argued with herself otherwise. Either way it was likely that she would be readmitted and rehoused if she let anybody know what she was thinking, something she couldn't allow to happen.

"W-we can't just leave him there, alone. He might need our help, Oliver," she pleaded, attempting to dig her heels into the ground as she tugged against his hold.

For whatever reason, when he had seen the man with that weapon, Oliver seemed to almost remember the other man. Perhaps if they stayed and helped, he might remember fully and she wouldn't feel quite so crazy.

"Have you seen the guy, Rose? I'm sure he'll manage."

Of course she had seen him. She'd done nothing but see him every night since she had met him.

She knew how powerful and muscular his body appeared, but that didn't mean she liked the idea of him risking his life in order to save theirs, or hurting himself by holding the other one back from them. The memory of his shouts and agonised cries when the doctors and nurses held him down imprinted on her brain, the pain on his face making her chest squeeze tight.

"Besides, he was the one who insisted I take you away."

"I never pegged you for a coward," she hissed, furious as she tried to pry his fingers from her wrist, not caring if her words might hurt his feelings. "You're a doctor. You're supposed to help people, not leave them alone to die."

Rosalyn may not fully understand what was happening, still unsure what to think of that man, but she couldn't just walk away knowing he could be injured, or worse. Surely three people stood a better chance than one.

It was possible the man with the weapon might even flee when he realised they were all prepared to fight back.

"I-I can't," Oliver stuttered, stopping dead in his tracks. His grip on her wrist tightening when his hands began to shake. Eyes filled with tears when he looked over his shoulder at her.

"When I was a student here, I was attacked in this parking lot," he muttered, his voice cracking whilst he spoke. "It took me two years just to gain enough courage to come back."

43

Rosalyn stared at him with her mouth wide open, unsure what she could say.

This whole experience had to be painful for him, bringing back all those unwanted memories, and here she was just assuming him to be a coward.

Still, she couldn't help but think of that man fighting alone, unarmed against the other one's blade.

"He needs us, Oliver," she pleaded quietly, squeezing his forearm gently with her free hand. "What happened to you was no doubt terrifying, but we can't leave him to go through a similar thing alone. Wouldn't you have wanted someone to come back for you?"

"Y-you're right," Oliver sighed, lifting his head with a look of determination. He released his hold on her arm.

Rosalyn smiled up at him and grabbed hold of his hand, giving it a squeeze before she led him back in the direction they'd come from.

She couldn't see or hear them anywhere, but she thought she could smell that odd floral fragrance she'd noticed before, both inside the hospital and out here before the man appeared. Not that it helped her. She had no idea how to use somebody's scent to track them down, nor could she see above the cars and vans that blocked their way.

"This way," Oliver called, already headed in the direction he'd pointed out to her.

No sooner had they both taken a few steps when they heard a piercing shriek echo all around them, making Rosalyn clasp her hands over her ears. Her knees buckled beneath her, the noise deafening and eerie, causing her skin to erupt with goosebumps.

Rosalyn forced herself to push on, unsure who that scream had come from, or what she would find, but soon wished she hadn't when she caught sight of two large silhouettes in the distance. One looming over the other.

"I told you to get her out of here."

It was him. The man she had begged Oliver to help her save. The man she thought might need them. A huge back sword gripped between his hands, poised above the other male that cowered on the ground.

In one fluid motion, he brought the weapon down, slicing it clean through the man on the floor's neck, causing it to fall and roll toward her.

Rosalyn screamed, holding her ears as she forced herself to look away, but it was too late. The images of what she had just seen played out over and over again.

Someone placed a hand on her shoulder, but she didn't wait to find out who. She ran. Pushing herself as hard as she could on wobbly legs, lungs burning as she fought for each breath. Her eyes stinging.

How could he?

To think, she had actually felt some attraction to such a man. A man so cold and callous. A murderer.

She felt sick.

Demon.

"No!" she shrieked.

He couldn't be a demon. There was no such thing. Only, she wasn't sure what she should believe in anymore.

There had definitely been something a little odd about that other man, what with the unusual haze she'd spotted inside the hospital, and the way he seemed to hide so easily among the shadows. None of the staff had seemed to notice him, or the other one either when they had browsed through restricted files.

"No," she shouted again.

What was she thinking? It was just her mind trying to find reason in what had just happened.

45

She was tired, overworked and seeing things. That man was a murderer. Nothing more.

"Rosalyn?" a male voice called from somewhere in the distance. Too far and muffled to be sure who that voice belonged to over the sounds of her own laboured breathing.

"Rosalyn!" the shout grew louder, more panicked.

She knew it was a bad idea to stop, but she paused anyway, listening for that voice, trying to figure out where she had run to, when she came face to face with him.

One emerald eye shone in the bright street light above, the other black as the night around them.

She forced herself to turn away, unable to look at him after what she had just witnessed. Her heart pounded in her chest whilst she fought back tears.

"I-I helped you," she began. Her voice shaking, trying to rein in her anger and sadness. Hands clenched tightly by her sides.

"You need to leave. Now."

"What?" she fumed, suddenly finding the courage to glare up at him. "How dare–"

"Enough," he roared, his eyes sparking to life when he took a step closer. So close that she had to crane her neck up high to look at him. Her traitorous body warming from head to toe with how close they stood together, without their bodies touching, her dreams fueling her desires.

"There isn't time for your arguments. More will come, brought here by it's scream."

As if on cue, the air around them grew heavy. The pungent scent of flowers assaulting her nose, making it difficult to breathe.

The man cursed loudly, spun around and held out his

arms on either side of him, almost like a shield in front of her. That nasty looking blade of his gripped tightly in his hand, dripping with a thick, dark, gunk.

Run, she yelled at herself, but her feet remained motionless on the ground, eyes scanning the darkness around them for more people like he insisted were coming. All the hairs on her arms and neck stood on end. Her knees drew together as her whole body trembled, unsure who she should be more afraid of.

"I'm trying to protect you," the man sighed, his eyes piercing when he glanced back at her over his shoulder. And damn it, part of her believed him.

Though it was possible he could have followed because she had seen too much, needing to silence her before she was able to call or find the police, it made no sense why he'd insisted she left the hospital earlier, or why he'd then told Oliver to take her away when that other man had appeared. Her mind in turmoil, unsure what to think or believe anymore.

Rosalyn tore her eyes away from the man in front of her and looked out into the darkness surrounding them. An inhuman noise sounded from all around, getting slowly closer and closer.

It was too late to flee now.

They were surrounded.

CHAPTER 7

Rayner was sure she would still attempt to flee. That look on her face when she had seen the Soulless's head roll to her feet imprinted in his mind. Her scream playing on repeat.

Great, he groaned internally. She would hate him now, wanting to get away from him as quickly as possible only making his job of protecting her ten times harder. Except, she didn't move. She stood behind him, searching from one side to the other, moving closer toward him whether she realised it or not.

Even after what she had witnessed, some part of her still felt safer by him than with them.

Very wise indeed.

But where had that doctor gotten himself to?

Better yet; where the hell was Lorkan?

He may be the youngest of them all, often distracted by almost any other task than the one at hand, but he was a good fighter, and he would need him now.

There were a lot of Soulless closing in. Far more than Rayner thought he could handle alone, especially with the female at his back to consider.

"Damn it, Lorkan," he grumbled under his breath, trying to count how many he could sense in close proximity.

Five.

This would be tough, but he crouched into position nonetheless, his sword gripped tightly in one hand, the weight of it a comfort as he waited to swing at the first one foolish enough to approach them.

"You really should have gone with the doctor," he commented before he leapt forward, plunging his sharp blade into one Soulless's throat, twisting it out on one side before the creature let out so much as a murmur.

Four.

Sword now poised in front of him, Rayner waited for the next of them to make a move.

These few who surrounded them appeared to attack much more like those he was used to. None of them carrying those needle-like blades the newer, unpredictable ones favoured.

He didn't need to wait long before another approached from the side and reached for the female, it's long, bony fingers grasping a strand of her hair.

Rayner swung his sword, slicing through its wrist with ease, making it howl and retreat, straight into Lorkan's dagger.

"About time you showed," Rayner grumbled, already spinning around and locking himself into combat with the next Soulless while Lorkan finished the other off.

Three.

"I found one inside with a sword like those the other night."

"Cameras?"

"Taken care of," he answered with his usual self satisfied smirk, lunging for the next Soulless, bringing it to the ground in a flurry of arms and legs.

In the middle of the fray, the female stood with her hands over her eyes, her entire body trembling. Unaware of the creature that was headed her way.

Rayner burst into action, leaving the Soulless he had

pinned to the ground in order to intercept the other, slicing his sword across its chest and putting himself between her and those still closing in.

He wanted to pull her to his side, knowing she would be safer if she were close and holding on to him, but he couldn't risk becoming weakened by the contact, especially with the Soulless still coming. Who knew how many more lurked nearby, close enough to hear the shrieks and come to their aid.

"Lorkan, stay close to her," he instructed with a sigh, wishing it could be him.

His need to keep her safe overwhelmed him, even if he couldn't quite understand why.

Spinning on the spot, Rayner lifted his blade up high and swiped it down quickly at the Soulless who dared to touch her, removing its head with a sickening squelch.

Two.

Lorkan gave him a questioning glance, but chose to remain silent before he grabbed Rosalyn and held her against him, his hand tight around her waist even as she fought to get away.

Rayner could feel the anger bubbling inside of him. A violent urge to rip his brother away from her and crush her lips against his, claiming her for himself, but he couldn't. It was dangerous to lose focus in a battle like this. And more importantly, he wasn't sure where these urges were coming from. He knew he couldn't touch her no matter how much he craved otherwise.

His solitude was clearly getting the better of him. His lust for her spiralling out of control. Desires he shouldn't be feeling for anybody, let alone her. A human. An unlikely partner for any Other. Yet, he couldn't deny his need to protect her, or find out more about her and her abilities.

For now, he would just have to grit his teeth and attempt to ignore the territorial thoughts that circled around inside his head.

Distracted, his eyes still glued on Lorkan with his arms around her, Rayner didn't notice the Soulless he had left on the ground until it was too late.

Back on its feet, the creature leapt forward and slashed Lorkan's arm with its long claws, forcing him to loosen his grip just enough that it was able to grab the female, and bolt. Her high pitched screams echoing through the alleyways.

Lorkan roared loudly, eyes now black as pitch as he slammed his uninjured arm into the remaining Soulless's face, knocking it to the ground where he plunged his dagger into its jugular, stomping down with the heel of his massive boot until the blade hit the concrete below.

One.

Retrieving his dagger, both of them gave chase.

Rayner's anger fueled him, pushing his body harder until he ran at full speed. His lungs and chest burning.

The Soulless's head start would not help it for long.

Pushing his limits, Rayner ran faster still, able to catch up with the creature and stopping just in front of it, aiming his blade toward its skill, above her head.

It paused, then smiled a toothy grin, wrapping long, misshapen fingers around her neck. Its sharp nails digging into her flesh, making blood trickle down her throat as she whimpered. Her big blue eyes locked onto him, pleading.

Lorkan wasn't far behind, circling around the creature, searching for a weak spot to attack without harming the female in the process, knowing by a simple nod of Rayner's head what he planned.

With a loud roar Rayner swung his blood soaked

sword through the air, taking the Soulless's head off at the same time Lorkan rushed forward, ducking below his arcing blade to yank the female to freedom, tucking her head against his chest to keep her safe and shield her view.

"Little late for that," Rayner scoffed bitterly.

"Let go of me!" she snapped, her eyes shimmering with unshed tears as she looked from one of them to the other, and down at the ground where the Soulless's body slumped in a heap.

"You're monsters. All of you."

Rayner didn't argue, knowing how this must look to her.

Men fighting and killing one another, never knowing the real truth or how much danger she'd been in.

The Soulless were usually only a threat to the Other, but with talents as strong and powerful as her own, she was in just as much trouble as them, her energy like a drug to them, something they must consume.

Then there was the fact that one had called her name outside the hospital; the nickname the doctor had given her anyway. *Rose.* Its voice still sent a shiver down Rayner's back.

There was a small chance that it had seen her name tag like he had, but Rayner doubted that was the case.

Not only was it concealed below her black jacket, he also didn't think it was possible for the Soulless to read, even those more intelligent ones. Those that were far more deadly than their horde like brethren.

For whatever reason, they had set their sights on her.

"You're not wrong there, sweetheart," Lorkan chuckled, retaining his grip around her waist despite her obvious struggles.

"Let her go," Rayner sighed, running a hand through

his mused hair.

It may not be one of his best ideas to allow the female to flee them, especially when he couldn't be sure how many more Soulless lurked nearby. There was a good chance that they could find and follow her home, or even find her at the hospital again, but he couldn't bring himself to take her against her will, no matter how much it physically pained him to let her walk away, knowing the danger he allowed himself to put her in.

Yet, when Lorkan released her with a scowl at him, she didn't bolt like he expected. She stood, staring at him with her brows knitted between her eyes, running her hands down her black smeared scrubs. Her own blood still trickling from the wound on her neck, making Rayner clench his fists and look down at the creature on the ground with renewed hatred, wishing he could kill it again for the pain it caused her.

"You're letting me go?"

"They'll know where she lives," Lorkan interrupted, pacing back and forth across the alley.

"H-how? The hospital doesn't leave personal information just lying around for people to go through."

"One of them knew your name, *Rosalyn,*" Rayner replied with a huffed out laugh, his tone anything but amused. Irritated that she couldn't grasp how much of a threat the Soulless were to her. Feeling like an arse when he saw her flinch and wrap her arms around her middle.

"Perhaps you're right and they don't know where you live, yet, but what if you're wrong?"

She froze, nibbling on her bottom lip, rubbing her hands up and down her arms, looking from each of them before she glanced behind in the direction Rayner assumed her home must be.

He may not be willing to force her to come with them, but he could at least attempt to convince her that she would be safest with them.If she still refused, he would just have to follow behind and make sure that no other Soulless got too close.

He couldn't let them have her.

"I don't mean to rush, but I suspect we won't be alone for much longer," Lorkan chimed in, wiping some of the black blood from his daggers across his thigh, holding them out ready in front of him rather than returning them to their sheath.

He was right. Rayner could feel it too, like a buzz of electricity across his skin. His head pounded as the voices tried to break through whatever it was she did to push them out.

"You expect me to just follow and trust you after what you've done? From where I'm standing, you're just as bad as them," she snapped, clenching her hands as she backed away. Her eyes like saucers when she gasped, having realised what she'd said, and who she thought she was talking to, her fear unsurprising, even if it stung.

"No."

She had seen too much.

Even without the threat of the Soulless looming over her, she was in danger from the Council if they found out about her, and his interference. Yet, all Rayner could do was watch as she put more and more distance between them, glancing back over her shoulder as she walked away, her pace not quite a run, but a very brisk walk, likely expecting them to give chase when she was far enough away.

"We're really just letting her go?"

"For now," Rayner sighed.

He hated it. Still debating running after her and hauling her over his shoulder, taking her with them despite the agony he knew would come from such an action. At least then he knew she would be safe. Protected.

Instead, he waited a few moments more before he headed in the same direction she had gone, Lorkan close behind him. Both of them keeping their distance as they tailed along behind in silence.

Rayner wasn't sure who would come for her first, but he knew she would need them sooner or later, and he would be ready.

CHAPTER 8

Almost a week had passed since Rosalyn witnessed that bloody scene outside the hospital, and still the police had no leads.

She felt like a liar. A lunatic even when they claimed not to have found any bodies at the scene, just some thick black matter and a powdery substance that were both still in analysis.

She plonked down on her bed and stared up at the ceiling with bleary eyes.

Another long shift ended. Another night that she'd had to wait around for almost an hour before a taxi was available to bring her home, no longer comfortable enough to walk the streets alone after the incident that nobody seemed to believe her about.

She brought a hand up to her neck and padded her fingers along the still healing wound there, wincing when she touched a particularly sore spot.

Demon.

"Get out of my head," she grumbled, draping an arm across her eyes. The man with the mismatched eyes appearing in her head despite her command, making her heart skip a beat.

He was at the centre of it all.

Everything strange that had happened recently only started after he had been brought to the hospital weeks ago.

"Rose, babe. How are you feeling?" Sara asked,

hovering in her doorway while she pulled her top over her head, shaking her long blonde hair loose when Rosalyn turned to face her.

"Tired."

"Pity. Oliver popped by to see you. I would offer to keep him company for you, but he was quite insistent and my shift starts in an hour," she commented, fanning her face with her hand before she gave a little smirk. "And can I just say. Damn, he looked hot in casuals."

"You answered the door half dressed, again?"

"Maybe you should try it sometime. It's thrilling. But hey, I've got to get going. Don't do anything I wouldn't do," she chuckled with a wink over her shoulder, and a small wave. Her footsteps receding down the hall before Rosalyn heard the front door swing shut.

"Rose?" Oliver called, peering his head around the open door before he stepped inside, eyes scanning her modest sized room.

"Nice place."

"T-thank you," she replied, her own eyes scanning the room quickly to make sure she hadn't left anything embarrassing out for him to spot, like the bra she flung over the back of her chair where she'd changed in a rush after getting in earlier.

With a gasp, Rosalyn jumped to her feet and rushed over to her desk, hiding it quickly behind her back and stuffing it into the wash basket by her bathroom door the moment he looked away, her cheeks burning when he turned back her way with a raised brow.

"I like the colour," he commented with a smirk, only making her cheeks burn hotter.

"Surely you didn't come here this late just to admire my underwear?" she asked, turning away to hide her no doubt blazing red cheeks, but not before she noticed his own brighten at her comment.

"No. Sorry," he muttered, clearing his throat before he turned the other way. "I came to see how you were doing after, well, you know."

"I'm fine, really," she lied, looking down, playing with the hem of her vest top before she sat back on the edge of her bed with her arms wrapped around her middle. "I just wish people would stop asking me."

It wasn't that she was ungrateful. Maybe a little unaccustomed to it, but certainly not hating it. It was just that every time someone looked at her with pity in their eyes, or whispered about what had happened to her neck, all those memories she'd rather forget came back. All those whispers about how the police couldn't find proof making her feel like a liar all over again.

Only, Oliver had been there too, at the beginning. He'd seen the man with the different coloured eyes and remembered him this time. He saw him kill that first man before they had separated.

He may not have witnessed all the other deaths, but he had to believe her, right?

"Sorry I haven't been able to check on you properly. It's been hell," he sighed, rubbing a hand across the back of his neck before he took a step closer. "Your neck looks a lot better than it did. Another week perhaps and you'll barely notice it anymore," he continued, crouching down in front of her, his head tilted to the side to examine the wound a little more closely. His ever present smile back in place, easing some of her discomfort. "Have they managed to find him yet?"

Rosalyn shook her head, unsure whether she should be terrified that he was still on the loose, or relieved that he hadn't been seen anywhere in the area since.

And yet, some crazy part of her was unsure what had really happened, and why she believed his words when he said he was protecting her.

Just because he had made that claim, didn't make it true, and she was positive that he was the kind of man she shouldn't rely upon or trust, but she couldn't deny how she'd felt getting separated from Oliver, when he'd stood in front of her like a shield. Or when he'd told her to stay by his friend for protection. And how they'd both given chase when she'd been grabbed and hauled away, only to have her throat cut by that man with the abnormally long nails, allowing her to leave even after all she has seen.

She'd felt somewhat safe, despite her fear.

Her mind still tried to process everything she had seen. Struggling to find reason with that odd haze around those men, along with their bloodshot eyes and pointed teeth.

There was something about those men in and around the hospital that wasn't quite normal. Her foolish brain trying to insite they weren't human, just like she thought the others were demons. The one with the golden eyes who had come to take his friend from the hospital flashing before her eyes. His eyes had changed black just like those from the past. The one with the purple eyes that night doing just the same.

Thoughts and memories from back then that terrified her even more than the events that had taken place last week.

She couldn't go back to Greenbryer institute and residential, all those people judging her, believing she was crazy, again. But how could she explain what she was seeing, and the lack of evidence the police were able to find.

Perhaps she really was hallucinating; vividly.

"I wonder if he works for the government?"

"Well, it would explain a lot," Oliver continued when she turned to him with a bewildered look. "How nobody remembered him before, and how he seemed to magically disappear from the hospital car park surveillance tapes. People don't just disappear like that. Not without some connections."

No, they don't.

Believing he could be in some secret service like the MI6 was a lot easier to stomach than her own crazed thoughts, but that didn't explain those eyes, or that mist. Or even why they'd fought how they did.

So far as she was aware, the MI6 didn't make a habit of decapitating their targets.

"Oliver?" Rosalyn began, her voice quiet and unsure, "what did you see?"

"What did I see? I saw a huge guy cut the head off another with a sword before you ran off and I saw him chase after you, ignoring me completely."

Rosalyn flinched at his bluntness, but shook her head, forcing herself to continue.

She needed to know if he had noticed any abnormalities with those men like she had, or if it was really all in her head like she feared.

"What did they look like?"

"Well, he was tall and muscular. Like really big. Frightening, with odd coloured eyes."

"No. The other one."

"I don't know Rose. High I guess, what with his eyes all bloodshot like that."

Rosalyn's shoulders slumped.

Perhaps that was all it had been. An odd man high on drugs out looking for his next fix. Searching around the hospital for something he could use or sell, attempting to mug them in order to get some cash. But it didn't feel right. They'd acted strangely, even for someone who was high. The way they blended in with the shadows a little too easily, or how they had grouped together, circling them more like animals than men.

Where had they all come from?

The addicts she had known and come across over the years tended to keep to themselves, and though some had carried weapons, none of them had looked like theirs had. Long, thin and circular. Unlike anything she had ever seen before.

"Rose, are you sure you're alright?"

Rosalyn opened and closed her mouth a few times unsure of how to answer, or how much she wanted to admit to him, short of her fears that they were monsters and that she was going crazy.

Instead, she shook her head and let out a long sigh.

She needed to just let go and let the police handle it.

"Stop trying to make sense of what happened, Rose. There was no reason behind that man's actions, and you'll only worry yourself to death trying to find one," Oliver sighed, cupping her cheek in his hand as she looked up at him with a faint smile.

"But none of it adds up."

If he were just some merciless killer, or even a demon, or whatever else, why had he let her go? Why not kill her like all those other men, or take her along with him in order to keep her quiet?

His friend had been surprised by his choice which meant the one with the odd eyes had to be in charge somehow. But in charge of what exactly?

"You're not a killer, Rose. Of course none of this adds up to you." Oliver shrugged. "Perhaps you feel betrayed after risking yourself to go back and save him."

"Maybe, but why tell us to leave the hospital quickly, then just leave us like that. Why did he let me go?"

"You're going to make yourself go crazy like this."

"Perhaps I am already," she snapped, shoving at his chest to give herself some space before she stood and made her way across the room, leaning on her dresser for support.

"You're in shock. You'll be back to normal soon."

Normal? Rosalyn had never felt normal.

Rosalyn swayed, her emotions running out of control, bracing herself to tell Oliver to leave when she spied something move in the mirror in front of her, making her spin and stare out into the darkness. A shadowy mass moving across the window, too slow to have been caused by a passing car.

Suddenly the bottom floor apartment she'd picked wasn't seeming like a good idea.

Having noticed her stare, Oliver glanced back over his shoulder with a raised brow, before turning back to her with the same look she was getting tired of seeing. Pity.

Clearly he thought she was being jumpy and seeing things that weren't there. She wasn't too sure she hadn't, until she saw it again, this time moving by even slower. The outline of a person.

"I'm sorry I lost sight of you when you ran. I could've–"

"Shh," Rosalyn interrupted, taking a step forward to have a closer look and make sure that her window was locked, unwilling to take any chances.

"Rosalyn. Really, there's–" Oliver began, only to silence when he saw it too.

A pale face at her window, blurry and flickering in and out of focus.

A man with his lips curved into a feral looking grin full of large, yellowing teeth. His bloodshot eyes staring straight at her as it scraped on the window with an abnormally long, sharp claw.

The sound sent a shiver down her spine.

"What the hell?" Oliver gasped, jumping to his feet and stepping toward her, pulling her a few paces back from the glass when another face joined the first.

Perhaps deciding not to go with that man hadn't been such a good idea after all.

He said they would find her, but she didn't believe him, how could she? But here they were. The sheer look of terror on Oliver's face as he shook his head and continued to back away only confirming how unnatural those men appeared.

They weren't human. She was almost positive.

"*Let us in, little, Rose,*" one of them mocked through the glass. Its voice muffled and distorted, making all the hairs on her arms and neck stand on end as it continued to scrape with its nails. A scratch appearing in the glass as he repeated the same action again, and again, a little harder with each stroke.

The grin on his face soon vanished, only to be replaced by a furious sneer.

Rosalyn covered her ears and spun around, squeezing her eyes close when Oliver guided her toward the door with a hand on the small of her back.

Suddenly he stopped and wrapped his arms around her, pulling her to a stop at the same time a breeze hit her, wafting some of that floral scent to her nose.

Heart pounding, she peeked beneath her lashes expecting to come face to face with one of those terrifying things.

"Now are you ready to come with me?" a familiar deep and gravelly voice asked as she lowered her hands, noting the black gunk smeared across his face and clothes. A new slice cut through his chest that leaked blood down his black t-shirt, making it stick to his powerful body.

Rosalyn couldn't speak. Her throat closed up, her body trembling, but she nodded just as they heard the sound of glass shattering behind, making her leap forward and cling to the man's sleeve, soon realising what she'd done when she heard him grunt, dropping her hands from him in an instant.

She may not be entirely sure what was happening, or how she had gotten herself involved with all of this, but she knew for certain that he had come back for her. Likely that he had been trying to help all along, just like he claimed.

Those men, or whatever they were, weren't normal.

"I'm not going anywhere with you, you murderer. And neither is she," Oliver snapped, yanking Rosalyn back and holding her against him while he pulled his phone from his pocket.

"Then perhaps you'd prefer to stay here, with them," the man scoffed, nodding his head to the door behind them as the two creatures that had been at the window barreled across the room with their odd looking blades in their hands.

"Move," the man growled, stepping around them as he drew his own sword, blocking them when they took a swing at Oliver's head.

Rosalyn didn't hesitate having learnt her lesson from

last time.

She knew she needed to listen to what this man was saying, bolting toward the open front door as fast as she could, only to collide with something solid.

Another male she recognised.

The golden-eyed man.

"Come with me, female," he commanded in a stern voice, before he looked over his shoulder at a very pale Oliver. "I guess you'll have to come too now."

Without another word, he spun on his heels and pulled out two strange looking curved blades from beneath his jacket, kicking out with his boot into the chest of one of those creatures that ran toward them, sending it flying as they followed him toward a parked car outside.

"Who the hell are you people?" Oliver asked when he was shoved roughly into the back seat of the car after Rosalyn had already climbed inside, asking the very question she was thinking.

"Name is Nikostratos, or Niko for short. How many were inside?"

"T-two," Rosalyn replied, her eyes drawn to the front door just like his, waiting for the other man to emerge.

"Shouldn't you go help him?"

"He can handle two, and I don't trust *him* not to steal my car."

Rosalyn continued to stare unsure what was taking him so long if he were able to handle them like this man suggested, remembering the slice she had seen across his chest.

Perhaps it had slowed him down, or those things had gotten the better of him.

She leaned forward ready to argue when she saw the other man finally emerge from the building, leaning heavily on the door frame to catch his breath.

"Get a move on before we have more to deal with," the man called Niko shouted from his window, earning him a scowl from the other man before he pushed himself away from the wall and headed toward the car, clutching his chest.

"All clear?"

"Clear," he grunted, plonking onto the seat in front of her, slamming his door shut.

"Then shouldn't we, you know, go?"

"Who's the male?" Niko asked, eyeing Oliver in the rear view mirror after his outburst. His golden eyes turning black as she watched, just like they did at the hospital.

Demon.

Only this time when the thought came to her, Rosalyn wasn't sure she could deny it.

CHAPTER

9

When they'd claimed to be driving them someplace safe, a small cabin on the outskirts of the town, bordering the woods was not what Rosalyn had in mind. Not that she really knew what a safe house looked like.

It wasn't everyday that you followed along behind a man you knew had killed others. Or men you thought could be demons, Niko's eyes having changed black on more than one occasion on their car ride here. The sight of it still jarred, making Rosalyn uncomfortable.

For years she thought she'd seen supernatural creatures roaming the streets unnoticed by anybody else. All those people she'd thought were her friends laughing and judging. Mocking her face to face, and saying far worse behind her back. Years of being bullied in primary school, and on her way to and from whatever house she happened to be staying in at the time, until eventually her Aunt had enough and shipped her away to Greenbryer for her '*own good*', washing her hands of her the moment the nurses took her inside. She severed all contact after her eighteenth birthday when she was no longer required as a legal guardian, and they no longer got paid.

The staff there drilled it into her head that there was no such thing as monsters. That everything she had seen was just her imagination. That she needed a means to focus and forget about fairy tales and myths.

It had all been going so well.

She'd found herself a good college. Passing with one of the highest grades in her year. Later being accepted into a top university where she was able to join a hospital of her choosing and learn whilst she studied.

Then he had shown up, and everything changed.

Now she was back where she started. A mess that believed in demons. Unable to forget about him when it seemed that everybody else around her had.

Seeing him repeatedly in her dreams. Fantasizing about him even.

Then those other men appeared. Men that were far from normal. Everything about them put her on edge. From the way they moved and their appearance, to the way they sounded, and that sickeningly sweet smell that hit the back of your throat and made you retch.

Rosalyn thought she was losing her mind all over again, terrified that she would need to be readmitted. Unsure how long it would take this time around after her nine, nearly ten years previously in the residential complex.

Except this time Oliver had seen something too.

Something about those men at her window had frightened him enough that he agreed to come along with a man he thought was nothing more than a murderer.

Perhaps this time it wasn't all in her head.

"It was Rosalyn, correct?" Niko asked, taking a seat opposite her. His golden eyes locked with hers before they flickered black.

He made no sign that he noticed her flinch, but still she couldn't bring herself to look at his face for too long.

He seemed quite friendly, for a killer at least. Another thing she hadn't expected especially after their first encounter at the hospital.

He'd been in a hurry then, rushing to get his friend out, only now she thought perhaps she understood why.

The incision in the other man's chest matching the type of blade those creatures carried. His rapid healing likely to have shown up as an anomaly on the various tests Oliver had ordered to be run on him. His memory of him only vanishing after Niko had shown up and the pair left.

If these men were indeed demons, it made sense that they needed to get out and away before anybody started asking questions.

But Rosalyn still didn't understand how she had gotten swept up in it all.

"I'm sorry you got involved," Niko sighed, his timing scarily accurate, as though he'd read her mind, which she supposed may not be impossible for a demon if any of the stories she'd read or watched were true. "My *brother* should not have returned to the hospital."

"If I hadn't they would have gotten her already," the one with the mismatched eyes growled in response, snarling from across the room as he yanked his blood soaked t-shirt over his head, revealing all those lean muscles across his back. His arms flexing and bulging with his every movement; but it wasn't just the sight of his magnificently sculpted body that drew Rosalyn's attention, it was the designs across his skin that seemed to writhe and move below the surface, just like she had seen in her dreams. Glyphs that almost glowed in the dull light while she continued to stare, only they hadn't appeared to move when she had seen them in the hospital.

"They're– She's–" Niko hesitated, struggling to find the right words it seemed. "What makes you think they went there for her?"

With a fresh shirt still gathered in the crook of his elbows, he paused and turned back to them. Those markings circling around his abdomen and chest, beginning just below his jaw, down the length of his arms, and disappearing beneath his dark jeans, the accuracy of her dreams somewhat frightening the longer she continued to stare at the pattern and movement, mesmerised.

"Because, she saw them," he answered, his eyes locked onto her. His nostrils flared before she tore her gaze from his body. The wound on his chest already partially healed not going unnoticed by her. The rate of his recovery even faster than she had thought.

With the amount of blood on his t-shirt, his wound should still have been bleeding without any stitches to hold it closed, yet he appeared to be almost healed. The only blood she had seen in that brief glimpse already dried against his skin. The slice thinner than before with the appearance of an old wound, his words finally sinking in when her eyes flicked back up to his.

Was she not supposed to see them? That might explain why nobody else in the hospital had batted an eyelid when they'd searched through files and things at the front desk, and why it had taken Oliver some time to notice them in both the car park and outside her window just now.

"Is that so, Rosalyn?"

Rosalyn nodded, noticing from the corner of her eye that the other man had finished changing, concealing his body and arms once more beneath a fresh, long sleeved t-shirt.

What was wrong with her?

She shouldn't be ogling a man like him. It was bad enough that she had fantasized about him when he was a patient, but now she knew he was a killer, and thought the possibility of him being a demon wasn't so foolish, taking the bad boy thing to a whole new level.

There was no way she should be attracted to him,

even if his body was enough to make her mouth water. His jaw finely chiseled with those deep hollows in his cheeks making her weak at the knees. And eyes that were hauntingly beautiful.

No, somebody like him should definitely not be attractive to her.

"You saw them when they attacked?"

"And before," she admitted, lowering her gaze to the ground whilst she spoke, unsure how Oliver would react to what she was on the brink of admitting.

He would likely think her mad, like everyone else in her life.

Back at the hospital he'd been concerned, insisting he run tests on her because of her so called hallucinations, but surely now he had seen something when he looked at those things. He'd believe her now. These men would believe her, wouldn't they?

"I saw them inside the hospital. They were searching through the front desk of the ward, rummaging through files, but nobody seemed to notice them," Rosalyn began, tucking her hands between her thighs so none of them would see her tremble.

"There seemed to be an odd mist, or shadow around them. And I saw them again when I was in the cafe with Oliver. I think that one of them noticed me staring when they walked past the windows."

"Y- you shouldn't have been able to see," Niko mumbled to himself with a frown, pinching the bridge of his nose. "The mist. It conceals them, enabling them to blend in with the shadows and move around unnoticed by most. If you saw them, that could explain why they switched their target to you."

Rosalyn almost sighed with relief.

He believed her.

No laughter or telling her she was mistaken. Just validation that she had seen something that perhaps she shouldn't have. Not that that was entirely comforting, but it did explain why those things had then decided to follow her home.

Finally something about all of this was beginning to make some sense, even if it was frightening to think they were after her now.

"Woah, woah, woah," Oliver interrupted, waving his arms through the air before he stepped in front of her, "are you trying to tell me that those things, that they aren't human?"

"Thought you would have figured that out by now, doc."

"What else do you see?" Niko muttered quietly, making her flinch when she noticed how close he'd shuffled toward her, almost whispering the words, ignoring Oliver entirely.

"I..." Rosalyn began, her throat constricting as she tried to get the words out.

After years and years of name calling. Being laughed at and conditioned to believe that it was all a fabrication of her mind, the words wouldn't come.

Her focus lost, she blinked back tears, unwilling to risk the humiliation all over again.

Oliver was already struggling to make sense of whatever he had seen back at her apartment. How would he ever believe the other things she saw?

And these men; what if they weren't demons at all? What if they were from the government dealing with some rogue experiment like Oliver had mentioned before? They would laugh at her.

"It's alright," Niko spoke softly, holding onto her forearm before he placed a hand to her forehead, his skin warm and somewhat soothing despite the sight of his eyes clouding over. No longer golden in colour, or even black, but a murky white. A strange throbbing in her head making her wince and attempt to pull back.

Niko lowered his hand with a frown. The golden shade of his eyes returning after he blinked across at her several times.

"Impossible."

"Yeah. I meant to tell you that wouldn't work," the other man remarked, his brows dipped between his eyes as he scowled in their direction. His hands clenched into tight firsts that he attempted to hide by crossing his arms.

"Your memory alteration had no effect either."

Rosalyn wasn't sure she followed what he was saying, but the more they spoke, the more confident she felt that these men weren't human.

Perhaps she had never been crazy, it was just that the rest of the world couldn't believe in anything different, or more superior than themselves. Or that there were people out there somewhere that had to keep it a secret to prevent mass panic.

"You're, demons?" she asked at last knowing how ridiculous she sounded speaking the words aloud even though she felt like a weight had been lifted from her, her gaze instinctively seeking out Oliver to gauge his reaction. Unsurprised when she saw his raised brows and that curve of his lips where he tried to hold back his laughter.

"Really, Rose? Demons? Are you sure you didn't bump your head?" he snickered, crossing his arms over his chest as he looked down on her with a mixture of amusement and pity, making her feel small and pathetic.

73

Stupid even.

Perhaps she should have just kept her mouth shut and tried to figure this all out on her own, like she was used to. At least then she wouldn't be getting these looks that made her heart ache as it beat frantically in her chest, struggling to catch her breath.

"Demons? Shouldn't they have horns, or wings? Scaly skin perhaps?"

"Only on weekends," the man with the mismatched eyes scoffed. "Don't believe everything you read or hear in stories, doc."

At first Rosalyn thought that he was joining in, mocking and having a laugh at her expense. Nothing she wasn't used to. But his sneer wasn't aimed at her, but at Oliver instead.

"What makes you think that?" Niko asked, his eyes open wide, flickering between his golden shade and black as she tried to force herself not to turn away.

"Your eyes," she whispered, finding it impossible to keep eye contact no matter how hard she tried.

Those black eyes reminded her of all the creatures she'd seen growing up. All the creatures other people had told her were not real, insisting she was wrong. "T-they change."

"She sees through the glamour?" the other man asked, taking several steps in their direction, his own eyes different from Niko's. Never changing. And yet, she believed him to be a demon from the moment she met him.

"Careful, brother."

"She already knows, Niko. What's the point in denying it?"

Niko pinched the bridge of his nose and shook his head. His eyes the shade of pitch when his gaze returned to her.

"I could–"

"No. It didn't work, remember? Nor should it be repeated. She deserves the truth."

Rosalyn struggled for breath, looking from one man to the other while her whole body shook.

Finally someone believed her. But not only that. He wanted to tell her the truth.

All those who had told her she was a liar. That no such thing existed. They were the ones who were wrong, not her. Demons existed. They were right in front of her.

"The Council won't be pleased if they discover this."

"Then we just need to make sure that they don't."

"You're all insane," Oliver snapped. "There's no such thing. Demons don't walk among us. They can't."

Rather than responding, the man strolled toward Oliver, drawing his sword. The sound of the metal scraping against its sheath making Rosalyn gasp and plaster her hands across her mouth, unsure what he planned to do with it.

"I have no need to prove myself to you, human," he sneered, glancing in her direction before he shoved the sword into Oliver's hand. "But for her, I will."

The weapon now in Oliver's grasp, the man gripped the blade and forced Oliver's hand to move, slicing across his own hand, flashing a satisfied smirk when he let out a little shriek and stumbled backward, watching the blood bead on the surface of his palm.

The man then yanked the sword away and pressed it even deeper, letting out a grunt as it split his flesh, the blood now oozing from the wound as Oliver looked on in horror.

Rosalyn jumped to her feet, her instinct taking over

at the sight of so much blood. But there, before her eyes, she saw the bleeding slow and his skin close leaving nothing but a small red line across his palm after he wiped the blood away on his jeans.

"That's – That's not possible," Oliver stuttered, his eyes open wide when he turned to her and Niko, gasping and stumbling backward when Niko's eyes changed colour. Both of them giving him, and her, proof in their own different way.

It was an odd feeling knowing that she had been right all along, unsure how she felt learning that demons really existed, and that she had wasted so many of her years in Greenbryer when there was nothing wrong with her.

"What else do you see?" the man asked, mimicking Niko's earlier question as he crossed the room toward her, stopping alarmingly close considering his reaction to touch.

Rosalyn gulped down the lump in her throat, unsure how to answer him as she stated up into his eyes, astounded by how wrong she had been about them before.

They weren't just different colours, convincing herself that his dark eye was merely a deep brown instead of the black she had come to associate with demons.

It was definitely black, like an onyx gem. Only instead of his iris being a solid colour like Niko's when they changed and doubled in size, his appeared to be shattered. Littered with white specks that reminded her of a night sky. More beautiful than she would have ever thought possible.

"Y-your skin is patterned, " she whispered, averting her gaze in an attempt to hide the blush burning in her cheeks, unsure whether the pattern was visible to others or not. Getting her answer when he raised a brow and the

76

corner if his mouth lifted into a knowing smile.

"A-and your eyes," she rushed to add. "They don't change like his."

"Mine are broken," he sneered, that smile gone from his lips before he turned away from her abruptly and plonked down on a nearby seat. His fingers digging into the soft armrests.

His eyes were clearly a sore subject for him. But instead of backing away from him like she knew she should, Rosalyn followed, perching on the edge of the table in front of him, staring at his sleeved arm.

It didn't take him long before he sighed and rolled up his sleeve, revealing the pattern to her once more.

"They move," she gasped, scooting a little closer, reaching a hand toward him, flinching when his chest rumbled with an animalistic growl.

Careful not to touch, she hovered her hand above his skin, following the pattern with her fingertip, tracing it in the air.

"So, are we allowed to leave?" Oliver asked the moment Niko returned to the room, sipping from the bottle he held in his hand.

Rosalyn had wondered the same thing herself.

She was grateful to them both for arriving at her apartment when they had, as well as getting her and Oliver away from those creatures back there, but she wasn't sure if she was ready to step into their world just yet, giving up on the life she had finally begun to make for herself.

Though seeing unusual creatures wasn't exactly new for Rosalyn, her life had been going smoothly and relatively normal for the last few years.

She had friends for the first time in what felt like

forever, and a place she was able to call her own. Goals that she was working toward and making good progress on. The thought of becoming a doctor someday the only thing that kept her going through some very dark, troubling days.

She didn't think she was ready to give up all of that.

All her life she had been dictated to. Told what was right for her and what was wrong. Never feeling like she had a home of her own, or a place she felt like she could belong.

Finally everything was going according to her plan and then all of this happened. Now she felt conflicted.

Part of her wanted nothing more than to forget about everything that had happened and just go home, carrying on with the semi-normal life she had built up around her whether it was real or not. Unsure whether these men, these demons, were trustworthy. Terrified of what other creatures lurked out there after coming face to face with something so strange and frightening as those she had met tonight, and over the last week.

The other part of her was curious. Relieved even.

What were those creatures, and where had they come from? How many more creatures were out there that she had never seen or heard of before?

Growing up, Rosalyn had seen so many different people. Some she believed to be demons. Others vampires, animal shifters, and even some faeries. Some of them had frightened her, others were just in passing. But the more people told her they weren't real, the more terrifying each encounter became. She was just a child, she didn't know how to make it stop.

Now she knew they were real and she wanted to know more.

She wanted to know about Niko and the other two

demons she had met.

Brother he had called the one with mismatched eyes, whether that was by blood or some other bond, she wasn't sure, but she wanted to know.

But most importantly, she wanted to know why.

Why her? Why could she see these creatures when it seemed that nobody else could unless they chose to show themselves?

"Be my guest, doc," Niko shrugged, slouching into the chair before taking another long swig of the drink in his hand, "but I wouldn't suggest returning to the hospital, or your apartment. At least, not yet."

"But your friend already dealt with those men, didn't he?" Oliver asked.

"They're not men," Niko grumbled, shaking his head before turning his attention to her. "We call those creatures Soulless, and yes. My brother took care of those at Rosalyn's apartment just now, but that isn't all of them."

Rosalyn shuddered at the name he gave them, her heart racing the longer he watched her.

The thought of more of those things out there waiting sent a chill down her spine.

She would prefer never to have to see another one of them again. Their smiles were beyond creepy. The way they moved, odd and disturbing, reminding her of how spirits flicked around the room in movies.

"Didn't you say they were only after me because I saw them? Surely I am safe now that those in the hospital are gone?" Rosalyn muttered, unsure of herself.

She didn't want to think of those creatures still chasing her, but she couldn't bring herself to believe it was all over yet. She had never been that lucky, why would her luck change now?

"It's possible," Niko commented, staring at the bottom of his bottle, swishing the remnants around, "but I can't be sure. Those Soulless tonight, those that use the blades and can somehow speak are new to us. We don't know how many of them there are, or what they want, or even how they communicate."

"So, we can't leave?"

"On the contrary. You're free to go whenever you wish," Niko groaned, gesturing toward the front door with an outstretched arm, "but my brothers and I won't always be able to protect you. We have other things we must do."

Oliver didn't hesitate, already headed toward the door while Rosalyn remained frozen in place, still unsure what choice to make.

She could think of no reason for these Soulless creatures to seek her out again, but her feet were planted to the ground unwilling to budge.

Her head told her to leave, but it was her instincts alone that had gotten her this far, she wasn't prepared to ignore them now. Something insisting there was more to it.

Why had they been at the hospital in the first place?

"Great, thanks. You coming, Rose?"

"Could we not wait until it's daylight?" she mumbled, wrapping her arms tightly around her middle, trying to ignore both their stares.

The dark had always made her feel more alone and vulnerable. The majority of those creatures she had seen when she was younger showed up when the sun went down, whether that was because they preferred it when less people were nearby, or because she was more jumpy and always looking over her shoulder, she wasn't sure.

Either way, she didn't feel comfortable about heading back home. At least not yet.

CHAPTER 10

Rayner lay atop his bed, staring up at the wood beamed ceiling.

Yet again, he couldn't find sleep.

He'd thought that having the female in the next room might help, putting his mind at ease knowing that she was safe now, but if anything it just made it worse. It was torture.

Now all those thoughts and images of her that ran through his mind daily were accompanied by a burning need deep within him to touch. To hold her against his skin and lose himself to his desires.

What an idiot. He needed to focus, not think about some crazy fantasies that would never happen.

Not only would he have to suffer the agony that her contact would cause him, she was petrified. Not that he could blame her. It wasn't every day that you were chased by creatures like the Soulless, or saved by demons. Though if Rayner were honest, he suspected that all of this wasn't entirely new to her.

She'd known there was something odd about those that had chased her, and she had known they were demons before he had been aware of just how easily she was able to see them.

From the moment he had woken in that hospital he'd known she was unique, and not just because of the silence. Only now he was beginning to see just how unique she truly was.

Someone like her shouldn't even exist, yet here she was. Able to see Niko's eyes shift despite the glamour he kept in place, and the glyphs on his skin that only the Other should be able to see.

She'd even seen the Soulless through their mist, before they had attacked, something that even they struggled to do at times, relying on their senses to know when they were close, and where they hid.

Then there was her mind. So tightly sealed that even Niko with his superior psychic abilities was unable to penetrate, claiming he had never seen such complicated shielding before. His mind alteration on their first encounter having had no effect on her. Something that had never happened before.

She was a mystery, and Rayner was fascinated by her, and his reactions toward her.

"What do you want?" Rayner asked, not bothering to face Niko when he heard him open the door, not until he caught the scent of wild berries lingering in the air, causing his body to stiffen. His attention focused fully on her when she appeared, shifting her weight from one foot to the other. Her eyes darting between them.

"It's time to return them home."

"What?" Rayner growled, kicking his legs over the side of his bed to sit and face them. His fingers buried deep into the sheets below him, clenching tight.

He suspected something like this might happen, especially after bringing the damn doctor along, but he had hoped he was wrong.

Damn it. She couldn't return there.

Niko might believe that the Soulless had only targeted her because she had seen them back in the hospital, but Rayner wasn't so sure.

There had to have been a reason for them to go to the hospital in the first place, and he didn't think it was because of him. Nor did it explain why they had followed her and attacked her at her apartment, not when he and Lorkan had already taken care of those that had seen her in the hospital.

Henry had warned him not to return to the hospital for whatever reason as well, and he needed to know why, and what he knew.

Rosalyn was more involved in this than either she or Niko believed, he was sure of it.

"They wish to return and we can't keep them here."

"Like hell we can't," Rayner spat, pushing away from the bed to stalk toward Niko with a deathly glare, freezing when he saw her flinch and shrink away from him, behind Niko.

Niko made no attempt to move, just stood still, frowning at him, but he wasn't the only one surprised by his reaction.

Rayner wasn't the sort to be protective over anybody beside his brothers, but with her things were different. He gave a damn about whether she lived or died. The thought of her so much as being injured filling him with rage.

"You know what the Council will do if they find them here, with us."

Niko was right. Damn it, he always was. But that didn't make it right.

If they took her home, the Soulless could easily come back, and he wasn't able to wait around forever to keep an eye on her despite his wish to do so.

There were too many Soulless around town for him to ignore, and there was always a risk that a rogue Other would turn up.

He was still a Warrior after all and would suffer punishment if he didn't do his job.

And as Niko so rightly pointed out, there was the threat of the Council.

If they discovered her abilities, if they weren't aware of them already, they would kill her, or experiment on her to discover more information.

He couldn't let them have her.

"We cannot force them against their will."

Rayner growled loudly, running a hand through his hair before he squeezed his eyes closed and clenched his teeth.

Neither option was satisfactory, but at least, staying here, with them, he could have kept her safe and hidden. Sending her home back to her apartment was asking for trouble. But yet again, Niko was right. Rayner hadn't been able to force her to come with him back then, and he couldn't keep her here now either.

He would just have to keep an eye on her as he had before and hope that he wasn't too late like he had almost been this time.

"Fine," he snarled, snatching his sword from the cabinet beside his bed, fastening the strap across his back.

As far as bad ideas went, this had to be one of Niko's worst.

He may not be able to sense any Soulless nearby, or inside, but he could see that her window had merely been blocked by a few flimsy looking boards that stood no chance against another attack, her front door cordoned off by police tape.

The female that Rosalyn shared her apartment with had likely gone to stay with friends or family whilst investigations were carried out, leaving her alone in this place.

"Would they have gone after Sara?" Rosalyn asked, peering around him toward the front door, her hair tumbling over her shoulder, hands clasped tightly together in her lap as she nibbled on her lip. Tears in her eyes.

"No."

He lied of course. He wanted to put her mind at ease, and truth be told, he had no idea whether they would follow her friend or not.

The Soulless he knew before wouldn't have unless they were starved. Humans didn't have enough energy for them to bother with so they tended to go ignored. This new breed however, none of them knew their aim, or if they fed in the same way as the others. They hadn't seen it.

Somehow though, she saw through his lie, scowling across at him before he turned back to the front door with a sigh.

"She wasn't here when they appeared, so it's unlikely."

She seemed more satisfied with his response this time, nodding absentmindedly when he turned his attention back to her, noting how she stared at the tape blowing in the breeze.

"Is there somewhere else you can stay? With family or another friend perhaps? It's not safe here."

Staying somewhere else with other people might not be as safe as staying with him, but it was better than allowing her to return here, especially with nobody around and the building even less secure than it was before thanks to the Soulless, and him.

"No."

His hands clenched around the steering wheel unsure

whether he was angry at her defiance for wishing to head back inside after all she had seen, or at the tears he could see on the verge of falling from her red, glassy eyes.

"Then you should stay with us. At least until your house has been cleared. It could take weeks for them to arrange another apartment for you."

She turned to him slowly, her brows furrowed between her shimmering blue eyes as she watched him. Some of that sadness he'd glimpsed before seeming to dissipate.

"You may not trust us, which is understandable, but surely you know staying here would be foolish."

She didn't answer. He didn't expect her to.

Her eyes just flicked back toward her front door, hands tucked between her thighs.

"Our job is to protect others from creatures like the Soulless. We aren't going to hurt you, or keep you prisoner. Should you wish to leave at any time, we can bring you back here, or wherever you wish to go."

Trying to reason with her before hadn't worked, but she'd been frightened of him and Lorkan then. Perhaps now she had seen they weren't necessarily the bad guys, what with the terror she must have felt when the Soulless invaded her home, a more gentle approach might work.

Niko may not have been able to sway her, but Rayner doubted he had the same level of determination that he did, and with the doctor not here to make things more difficult, she might listen.

He could tell that she was no fool. Stubborn, he could believe as she looked around him once more, weighing up her options, but he would be damned if he let her stay in that building.

"I don't really have a lot of choice, do I?" she

mumbled, letting out a long breath, leaning back in her chair defeated. "I'll need to leave Sara a note though."

"No," he snapped, brushing some of the loose strands of his hair back from his eyes.

"She needs to know that I'm alright, otherwise I'll just have to wait around here until I can tell her myself," she argued a little firmer than he had expected, his smile impossible to hold back after witnessing a little more of that courage she had shown before.

She had every right to be afraid. The Soulless were damn creepy. Then there was them.

It wasn't everyday you found yourself in the company of demons, and what with their silly superstitions and movies making them out as monsters, she had to be wary of them as well. But she was far braver than he thought even she realised.

"Alright. I guess we will need to head in and grab you a few bits anyway. Just make sure not to mention where you are, or who you're with. You might want to inform the hospital that you need some time off too."

"Wait, those things can read?"

Rayner shrugged. It hadn't been too long ago that he had wondered the same thing, but honestly, he didn't know. None of them did.

If she had asked him a few months ago, he would have likely laughed at the idea. The Soulless they fought then nothing more than brain dead creatures, much like the zombies humans found so fascinating. Food being the only thing that drove them. Their tastes aimed toward the Other and their more powerful energy that sustained them for longer periods. Now things were different. The rules had changed.

These evolved Soulless were smarter and much more

organised. Searching for something and fighting them every step of the way. A war waging between them.

Slowly Rayner glanced across to her, hoping he was wrong, that she wasn't involved in some way. That it was all just a case of her being in the wrong place at the wrong time. This odd sight of hers, her shields and her ability to silence the thoughts in his head just making her a target they stumbled across.

This war between the Warriors and the Soulless was only just beginning. More and more of them were emerging all the time. He hated the idea of her being stuck in the middle of it.

"Lets go," he grunted, climbing from the car, waiting for her to join him. "Stay close."

He wasn't sure that she would listen, but she did as he instructed, moving even closer than he had anticipated, her hand grasping the hem at the back of his t-shirt, making his body tense.

"Is this, ok?" she asked, her big eyes searching his face.

Unable to breathe, let alone speak, Rayner nodded, staring back into the deep blue of her eyes before he blinked and forced himself to turn away.

It was dangerous to allow her so close to his skin, especially if it turned out that he was wrong and there were Soulless inside, but instead of doing the smart thing and insisting she remove her hand, keeping her at a safe distance, he found himself longing for her to move closer. To touch him.

Idiot, he growled to himself, realising the sound hadn't been as silent as he thought when she tugged slightly on his t-shirt at the noise.

"I think it's clear," he commented, clearing his throat

before he tore through the police tape and pushed the door open, stepping inside first to make sure that nobody had managed to hide from him.

"Still, let's make this quick."

CHAPTER 11

It wasn't the first time Rosalyn had come back to the apartment when nobody was home. Sara was often on a different shift to her, or she would be out for the evening with some of her other friends, or the next guy, but for some reason this felt different. Empty.

The demon Niko had called Rayner stood close to her as they made her way through the living space.

Unusual dust piles littered the floor and black gunk that she assumed came from those creatures, the Soulless, their name alone sending shivers down her spine. Each stain on the carpet highlighted with little numbers were the police had come to take evidence.

"They won't find anything," the demon commented, following her gaze to the red mark on the floor, likely to be his blood from the wound he'd had across his chest.

Though she didn't doubt his words, not after the police hadn't been able to find any bodies or clues outside the hospital, and down the streets she'd attempted to flee, it was somewhat relieving to hear him say it.

All those officers had given her a variety of expressions, all of them skeptical and mocking in their own way. Their words may have been chosen carefully and lacking in judgement, but they couldn't hide the pity in their tone. Not one of them believing what she claimed to have seen.

"The Soulless don't leave fingerprints, and their

blood won't show much information in any forensic tests your police might run," he continued, disturbing a pile of dust with his boot. "This is all that remains of them once they die."

Rosalyn nodded absent-mindedly following her feet toward her room, hesitant when she saw more tape secured across her door.

The demon paused too, glancing briefly at her before he gripped the hilt of the sword strapped to his back and tore through the tape, stepping into the room before her.

Inside was carnage. Nothing like out here.

More stains marked the carpet and her sheets. A couple more dust piles near the doorway. Almost all of her furniture toppled over. The contents of her draws and the wardrobe pulled out, most of the items torn or broken. Shards of glass still shining on the ground below the window, catching the light that broke through the cracks in the thin wooden strips they'd used to board it up.

With trembling hands, Rosalyn stepped further into the room, that same strong scent of flowers she'd noticed when near those creatures irritating her nose.

Making a mental note to ask him about that later, when her heart wasn't in her throat and she was able to think more clearly without the fear of those things coming back, Rosalyn began to fumble through her belongings, searching for anything she could salvage and take with her.

She still wasn't sure she was doing the right thing by returning to that cabin with the demon, but she couldn't stay here. It would be far too easy for someone, or rather, something to get in with the front door barely holding on to its hinges after he'd kicked it in, and the flimsy wooden boards the police had used to cover her broken window. She wouldn't be able to relax, and she certainly wouldn't be able to sleep.

Just being here now was putting her on edge, wondering whether they would come back while they were here. In fact, she wasn't sure she would ever feel comfortable here again. A new apartment in a different building would perhaps ease her mind, but this particular one, no. Those creepy faces banging and scraping on the glass would forever haunt her dreams.

All of those unusual creatures she had seen growing up never prepared her for something like them.

Maybe if she had believed in the things she saw. If people hadn't convinced her that it was all imaginary, things might have been different.

They were real. All of them, the demon behind her a constant reminder of just how wrong all those people were.

With a deep breath, Rosalyn looked across at him, watching his movements.

Everything about him appeared so human, and likely to everyone else who met him, he was. Oliver had believed as much, but she could feel something different about him, even more now than she had before. Whether that was because she knew what he was and had decided not to argue it any longer, or whether the power that seemed to radiate from him seemed to be stronger whilst he was in this defensive state.

Unlike Niko whose eyes changed black, the same as all those other demons she believed she had seen in the past, his remained unchanging. *Broken* he'd called them, and she believed him. That shattered effect she'd noticed both beautiful, and breathtaking, unlike anything she had ever seen before. And also, a little sad. Her previous judgement and snappy comments seemed a little unfair now that she knew what he was.

He and his brothers weren't just some monsters killing men for no reason. They were demons, dealing with creatures terrifying enough that even they seemed on edge around them.

Perhaps once all of this had sunk in properly, able to come to terms with the fact that she had seen these creatures for years, never believing in herself, she might attempt to learn a little more about them and this world she seemed to have been sucked into since she was a child. Maybe then she might come to understand how and why she was able to see them when nobody else could.

Rosalyn was just beginning to relax on their car journey back to the cabin, her eyes growing heavy when he stopped the car in the middle of nowhere.

Trees surrounded them in every direction, the canopy of leaves above blocking out what little sunlight remained as the sun dipped lower beyond the horizon, painting the sky orange and purple.

"Why are we stopping?" she asked, her pitch a little higher than she would have liked, showing just how nervous he still made her.

She may be coming to terms with the fact that he was a demon, like her brain had insisted from their first encounter, and she now understood his actions outside the hospital when he had killed those things she had thought were just unusual men, but she couldn't help but feel as though there was something else he was keeping from her, putting her on edge.

"The car could have been followed," he answered, reaching behind him to grab the small bag she'd filled earlier from the back seat of the car, tossing it over his shoulder before he climbed from the car.

"We switch between two cars that we leave in one of four different areas in the woods, keeping track of which car is where in case we need to leave suddenly. It isn't wise to leave them outside the cabin, drawing attention like we did last night," he explained when she joined him on his side of the car, her heart hammering in her chest as she scanned the trees around them.

Normally Rosalyn adored the woods and nature, enjoying a stroll through them, seeing what hidden things she could spot when she got the chance, but with those things still out here, and the rapidly darkening sky, she wasn't sure she liked the thought of being outside.

Keeping her thoughts and fears to herself, she followed along behind him, her eyes darting this way and that, checking over her shoulder every time she heard a sound. Her heart pounding even faster as she squeezed her hands tight and practically ran to catch up with him each time she felt that the distance between them was too great.

"Am I going too fast for you?" he asked, his sudden question and abrupt stop startling her.

"N-no."

"You're afraid of the dark?"

"No," she snapped, frowning up at him, "just a little concerned about what might come out of it."

"The Soulless move just as freely during the day as they do the night," he commented, his admission not helping her tattered nerves in the slightest.

At least before, believing they only came out at night had helped her feel safer during the day. Now, not so much.

"Thanks," she huffed, hugging her arms around her middle when he started to walk again, keeping a little closer to him than she had before, careful not to get within touching distance, despite her longing to grab hold of his arm in order to feel a little bit safer, and steadier on her feet.

"Has it always been that way?" she asked, both a little curious about him, wanting to learn more, and needing a distraction from their current predicament.

"What?"

"Your *Dermatographia*?"

"What's that?"

She was positive she had pronounced the term correctly, remembering what Oliver had muttered when he noticed the marks on his skin from the doctors and nurses touching back at the hospital, looking up what the condition was for herself in the days that passed after, when she'd been unable to forget their encounter. Perhaps he had just never been diagnosed, or it was something else entirely. He wasn't human after all. Though it couldn't be something that all demons suffered with. Niko had been able to touch her and retain contact without any discomfort. And that other demon outside the hospital, he'd grabbed her and held her against him without the same reaction.

"It's a condition that makes the skin inflamed and sore with contact, also known as skin writing."

"It's not some condition, it's a damn curse," be growled, his hand clenched around the handle of the bag slung over his shoulder. His jaw set hard when he glanced back at her rushing to keep up with his much longer strides. "And no, it hasn't always been this way."

"O-oh."

Rosalyn wasn't sure what was worse. Having never experienced the closeness and pleasure of another person's touch. Anything from a simple brush of the hand, or a lover's embrace, to something a little more intimate; or having known all of those things and having it all taken away from you, never able to feel them again. Stuck with nothing but memories of the times you were able to get close to another, only now for it to cause you pain. And it didn't appear to be the kind of pain you could brush off or take some medicine for either. It had looked excruciating. The simplest of touches, even a mere brush making him hiss or growl. Which made her wonder why he had allowed her to hold onto his t-shirt before, knowing what he would have to endure should either of them slip.

Perhaps he wasn't this cold, killing machine she had thought him to be, allowing her to take some comfort in him when she had needed it.

How selfish of her to think of him in such a way, putting him through that unnecessary stress just to put herself at ease.

"Thank you," she whispered, walking in step with him after he had slowed down a few paces, clearly having noticed her struggling, again proving that he wasn't as uncaring as she'd first thought.

"What for?"

"I realised I hadn't actually said it before," she sighed, turning from his gaze to hide her blazing cheeks.

She hadn't meant for him to hear her, even though she did want him to know that she was grateful for everything.

"I know you were only trying to help us against those, Soulless things."

"You."

"Pardon?"

"I was trying to protect you. The doctor just got in my way."

97

"O-oh."

She hadn't expected that, his answer deepening the blush of her cheeks as she instructed herself not to read too much into his comment when he glanced in her direction.

It wasn't as though he had some personal interest in her, why would he? She was just a human, and he wasn't.

No, it was only his job that made him feel the need to protect her. That and the need to keep their secret safe, not only from her now knowing the truth, but because of her ability to see them so clearly.

CHAPTER
12

"Finally decided to show, did you?" Henry sneered the moment Rayner entered the Great hall and made his way across the room.

"You were summoned three days ago, and only Niko'stratos and Xander bothered to appear before us."

"We've been busy, or did it perhaps slip your mind that there were Soulless gathering in the streets? It wasn't wise to all come at once."

Henry made a snarling noise but decided not to argue any further about his tardiness, bringing a smirk to Rayner's lips.

Of all the leaders on the Council over the years, Henry was by far one of the worst. A tyrant that believed he was untouchable, angering even his own members, leaving the Council more divided than it had ever been. Those that supported him and his reign sitting by his side while more and more that opposed him joined with the resistance. A group formed before his time, led by a powerful vampire Lord by the name, Lothaire.

Once the Council had been a great thing for their kind. A strong group of men and women who governed all Other, working together to keep them secret and safe from the humans. Integrating themselves into high positions in human society in order to keep tabs on their world, and how much information they had discovered. Hiring the Warriors all over the world to act as a police of sorts, taking out the rogues that threatened exposure, and dealing with the threat of more bloodthirsty creatures, like the Soulless.

But over the last decade, things have shifted.

More and more leaders grew hungry for power, corrupting the Council at its core. Killing and bribing in order to get to the top and make some changes of their own, often for the worse. Henry just like those before him, taking out the competition until he reached the top.

The majority of the Council turned a blind eye to his deeds in favour of a more strict leadership. The rest of them joined Lothaire.

Rayner and his brothers had attempted to keep out of all the politics, just continuing with their duties as they had for the last few decades. Once proud to be called elite soldiers, tasked with keeping the Other safe, until their brother, Helmer, was taken from them. Killed in cold blood like their predecessors.

All of them believed Henry and a handful of his followers were to blame for the incident.

Helmer may have been one of the most unstable of them, often being reckless in their hunts, but that didn't mean he deserved to die.

For years they had hunted for the proof they needed to bring Henry down, but he was too clever and hid his tracks well, killing some of his own in order to keep their lips sealed. Punishing Rayner and his brothers when they refused to continue their work under his reign and lashed out at the Council when they discovered the news.

"I'm here now, so what was so important that you called all of us?" Rayner grumbled, crossing his arms over his chest, fighting the overwhelming urge to pull out his sword and run it through the old vampire's heart, putting an end to all their worries.

"We were wondering whether you had made any progress with these new Soulless?" Karl answered, his fingers steepled in front of his face, shaking his head gently from side to side.

Since their brother's death, each of them had paid the resistance many visits in order to gain more information, Kael being a top ranking member who had earned their respect. So when the shifter warned them like he was warning Rayner now, they tended to listen, even if it was difficult.

With Rosalyn waiting back at the cabin for him, his emotions all over the place, threatening to consume him.

He needed to get this meeting over with so he could leave sooner rather than later, so he had to bite his tongue and answer the questions asked and listen to Henry.

"They're more intelligent than we first thought. Not only able to use these weapons, but also able to speak."

Many gasps filled the silence, followed by their hushed whispers, some of their voices reaching Rayner's mind when they dropped the concentration on their shields, making him wince and rub his temples, but not Henry he noticed. He sat above the rest of them as always, a half smirk on his thin lips, taking great pleasure in seeing Rayner suffer.

"We need to capture one and see if it has any answers for us," one member chimed in, shifting uncomfortably in his seat.

"Don't be absurd," Henry spat, his eyes crimson when he turned his glare back at Rayner, "your job is to kill them, so get on with it."

"We would, but we keep getting summoned to these pointless meetings," Rayner bit back, unable to hold his tongue for much longer.

"Sure, but don't we need to know where they're coming from? What they could be after?"

101

"More will come, they always do."

"We need answers."

Henry stood from his seat and slammed his hands upon his desk, silencing all the questions and chatter, pointing toward the young Fae who first spoke out.

A handful of guards stepped forward and dragged him away.

Rayner gritted his teeth in order to keep silent, knowing exactly what the bastard had planned for anyone who spoke against him, the glyphs over his skin itching in reminder of his own disobedience.

"Your job is to come when called, Warrior, not to ask questions and rile up my Council. You do as you're told, like the good *pet* you are."

Rayner snapped.

No amount of pleading and cues from Kael would hold him back enough to rein in the fury Henry had unleashed within him with those words.

He pulled his sword free from behind his back and launched it through the air toward Henry's head. The tip embedding deep into the plush cushion of the seat mere inches from his cheek.

The vampire opened his eyes wide, his face more ashen than normal as he stumbled away, glaring at the sword and Rayner.

"Let me make this perfectly clear," Rayner snarled as he stalked forward, jumping up onto the desk to pry his sword free, leaving it to hover in the air between them while he stood face to face with Henry, ignoring the remaining guards who circled in on him from behind. "I am nobody's pet, especially yours."

"You're still a Warrior, and I am–"

"You may lead the Council for now," Rayner

sneered, glaring over his shoulder toward the guards, making them freeze in their tracks before he turned his fury back to Henry, closing the distance between them, knowing full well that he wouldn't dare to touch him and risk revealing any of his own secrets, "but you do not control me, and you never will."

Rayner hopped back down from the desk, and was immediately set upon and grappled by the guards, causing him to roar in agony, sending several of them flying across the room before more came and they were able to overpower him.

"T-take him to Deyanira," Henry shouted above Rayner's howls, some of the colour returning to his cheeks when he sank back into his chair, smoothing his hair and suit back into place. The crash of voices in Rayner's head now becoming unbearable as more and more hands tried to pin him down, struggling to restrain him, until the pain became too much and he succumb to the darkness, the room fading to black; but not before he caught sight of Kael pinching his nose and shaking his head.

CHAPTER 13

"You look rough," Niko commented when Rayner entered the cabin and slumped onto one of the worn out arm chairs, his head still pounding after all those voices had bombarded his mind. The constant back stabbing and bickering of the Council laughable.

"That's just his face," Lorkan chuckled, earning himself a glare from both of them, which only made him laugh harder.

"The usual. Henry and his overbearing self. Being dragged out by the guards," Rayner sighed, wincing as he reached forward for the glass of water in front of him. All the burns across his body stinging with the movement.

"You need to learn to control your anger better, Rayner. We can't lose another brother."

"Did he send you to Deyanira?" Lorkan mumbled, all hint of his earlier amusement vanished when he noticed the brightness of Rayner's markings across his stomach where he leaned back and draped a hand across his eyes to soothe his aching head, exposing some of his skin, the cool air soothing the burns slightly.

Rayner nodded, a shudder working its way through his body at the memory of her hands caressing his skin, focusing more and more of that spirit magic she used into his glyphs, making them stronger and spread further across his body. Toying with him and taking great pleasure in being the only creature able to touch him without him screaming out in pain.

"As if you need to ask," Niko snarled, slamming his

104

own glass to the table with a deafening thud. His own distaste for the half breed as clear as day upon his face. "It's difficult knowing who is working for who with those two."

"I always got the impression that she was in charge," Lorkan snickered, chugging a can of beer while he slouched in his chair, glancing in Rayner's direction every now and then. "It's a shame though, If she weren't so twisted, she'd be damn hot."

Rayner scrunched his nose in disgust, finding it impossible to ever think of her as attractive after all she had done to them.

She may have been beautiful to most men, human and Other alike, but certainly not to him.

The only creature Rayner felt any desire for was Rosalyn. Her wild berry scent lingering in the air, making his body stiffen even now as it enveloped him.

Taking a deep breath he leaned forward in his seat, expecting to find her standing at the entrance to the room.

Nothing.

Niko froze too, holding a hand up to Lorkan before he had a chance to open his mouth and say any more.

"Rosalyn?" Niko called when they heard clumsy footsteps from down the hall, followed by a bang and a whimper.

Rayner was already off his feet and headed down the hall at the first sound of her distress, able to pinpoint her exact location now there was no noise in his head to distract him.

"R-Rayner?" she whispered, her cheeks stained red when she stumbled toward him. Her hands brushing against his chest making him grunt. Her usually beautiful deep blue eyes now pale and milky white as he stared down at her in disbelief.

"What's happening?" she choked, biting down on her bottom lip to stop it quivering. Her hands clutching hold of his t-shirt and tugging him slightly closer until she bumped against him, dropping her hands at his sudden intake of breath. Not that it hurt him as much as he thought it would, the material between them softening the contact. Her touch was more like an electric pulse against his skin that took his breath away. So unlike the pain he'd felt earlier with all those hands on him, leaving his skin tender and sore.

"You had a vision?" Niko mumbled beside him, taking her face between his hands and titling it up toward the lights above so he could see more clearly, her pupils not responding to the sudden change in brightness.

"It's alright," Niko cooed, brushing the bloody tears from her cheeks with his thumb, making Rayner feel useless, unable to do a thing to help calm or soothe her.

"It's not alright, Niko. I can't see!" she shrieked, punching at his chest with her small fists. The way she could tell them apart despite her lack of sight astounding considering the short time in which she had known them.

"I know you're right in front of me. I can feel you there. Yet all I can see is a blur."

"Have you had visions before?" Niko asked, ignoring her pummeling fists as she continued to fight against him, before he gripped her by the upper arms and held her still.

Rayner clenched his fists.

He knew that Niko was the best one for the job. All his life he had dealt with visions. The ability, like Rayner's and the rest of them turned against him after they refused to continue their work for the Council after their brothers death. He would know what was happening to her better than any of them, able to make some sense of it and help her should she trust him enough to do so, but Rayner couldn't help feel angry.

Angry at Niko for stepping between them. And angry at himself and his damn curse for not being able to comfort her when all he wanted to do was wrap her in his arms, making it all go away.

"Not since I was a child," she muttered, shaking her head. Fists now hung loosely by her sides while more red tears flowed from her eyes.

Rayner grit his teeth and turned away.

He wasn't sure why her pain and suffering bothered him so much. All he knew was that he hated it. His shoulder taut and his jaw ached from the pressure of his grinding teeth, wishing he could make it stop.

"Were they frequent? Then I'll wager that this is due to you repressing them for so long, causing them to build," Niko sighed, tipping her chin up gently at her nod. "You can't force them away for long. They will find a way to come through."

"But, I–"

She sounded so broken. So fragile, even though Rayner knew that wasn't true.

He'd seen her courage even when she was afraid. The way she didn't back down, and how she stood her ground. Even her punching Niko's chest just now knowing what he was and what he could do. All of it proof of how brave she really was.

"I imagine your sight will return. You just need to rest your eyes and stop trying to control what you allow yourself to see. Trust yourself."

"How can you be so sure?"

"I speak from experience."

CHAPTER
14

The room was a blur of colour as Rosalyn sat on the edge of the bed, not wishing to move even though her mouth was dry and her legs ached.

She thought that perhaps after some sleep, her vision might return, Niko insisting that all she needed was time.

It hadn't worked.

She knew it was daytime now by the brightness around her, but everything else was still out of focus. Vague shadows and shapes everywhere. But she couldn't sit here forever. She needed a drink and some food, her stomach churning painfully when she attempted to stand, only to stumble when she missed her footing. Her cheeks wet with fresh tears, fearing that this would be her life from now on.

"Shame," a male voice sighed from behind her, making her gasp and fall to the ground with a loud thud, sending shockwaves of pain up her arms and back.

"What does my brother see in you? You're not nearly as strong as I thought you were. Nothing more than a weakling," the voice drawled, a dark shadow looming over her, blocking out some of the light behind him.

"W-who are you?" she asked when he moved closer, an unusual sweet and spicy fragrance tickling her nose. A scent she was almost positive she recognised, but couldn't quite place.

"It's too late. They should have come when they had the chance."

No sooner had the words left his mouth, his breath fanning over her face as he crowded over her, he was gone, leaving her alone on the floor breathing rapidly. The sound of the door suddenly opening drawing her attention to the other side of the room.

"Are you alright?" Rayner asked, Rosalyn easily able to recognise the deep timbre of his voice despite not being able to see him clearly.

"No," she muttered, bringing her knees up to her chest and wrapping her arms around them, wincing when she grabbed the wrist she'd landed badly on.

"Do you need to have that looked at?"

"No," she grumbled, feeling ashamed enough already that he had seen her on the floor like this.

Having more people come in to witness it would only make her mood worse.

All she wanted to do was get back in bed and lay there, hoping that her vision would come back sooner rather than later. She couldn't deal with this much longer. She hated it. This feeling of being completely useless and dependent on those around her.

When she was younger and everyone had turned their backs on her, calling her a liar and a fake that sought attention, she had wished she couldn't see all of the creatures that she did, believing some days that it would be best if she could see nothing at all. Now she knew how wrong she was.

Being unable to see anything in front of her, aside from those indistinct shapes was far more frightening than anything she had ever witnessed growing up. Even that Soulless's face at her window that still haunted her dreams, or that vampire who lead to her being stuck in Greenbryer was better than this. At least before she had been able to see them coming, knowing which way to run.

The man who had been here only moments before

nothing more than a gravelly voice and a scent to her. Unsure whether he had even existed, or whether it was just another vivid vision.

Suddenly something warm and heavy fell over her, causing her to jump. Rayner's shadow hovering above her much like that other males had, their size similar, making her cower and squirm a little closer to the bed behind her. Unable to distinguish the difference between the two without her sight. Until she realised that warmth around her was nothing more than a blanket he had draped over her shoulders. The soft fabric brushing against her cheek when she moved.

"Thank you," she whispered, hugging it close as his dark shape moved a little close, making her grip tightly on the fabric, letting out a small groan when a burning sensation tingled through her hand and wrist.

"Would you like a hand getting back up?" he asked, the concern in his tone bringing a small smile to her lips, wishing she could see the expression on his face to make sure she wasn't imagining it. Curious why he would even care.

"I'll be fine down here, for now."

She stared up at his shape, trying to find something within the dark mass that proved to her that it was really him and not another figment of her imagination.

She reached out a hand where she thought his leg must be, guessing that the dark jeans he tended to wear would be enough to stop her touch being too painful for him, when she heard his sharp intake of breath. A green light shining up high, seeming to break through some of the darkness, exactly where she imagined his head would be.

This had to be him, and now she felt awful for having to hurt him just to make herself feel better.

"I'm sorry," she mumbled, hanging her head. "I wanted to be sure it was really you."

"It's alright," he replied in a breathy whisper when she attempted to pull her arm away, only to be stopped by his hand wrapping around her arm. The blanket between them, cushioning the contact as he held her in place.

"Doesn't it hurt?"

"No," he replied in that same breathy whisper. The green light she had seen earlier glowing even brighter the longer she kept her hand against the coarse fabric of his jeans, his shadow shrinking, the material scraping against her palm as he crouched in front of her. Her hand now rested against his bent knee.

"It's more like a buzz against my skin."

Rosalyn was at a loss for words, remembering all those vivid dreams she'd had after he'd been brought into the hospital that time. Her hands had stroked his body, and their lips met in a passionate kiss. His hands roamed over her, making her feel tremble.

The memories made her cheeks feel like they were on fire, forcing herself to look away from him before he noticed her reaction.

"So, it's just skin contact that hurts? The clothing protects you?" she asked, trying to distract herself from her lustful thoughts, even though she couldn't quite bring herself to remove her hands from his knee as those images continued to flash through her mind. His warmth seeped into her skin, chasing away the horrors of the past few weeks, comforting her. A ridiculous thought seeing as it was a demon of all creatures that she was touching. A monster most would say.

"Not usually like this," he admitted, taking a deep breath when she scooted a little closer so she could relax her outstretched arm, brushing her palm against his thigh when she slipped forward.

"Normally the first brush of contact is a sharp jolt that makes me, or them back off. I tend not to allow more prolonged contact than that, not wishing to test how long it lasts."

So why was he allowing her to touch him like this now? He said it wasn't painful, and she supposed he must miss contact with others, remembering that he said it hadn't always been this way, but still, he must be anxious that she would slip and touch his bare skin. Or that the pain would eventually reach him through the clothing.

"Something about you is *different*."

For once in her life, Rosalyn was glad to be called different. The way he said it, not some sneer or snide remark, but a compliment that made her feel special.

For a long time all she had wanted was to be normal, like everyone else. Not having to see things or have visions that others didn't. Not being forced into a world that she didn't understand, with creatures and things that terrified her. Never having anybody to teach her about any of it. But right now, with Rayner in front of her, she felt a little grateful for her differences.

At first she had blamed him for being pulled back into this world that she didn't want to be a part of. The Soulless only coming after her because of her connection to him, but she knew that wasn't really fair.

She had seen creatures for as long as she could remember, and that had nothing to do with him, or the rest of them. They just happened to appear in her life and forced her to remember who she was, whether she wanted that or not.

Niko was right. There was no escaping any of this.

She'd tried so hard, for so long, and look where it had gotten her. Nowhere. Blinded because people told her that she was a liar, when it was them who had been wrong all along, their judgement of her forcing her to shy away from everything that made her, her.

The more she thought about it, the more she wondered why the Soulless had been at the hospital in the first place, and why they had bothered to follow her home, somehow knowing her name.

Perhaps it wasn't Rayner's fault that they had come, but hers instead.

Niko believed that they had only targeted her because she had seen them snooping inside the hospital, but Rayner seemed to think differently. Why else would he have returned to the hospital after apparently wiping all their memories, including hers?

"Why?" she asked aloud, clenching her hands a little, only to relax them again when she heard him take another deep breath. "Why did you come back that night? To the hospital I mean."

She didn't expect an answer, her hand falling through the air when he moved away and stood in front of her, already missing his body heat, before she heard a thud beside her and felt the bed move back slightly as he sat beside her.

"You're not like other humans."

That was an understatement if she had ever heard one.

The only people who ever treated her as normal were her parents before they had been taken from her. And even then she couldn't be sure. She was so young when they died, unable to remember if those memories of them she held dear were real or not.

Everybody else had thought she was odd. A freak. Able to see things they couldn't. Calling her a heathen. Having visions of things she didn't really understand. People laughed at her whenever she tried to ask for help, until eventually she learned to remain silent and keep it all hidden. Never speaking to anybody about it, until eventually she learnt to lie even to herself. The lie taking hold and making her ignore everything even a little odd around her just so she could fit in and feel accepted.

That was, until he had come into her life and changed everything. All her past coming back to haunt her.

"You, intrigued me."

What does my brother see in you?

That man's voice echoed inside her head.

Could he have been talking about Rayner and his interest in her being an anomaly among humans? Or was she just reading into something that wasn't even real?

"How many brothers do you have?" she asked, curious whether this male she had seen was linked to him in any way.

"I had four brothers Niko and Lorkan you have already met. Xander, you haven't, for good reason."

"And Helmer," he sighed just when Rosalyn was about to say that he had only named three people. Her body erupting into goosebumps, sending a shiver down her spine when she heard that name.

It was him. Helmer. It had to be.

A pressure building inside her head as she tried to picture that man's shadowy figure, looking for anything that would help her distinguish him other than his scent, but there was nothing. No colour other than the blacks and greys of his outline, and a voice that she doubted she would recognise if she heard again.

"He died twenty five years ago."

"Oh."

"Why do you ask?"

"I thought I saw him before you came in," she admitted, not sure how much she should say, still unsure what she had seen and how he would react to her claiming to have met his dead brother.

Rayner remained silent, but Rosalyn could feel the intensity of his eyes boring into her, making her nervous and wish she had just kept her mouth shut. She was normally so good at that. Why had she bothered to say anything?

She didn't know what was happening to her, or what she had seen. Whether it was a vision, or maybe some crazed dream. Never really understanding how the visions worked, or what was happening. But to see someone who was dead was new, even for her.

All she did know was that his words made her feel uneasy.

It's too late. They should have come when they had the chance.

CHAPTER 15

Rosalyn lay staring up at the ceiling, not really able to tell whether her eyes were closed or not. The dark room looked the same no matter what she seemed to do.

Already another day had come and gone, much of it wasted with her resting in this room, hiding and wishing she was back at the hospital doing something, anything, while the demons around her continued to hunt the Soulless. Creatures she still knew nothing about other than that they turned to dust when they died, and that their blood was a thick, black gunk.

She'd meant to ask Rayner and Niko more about them so she could learn what they were, but with losing her sight and all the visions bombarding her it had slipped her mind.

Unable to sleep, Rosalyn kicked her legs over the side of the bed and pulled herself into a sitting position, gazing around the colourless room with a sigh, when she heard a ding beside her, followed by a vibrating noise. A blue light shining brightly in the darkness.

"It's not like I can read it," she grumbled, reaching her hand toward the light, her fingers padding over the cool glass screen of her phone as she lifted it up to her face.

It was bright, despite her blurry eyes, making them water the longer she stared. The phone vibrated once more as she continued to hold it in front of her, only this time it continued to vibrate.

Part of her was curious who would be calling her in the middle of the night, even though she had no idea of the actual time. The other part was saddened, unwilling to talk to anybody right now. The thought alone made her chest feel tight while she clenched the phone in her hand, before tossing it to one side.

"Leave me alone," she sniffed, wiping her hands across her stinging eyes with a frustrated shout, when she heard a rap on the window behind her.

"Rose." She heard a muffled voice call. "Rose. I can see you. Open the window."

Impossible. The voice sounded like Oliver, but why would he be here? Niko had taken him back to the hospital nearly two weeks ago. She had to be imagining it.

"Rosalyn. Come on!" he shouted much louder this time.

There was no mistaking his voice now, but how had he gotten there. He couldn't possibly remember where they lived, could he?

"O-Oliver?" she called back, spinning around on the bed to where she seemed to remember the window being.

"Are they in there?" he asked when she attempted to walk toward him, stumbling every few steps.

"Who?"

"Those men, of course."

"No, I don't think so. What's wrong?"

"Open the window, Rose."

Rosalyn stumbled forward a little more, bashing her shin against the small table by the bedside, making her groan out loud and curse under her breath, but still she pushed herself forward, a little slower this time with her hands out in front of her, searching for the wall, and the windowsill.

A few more paces forward and her fingertips met something solid and grooved.

117

Stepping to the side, sliding her fingers along the surface, she felt her way across the room, bashing her toes on something hard, bringing tears to her eyes, until eventually her hand landed against the cold window pane.

"Rose?"

"One minute," she snapped, fingers padding along the icy surface, hunting for the lock so she could slide the window open.

"What took you so long? Why were you walking like that? It's freezing out here, and creepy as hell in these woods, Rose."

Rosalyn ignored his grumbling, and attempted to step to one side while he climbed inside, grunting and lifting himself through the now open window.

"Where are your things?"

"Pardon?" she asked, looking in the direction she thought he was standing with a frown.

"After that guy dropped me off at the hospital, I phoned the police and then went straight over to your apartment, but it was already sealed with police tape, and Sara had no idea where you were, though she mentioned a note you apparently left behind. Then the hospital informed me that you've taken some time off and I wouldn't be needed to train you for a few weeks."

"The apartment was a mess, so they said I could stay here, with them."

"They let you? Rosalyn, those men are murderers. They manipulated you. Tricked you into staying with them. No doubt they were the ones who trashed the apartment just so that you would agree."

"No."

Rosalyn may still be confused about a lot of things in this supernatural world she was a part of, but deep down

118

she knew these men, these demons were helping her.

Oliver may not have been able to see it, but he hadn't been here the last twelve days like she had, and though some of that time had been in darkness like it was now, she knew they meant her no harm. That they weren't manipulating her.

If they had meant to hurt or kill her, they would have already done so by now. It wasn't as though she could really defend herself against them, even if she wasn't in this state. And Rayner had even left her phone in her room, something he wouldn't have done if he didn't want her to have any freedom.

Nor had Rayner been left inside long enough to cause the amount of damage in her apartment like Oliver seemed to believe. And neither he or Niko had been back there during the night before she was taken back.

She hadn't really had much of a choice when she decided to come back with Rayner, having nowhere else to go, but she didn't regret her decision.

When she had woken, unable to see anything, stumbling out into the hallway, they had come to her and comforted her in their own, odd way. Niko even allowed her to punch at his chest, not realising what she was doing in her frustration and fear until afterwards. And Rayner, despite the pain he faced, he allowed her to actually reach out and touch him, something he admitted that he didn't allow others to do.

"They're all mad. Demons, Rose. Really?"

"They're not mad, Oliver."

"How can you believe them? There is no such thing."

"How can you not?" she snapped, shouting louder than she had intended, pushing out with her hands when he

119

attempted to pull her toward him.

"After everything you have seen, and they showed you, you still don't believe them, or me?"

"You're just–"

"No, Oliver," she interrupted, pushing him back once more when he rested his hand on her shoulder. The action patronising, making her lose her patience with him. "I've had enough of people telling me I'm mad. That what I see isn't real. I don't want to hear it from you too, not when I know you have seen it as well."

She was done with people making her feel like a liar, or some crazy person. Done with trying to hide what she was able to see before she had lost her sight.

He and all the rest were wrong, not her.

She understood that it may be difficult to come to terms with things when you have never believed in them before, and knew that coming from a scientific background that Oliver would struggle perhaps more than most, but she didn't understand how he was still able to deny it when nothing around him was making sense anymore. When there was no logical explanation for the things they had seen.

"W-what have they done to you?" he asked, seeming to ignore her outburst. His fingers digging deeper into her shoulder when he held her still. His breath fanning over her face as he leaned in close. "Your eyes. They did this to you?"

"No, Oliver. I did this to me," she sighed, struggling to break free of his hold before she managed to push him back, needing her space.

Letting him in was suddenly feeling like a very bad idea.

"You did this to me, and everybody else that told me

120

I was a liar. A freak."

Instead of the despair and self loathing that she had been dealing with the last few days, and the majority of her life, Rosalyn felt angry.

If it wasn't for all those people claiming everything was all in her head, and the staff at Greenbryer insisting she was wrong, she wouldn't have repressed and buried her sight or the visions she had. If it wasn't for them, she would have been a little more prepared for the world she was now thrust into, and likely wouldn't be blinded like she was right now either. Niko's theory that it was her visions that overwhelmed her after so long, breaking through despite her forcing them away actually made some sense.

"I don't understand."

"Exactly," she groaned, finally using enough force to push away from him and head back toward the bed, only to bash her toe on the corner, making her pause and take a deep breath.

"Just because you don't understand it, doesn't mean it's not real. There are so many illnesses and diseases in the world that scientists still don't know how they work, or how to treat them, yet they don't deny their existence. Nor do you deny the existence of creatures from the deep oceans or countries you have never been before. Why is it so much harder for you to believe me?"

Oliver remained silent, but she could feel his eyes on her as she felt her away around the bed, making her way toward the top so she could take a seat.

"You, really can't see, can you?"

She felt the bed dip beside her after her nod, and heard the soft thud when he dropped something heavy to the floor.

"It was my choice to come back here after Rayner

121

took me to the apartment. I had nowhere else to go, and he said I could stay as long as I wished."

"Of course he did. I've seen the way they all look at you."

Rosalyn was curious what he meant by that, but decided to let it go for now.

Asking too many questions would only make him suspicious of her relationship with them, and Rayner in particular.

No matter how hard she tried to push the thoughts away, he meant something to her.

She was drawn to him. Lusting after him despite everything. And when she had touched him the other day, she'd felt something she couldn't explain, or even describe. It just felt right.

"Those creatures destroyed my apartment, and seem to be following me for whatever reason. At least here, I'm not alone."

"And you think these *demons* will keep you safe?"

"Yes."

To her, it was that simple.

She admitted that at first they had frightened her too, and part of her was still a little wary now, but even when she had witnessed Rayner kill those men, before she had known what they were, with Lorkan's help, part of her knew he was protecting her.

Both of them could have let her be taken in that alley. They could have washed their hands clean of her then, or even when she refused to go with them to begin with, but they didn't.

Oliver may think she was trapped here, or delusional, but she knew differently.

Rayner had already let her go once, and she knew

that if she asked him to take her somewhere now, he may not like the idea, but he would take her.

She couldn't guess at their motives, or why they seemed to care about what happened to her, and if she let herself think too much, it made her curious and a little suspicious too, but they had given her no reason not to trust them. At least, not yet.

"Nothing is going to change your mind, is it?"

Rosalyn shook her head, a small smile curving her lips when she heard him sigh and mutter under his breath, "not like I can compete with a demon."

"I know you're trying to look out for me, and I'm grateful, but I truly think here is the best place for me to be right now."

"Well, I guess they let me go, which they wouldn't have if they were that bad."

"Exactly," she commented, reaching over to place her hand on his arm, squeezing it gently. "So long as you don't tell people about them, I'm sure they don't care."

"Trust me, it's not like I plan on going up on the roof tops to shout about demons kidnapping me. That's the kind of thing that gets you locked up."

"Sorry," he sighed when she flinched at his words. "I didn't mean anything by that."

Oliver didn't know of her past, unless he had bothered to look into her files, but she of all people knew that it was pointless to tell others about anything different you saw, knowing they would never accept it.

She may be different, able to see things others can't, something she had never wanted to ask for, but at least now she knew she wasn't mad.

CHAPTER
16

"I take it that some of your sight has returned?" Niko asked when Rosalyn stepped into the kitchen and poured herself a glass of water from the jug on the table.

"It's still a little blurred at the edges, but I can make out almost everything now."

"The blur will fade just like the rest. You've improved a lot in just a few days," he murmured, tipping her head up by her chin the moment she placed her glass down.

"A lot of colour is back in your eyes too. Have you seen much?"

"The Soulless mainly," she replied with a shudder. Their faces still haunted her.

Rosalyn doubted she would ever get used to seeing creatures like them, and hoped she wouldn't have to deal with them for too much longer, what with Niko and the others leaving on their nightly hunts. Not that she really knew what they did each night, too afraid to ask for details.

"That's to be expected. They're likely the most prominent thing on your mind."

She had seen Rayner a few times too, though she suspected those to be just dreams and not visions.

She may not know how these visions worked, or even what caused them, but there seemed to be some truth to what she saw. Whether it was something that had happened in the past, or something that was going to happen in the future. But those that involved Rayner could never come true.

In them her hands roamed across the hard planes of his bare stomach and chest, tracing the patterns across his skin, while his hand tangled in her hair and he brought their lips together. The other wrapped around her waist, pressing her against his hard length, making her gasp and moan with the delicious friction. Taking her time as she climbed over his lap and enjoyed touching every inch of him. Rocking back and forth over his hips with her hands still exploring his body. His green eye shining brightly as he stared up into her face with a wicked smile, his fingers digging into her waist to hold her in place. Their moans of pleasure mingling.

None of that could be real, unless she was seeing something of his past with another woman, before his so-called curse. But it wasn't like she planned to mention those particular images to Niko, even if she was curious about them. Dream or not, he didn't need to know about her fantasies involving his brother.

As if on cue, Rayner stomped into the room, her cheeks burning hot when he glanced in her direction with a raised brow.

Get a grip, she told herself, looking down at the floor when she stepped back from Niko.

"You look like hell," Niko commented, leaning back against the counter, staring across at Rayner.

Rosalyn looked over too, watching him plonk down on one of the chairs, draping his arm across his eyes as he stretched out his long legs, the muscles in his biceps flexing and straining against the tight fabric of his long sleeved t-shirt. The smallest sliver of bare flesh exposed at his waist where the material rode up from his position.

He really was handsome. Dangerously so. The

memories of his body as he'd stripped and changed his blood soaked top weeks ago proving how accurate her dreams really were, fueling her desire.

"There were two more close by tonight. I told you that damn doctor would lead them back here," he growled, running a hand through his hair before he paused, eyeing the door.

"You know I couldn't wipe his memory again," Niko sighed, pinching the bridge of his nose. "But I admit, I didn't think he would be foolish enough to return after I took him back. I guess that was a mistake on my part."

Rosalyn hadn't expected Oliver to turn up at her window the other night, sure he had washed his hands of her after discovering that she saw supernatural creatures, but she wasn't the only one who was surprised by his sudden visit.

Rayner had been furious, telling him he had led the Soulless right to them by being foolish enough to drive all the way here, never knowing who could have followed him.

Niko on the other hand had remained silent. Rosalyn never realised he was in the room until he finally spoke, asking him what he had been thinking, and whether he planned to stick around this time.

Oliver claimed not to have seen any more Soulless whilst he'd been at the hospital, and he hadn't seen anything following him, but Rayner continued to curse beneath his breath, his heavy footsteps stomping around the room before he left and slammed the front door behind him. That night he had found several Soulless wandering in the woods close by, blaming Oliver for their appearance. Niko decided that it was best if Oliver stayed a few days to be sure nothing followed him here, or back to the hospital.

That was three nights ago now, and every night since Rayner had left to hunt for more, finding at least a handful of Soulless each time. Cursing Oliver whenever he returned.

"I won't make the same mistake again."

"Shh," Rayner hissed, holding a finger to his lips as he frowned and stood abruptly from his seat. His hand hovering over the sword he'd only moments ago placed on the table.

He must have heard something outside, but to her it seemed quiet.

Niko spun around too, staring out into the darkened forest though the small kitchen window. Rosalyn hovering in the middle of them both, not willing to move and risk making a sound when they seemed to be listening to whatever they'd sensed outside.

She hoped that it was merely an animal that had strayed too close, but she doubted that to be the case by their stern expressions.

"I'll grab the doc," Niko whispered, his footsteps barely audible as he slipped by Rayner and made his way down the short hall.

No longer feeling safe between the two of them, Rosalyn stepped closer to Rayner, longing to grab hold of his arm for comfort, but not wishing to distract or slow him down should he need that hand to reach for his sword. An odd energy seeming to charge the air making her head hurt and her vision waiver.

Not now, she groaned, knowing exactly what was coming after having felt the same thing everyday, sometimes multiple times in the past couple of weeks.

Worst possible timing.

The last thing Rosalyn saw before everything turned

black was Rayner looking back at her over his shoulder when she brushed her hand against his arm to gain his attention. His brows creased in concern when he seemed to understand what was about to happen. A loud sound ringing out, unsure whether it was him shouting, or part of the vision she was about to see.

Standing there before her was yet another Soulless, its face far too close for comfort. It's putrid breath even more powerful than the floral scent that seemed to emanate from them. Only this one didn't reach for her like all the others she'd seen, but for something else. A loud road of pain reverberating through her ears, drawing her attention to a figure struggling to remain on its feet.

Rayner. He was covered in black gunk and his own shimmering red blood. His t-shirt torn, revealing too much of his bare skin. The flesh there red and sore all over. Some of it even appeared black and blistered in places as though he'd been burnt. Still he continued to fight them off, her own image standing behind him, hovering between him and a dark doorway.

He was trying to keep them from her and suffering a great deal because of it. More and more of them poured into the narrow hallway to grab and tear at his skin. The deafening clatter of his sword falling to the ground making her cover her ears as tears cascaded down her cheeks.

"Rosalyn," he growled. Only it wasn't him. At least not the Rayner in front of her.

A gentle pressure on her shoulder made her gasp and open her eyes. Rayner's beautiful mismatched eyes mere inches in front of her.

She longed to lunge forward and wrap her arms around him as relief swept over her.

He was alright.

"She's back, great," Niko commented from somewhere behind her, drawing her attention away from Rayner when she realised they weren't the only ones there any longer. Niko was back to his position by the kitchen window, staring out into the darkness beyond. Oliver standing by his side with his arms crossed, glaring in her direction for some unknown reason.

"They're not making a move," Rayner commented, his gaze focused on the door with a scowl of his own.

"They?" Rosalyn asked, fearing she already knew the answer, but ever hopefully that she could be wrong. That the vision she had just seen wasn't about to come true.

She couldn't bear the thought of watching Rayner suffer like she had, unable to do a thing to stop it, other than putting him through even more pain if she tried to pull him away.

"Soulless."

No such luck.

Even now she could see him massaging his fingers over his palms after he'd touched her shoulder, her thin shirt unlikely to have given his skin much protection from the contact he'd made to wake her. The unusual patterns across his neck writhing beneath the surface while she watched, fascinated.

She'd hurt him already, and there were Soulless outside. A lot of them if her vision was anything to go by, Niko and Rayner's grim expressions only confirming it.

"If you had left my car outside rather than moving it, we could have made a run for it," Oliver grumbled, rolling his eyes. Rosalyn wincing, ready for the backlash she knew he was about to receive for his comment.

"If you hadn't come back here in the first place, we wouldn't be in this situation," Rayner snarled, grabbing him by the collar of his shirt, lifting his feet several inches from the floor. Gritting his teeth from more pain.

"Enough," Niko commanded, the boom of his voice deafening. "We haven't time for bickering, and what ifs aren't going to help us now."

Surprisingly Rayner snarled in Oliver's face, but released his hold on him and moved to the window on the other side of the room.

"Which direction is the Audi?"

"Dead ahead."

"Through the thick of them. Typical. What about Olivers?"

"Another few miles out from that."

Rosalyn tried to make sense of what was happening, when an odd high pitched noise sounded all around. A whooping noise that she could only associate with hyenas when they moved in on their prey, followed by cackles that made all the hairs on her body stand on end.

"So much for their declining numbers," Niko muttered, pulling his own curved blades free, never taking his eyes off the window. "We're not going to be able to make it to the car through this many."

Rayner was silent as he looked across at her, then back to Niko and Oliver, before he let out a long, shaky breath and closed his eyes.

"We'll have to use Xander's tunnel."

"That space is too narrow, Rayner. It'll be impossible to fight there."

"They won't get in."

Rosalyn's heart began to beat faster, an overwhelming feeling of dread coursing through her body as she looked between the two of them, sensing what wasn't being said.

She didn't want to go into this tunnel.

It wasn't the darkness or the cramped space that was playing on her mind as it would usually be, but her vision instead, and that dark doorway she had seen.

Over the years she had learnt to trust her instincts, even more so over the past few weeks, and right now they screamed for her not to go there.

"Isn't there another way?" she asked, gaining Rayner's attention with a small tug on his t-shirt.

"Did you see something happen?"

"I saw them all coming. Your skin–" she paused, unable to continue past the lump in her throat. Her eyes filled with unshed tears as she refused to look up at his face, trying not to remember his howls of pain.

"Did they get you?"

"No."

He'd pulled her from the vision too early to be completely sure, but she felt confident enough in her reply.

He had been in front of her, much like he was now, blocking them from her with his own body. The darkened doorway behind the only other thing she had been able to see.

"Then we proceed. That tunnel is our only way out."

Her heart skipped a beat. Tears built ferociously behind her eyes as she continued to avoid his eyes.

He couldn't do this.

Whether she was ready to admit it or not, she had some feelings for him. Not sure what they were exactly, but she knew she cared, she had done ever since she met him in the hospital. Only now those feelings had grown stronger. The thought of him dying, or seeing him in so much pain making her chest squeeze tight, his words foolish, even if they were a little touching.

Taking a deep breath, she raised her eyes to look at him, but before she had a chance to yell at him for being so damn stubborn, and how she wouldn't allow him to risk himself for her like that, they all heard a loud bang.

The front door slammed against the wall. Two Soulless carrying those thin, circular blades entered with nasty smiles on their faces.

A few other Soulless squeezed through either side of them, running toward them with nothing but their long, claw like nails swiping through the air.

"They brought the others too," Niko commented, coming to stand by Rayner's side. His odd looking curved blades swinging through the air in a large arc, taking two of the creatures down with one blow.

Both of their moevents so fluid that it seemed like nothing was going to make it past them.

"Expendable distractions," Rayner commented with a grunt, pushing more of them that approached back with a shove of his own blade.

More and more growling, crazed looking Soulless forced their way into the building, whilst those who had entered first stood back, watching. Menacing smiles still plastered on their faces, something about those two different from all the rest, almost like they were a completely different species.

"Keep close," Niko demanded over his shoulder, both Oliver and her complying at just the right time.

The window near to where Oliver had been standing burst inward with a crash. Shards of glass flew through the air, several of them scraping across Niko's cheek and chest when he spun and stood behind them, blocking the blow with his body, ready to attack those that climbed through the new entrance. Rayner let out a roar, drawing her attention back to the front as a couple of Soulless managed to grab hold of his arms before he cut them away. Angry red sores marking his skin below the torn fabric.

No. It was too late. Her vision was already happening, freezing her to the spot as the others seemed to all be moving around her.

"Rosalyn. Get near Niko. Now!"

Rosalyn didn't do as she was told, ignoring Rayner's command to step closer to him instead, tugging him back by his t-shirt.

She knew that he wanted her to be out of harm's way, knowing that Niko would be able to move her if he had to, but she needed to be by his side. She needed to make sure that he didn't do anything foolish.

There was a chance that she was playing into the vision, knowing that she had been close to him when it happened, but she feared what would happen if she left him to fight alone. Those Soulless in her vision piling up on top of him, and he didn't seem to care if he was injured, so long as they didn't get to her, his own pain forgotten if it meant he was doing his job.

Either way, it was too late now. The door was blocked by more and more Soulless pouring inside, filling the small living space. Several more lurking just outside the broken window. Their lopsided grins distorted and flickering as they squealed their hands against the fragments of glass, the sound causing her to shudder.

"Stubborn female," Rayner growled, lunging forward, taking her with him where she clung to his t-shirt, taking off the head of the Soulless that attempted to reach around him, toward her.

"If you won't go with Niko, then whatever you do, do not let go."

She had no intention of letting go even when he continued to advance forward, keeping her behind him at all times, sandwiched between his body and the wall behind them. More and more of those feral like creatures running at them before the two with swords made their move, running forward with their blades held out in front of them like spears, aiming for Rayner's chest.

He deflected the first blow with relative ease, causing the sword to embed in the wood not far from her shoulder. The second blade aimed straight for his heart.

Without so much as a second thought, Rosalyn put her hand on Rayner's back and shoved him to one side. The pain that he would feel from her contact nothing compared to that which he would feel if that sword pierced his heart. Only, she didn't act quick enough. The Soulless's sword may have missed his heart, but it caught his side, just below his ribs, making him roar out in pain as he swung his blade around, into the back of the creatures neck, causing its head to fall limply to the floor with a sickening thud.

"Thanks," he panted, brushing some of the muck from his handsome face with his shoulder before more of them rushed forward, followed by more and more loud grunts and squelching noises, making her shudder and try to hide her face behind Rayner. The sight of so much blood and gunk turning her stomach. Her fingers sliding on the material she held onto as more of Rayner's blood flowed between her fingers.

"Rayner?" Niko called, pushing another two back, attempting to make a path for them as her and Rayner backed up toward them. His eyes fixated on Rayner's side, hers doing the same, noticing that his blood was still oozing from the wound, making his t-shirt stick to his skin.

"Keep going," he grunted, wincing when he twisted and pushed her against the wall behind to stop another Soulless getting to her. Its long claws slashing through his arm making him roar and kick it backward. Her heart hammering knowing that could have been her if he hadn't moved her in time.

"Come on," Niko shouted, his own grunts and groans filling the air as Rayner came to a stop in front of a blank wall. Except it wasn't actually blank. A red pattern appeared across it when Rayner placed his hands upon it. Writing of some sort, like runes now pulsing before the shape of a large door appeared. Air hissed passed them as it slid open to reveal a dark, narrow space.

The tunnel.

Rosalyn looked into the darkness with a heavy weight in her chest, back to the gathering Soulless behind them. The space far too narrow for them to fight with their swords, just like Niko had said.

"Get inside," Rayner demanded, remaining motionless in front of the entrance. His sword held out in front of him, waiting for the Soulless to approach.

Oliver was first to enter, looking back over his shoulder when he stepped deeper into the darkness, almost engulfed by it, pausing to look back over his shoulder at her before Niko shouted at him to move, holding out his hand for her to take so he could pull her inside, mistaking her hesitation for fear.

Part of her was afraid to go into that confined space with the Soulless this close, and the almost solid darkness that she had never been keen on, but the real reason for her reluctance was her concern for Rayner who made no attempt to head toward the tunnel.

"Come on Rayner," she begged, tugging on his t-shirt.

He didn't respond, just stood and swung his blade at any Soulless that moved forward.

"Get a move on," Niko hissed, groaning while he held firmly onto the wall by the new doorway, his arm shaking under the pressure, the red glow around the entrance appearing to fade in and out.

Rayner took a few steps back, giving her hope that perhaps her vision won't come true after all.

She was wrong.

Rayner glanced back at her when Niko took her hand, giving the Soulless the only opening they needed to spring forward and grab hold of his arms, making him groan and spin around. Another jumping on top of him, slicing at his shoulders and back with its claws.

Rosalyn tried to step forward, only for Niko's hand around hers to hold firm, keeping her back as he pulled her toward the entrance of the tunnel, using his other hand to throw one of his two swords at the Soulless on top of Rayner. Releasing her to grab the other to slash at those he could reach whilst still keeping his foot in front of the door. The stone entrance groaned, slowly inching closed. Whatever Rayner had done to open it wearing off.

Niko wouldn't be able to hold it open for much longer.

Rosalyn looked up at Niko, then back toward Rayner, her mind already made up.

Oliver shouted and reached for her at the same moment she ducked below Niko's arcing blade, no doubt knowing what she was about to do as she ran back toward

136

Rayner, grabbing hold of Niko's other sword from the Soulless he'd hit only moments before. The blade jammed in place when she tried to pull it free. The Soulless shifted below her, attempting to get back on its feet.

"Rosalyn. Get back."

"I won't leave him!" she screamed, pulling with all her might to free the blade as more of them reached for her and Rayner. The Soulless below her moved sharply, its eyes and mouth snapping open. The creature's long claws swiped out at her shoulders, gripping on to them tightly, her energy seeming to fade away.

Rayner let out a loud roar and shoved hard at those crowed over him, his legs buckling beneath him as he stumbled toward her and balled his fist, her vision blurring as more and more of her energy seemed to seep away, until she was tossed to the floor.

Shaking off the lethargic feeling, Rosalyn looked up to see Rayner on top of the Soulless with the hole in its chest. The blade now discarded on the floor beside her.

Three more approached, grabbing at Rayner's arms while he fought in vain to keep them back.

Taking a deep, shuddering breath, Rosalyn snatched up the sword and swung it down onto one of their arms, loosening its grip on Rayner if only momentarily. It was still enough for her to grab his other arm and pull him back to his feet, yanking as hard as she could toward the door that still pushed against Niko.

Rayner's legs wobbled beneath him with each step, struggling to keep on his feet. His shouts and yells making her wince as she tried to ignore how much she was hurting him in order to get him out of there, his muscled body becoming too much for her to hold when he fell to his knees. The Soulless pulling him in the opposite direction, grabbing for him once more, adding to his already substantial weight.

One of them grabbed her arm, its nails digging in deep, causing her to whimper, but Rayner was there, letting out his own animalistic growl as he shoved hard with his elbow, using the remainder of his strength to knock it off its feet before he collapsed forward.

"Grab her," Niko ordered before she felt an arm wrap around her waist. Niko reached around her to take Rayner, pulling him the last few feet toward the door before he stepped back into the darkness, allowing it to finally slam shut, squashing those Soulless that had been hanging onto Rayner's side and legs. The squelch and crushing of bone making her retch while Oliver held her securely against him.

CHAPTER 17

"Will that hold?" Oliver asked, his arm still held tightly around Rosalyn's waist as the Soulless continued to battle with the door on the other side. Their fists and their nails slamming and scraping, sending shivers down her spine.

They were relentless.

"The door will hold, but I'm not sure how long the wall itself will last against so many pounding against it."

"Then how the hell are we supposed to get out of here?"

"The tunnel has no intersections. Just follow it and we'll come to the exit," Niko sighed, his eyes the only thing Rosalyn could see in the darkness around them.

"Is he still breathing?" Oliver asked, sliding his phone from his pocket to fill the space with a bright blue light, shining it toward Rayner who lay prone on the floor.

His eyes were closed, but Rosalyn could now see the shallow rise and fall of his chest as she struggled to free herself from Oliver's grasp and approach him.

"He's breathing," she whispered, more for her own benefit than anyone else's, needing to reassure herself that he wasn't dead. Her own legs wobbling below her, letting out a shaky breath.

"You were reckless, and foolish," Niko snarled, grabbing hold of her uninjured shoulder. "They nearly had you because you ran in like that. Rayner only just managed to get that one off of you before it was too late."

"What was that thing doing to her with its mouth

open like that?" Oliver asked, reminding her of how weak she had felt when the Soulless held on to her, seeming to take the energy from her.

"Feasting. They drain our energy to keep themselves going. The more powerful the Other, the more they hunger for them."

"It-it was feeding on her?" Oliver gasped, retching when he pressed the button on his phone again, shining the light down on the Soulless arms and torso's scattered on the floor by the wall they'd come through.

"Yes."

"I couldn't just leave him there to die," she snapped back, her hands shaking by her sides when her ragged emotions got the better of her. The fear of him dying outweighing her own need for survival and the terror of the Soulless. Needing to free him from their grip and not allow her vision to come true. Unable to stand by and do nothing while he cried out in pain. Her need to put an end to his suffering overruling her apprehension of getting in the way or hurting him.

Niko returned his attention to her, his face softening before he crushed her against his chest, holding on to her tightly. Resting his cheek against the top of her head.

"You were senseless," he said, his words muffled by her hair. "Not many would have bothered. Thank you."

Rosalyn was at a loss for words as he continued to hold onto her, her eyes drawn to Rayner still motionless on the floor.

"Sorry to interrupt the moment, but shouldn't we get going?" Oliver commented, clearing his throat before he pressed his phone again. The sounds of the Soulless on the other side of the wall growing louder. "I don't have much battery left."

"W-what about Rayner?"

"He'll be out for an hour or so at least with the amount of damage he's taken. His body will need time to heal all those wounds," Niko sighed, lifting his limp body over his shoulder, grunting under the weight as he nudged her forward with a hand on the small of her back. "Me carrying him will only make it take longer."

Though Rosalyn was unable to see his expression, she could hear the sorrow in his voice. The regret he felt for having to inflict even more pain on his brother in order to get him, and them to safety. Her own guilt stabbing at her, trying to ignore the sounds of his pain when she had pulled him back.

Perhaps if she had gone to Niko sooner rather than staying by Rayner's side, he might not have been distracted trying to keep her safe.

They might not have gotten that first contact on him which had slowed him down. But then, if she hadn't stayed by his side, she wouldn't have been there to push him away when that sword was headed for his heart, or pull him back when they started to swarm over him.

"How is your arm?" Niko asked, grunting and adjusting his hold on Rayner.

"It's alright."

"It doesn't appear to be too deep, but it's still bleeding."

"I'll deal with it later, when I can see."

Her vision was only just coming back to her, the edges still a little blurred, and now she was back in the dark again, not able to see and left stumbling, feeling the walls to know where she was going. Niko on the other hand seemed to be able to see clearly without a need to hold the walls. Not that he would be able to with Rayner over his shoulder, occupying his hands.

"What did you mean earlier? Not many would have bothered?" she asked, trying to distract herself from the sting of her wound and pounding of her heart, the darkness appearing never ending. All of her pent up emotions and fear of what had just happened, and might come squeezing her chest tighter with each step they made.

"We're expendable," Niko sighed, pushing her a little firmer when her pace slowed, the warmth of his hand on her back somewhat soothing amongst all the chaos and terror.

"We are Warriors. Our job is to keep the Other safe and hidden from the human world. The Council orders us to do as they wish. Neither of them generally care what happens to any of us along the way, so long as we keep doing our job."

"That's horrible," she whispered, some of the tears that had been threatening to spill finally falling down her cheeks.

She didn't understand how anyone could be so cold.

They were people too, even if it was their job to fight and protect.

"Though I still think you were stupid to go back, risking them getting hold of you. Not to mention the fury you will face when Rayner wakes. I wanted to thank you again."

"I didn't really do that much."

She'd barely been able to move him, and had really only gotten in the way. Rayner having to use his waning energy to save her several times rather than using it to defend himself.

It had been Niko who had grabbed him when they were close enough, pulling him through the door and securing them on the other side, carrying him to safety now.

"The door opens only once. The ritual would need to be re-applied to work again which would have been impossible. You getting him close enough was all it took."

"I saw them," she began, flinching when Oliver cursed and the light on his phone faded.

"Sorry. Dead battery."

"Keep going. Use the walls to guide you if you must," Niko instructed, his glowing gold eyes giving her a sliver of comfort as he stared dead ahead of them, his ever present hand on her back keeping her going when all she wanted to do was collapse to the floor, drained emotionally and physically.

"What did you see?"

"I saw them before me, piling on top of him. Clawing at him."

"You saw him die?"

"No!" she shrieked, stopping in her tracks despite his hand urging her forward. Both of him and Oliver stopping with her, their footsteps silent. "He pulled me out of the vision before it finished, but he won't, will he?"

"Unlikely," Niko sighed, his hand squeezing her upper arm gently, forcing her to turn back before he pushed her forward. Her heels digging into the stone, not happy with his answer, but his strength was too much for her to resist for long.

"He's suffered worse before."

Rosalyn wasn't convinced he was telling her the truth, but chose not to question him and carried on moving, glancing back every so often even though she couldn't see Rayner, hoping that he would be alright. That she hadn't been too late.

"Wait," Niko commanded. "We're here. Step aside."

Pressing her back to the wall so Niko could pass, Rosalyn spotted a small sliver of light down by his feet. The scent of pine and mildew reaching her nose. Sounds of metal ringing in the tight space around them as Niko pulled out his sword and pushed on the doorway she struggled to see. That smell growing stronger with each notch the door opened. More and more light pushing back the darkness around them. The moon shining brightly above them, breaking through the canopy of leaves overhead.

"It looks clear," Niko muttered, his voice still hushed as he adjusted his hold on Rayner, a small grunt escaping his lips when his stomach met with Niko's shoulder, the tiny sound filling Rosalyn with relief.

She had seen the rise and fall of his chest, knew he was still breathing, even reassured by Niko claiming that it wasn't enough to kill him, but to hear him make even such a small sound made her tense body relax a little.

"The car shouldn't be too far ahead," Niko continued, already headed in the direction he had just nodded. "Stay close, and keep as quiet as you possibly can."

Rosalyn had no intention of doing otherwise. She didn't want to draw the attention of more Soulless if there were any nearby.

For whatever reason, they seemed to have taken an interest in her. One she doubted had anything to do with her spotting them in the hospital any more. But what else could there be?

Yes she could see them, and other creatures despite the glamour Rayner had mentioned what seemed like a long time ago, but she didn't understand why they would follow her so tirelessly for something like that.

144

Niko said they only hunt the Other, so why were they bothering wasting their time and efforts on her? She knew she was different, never really understanding why, but still, she wasn't like them. She wasn't Other.

"Damn it," Oliver grumbled, stumbling on yet another tree root, his elbow scraping against the bark when he attempted to catch himself from falling. "Where did you say the car was?"

"There."

In front of them Rosalyn could make out the shimmer of metal, moonlight catching on the black paintwork. Only, the car wasn't the only thing there.

Hovering around the car she could see at least five silhouettes moving back and forth, circling. Three of those shapes carried something shiny. Blades most likely. The other two scouting further out, making an odd noise. Not one of them appeared to be those more feral types of creature she had seen back at the cabin.

"I count six."

"Is that bad? Can you take six?" Oliver asked, his eyes flicking between them and Niko. Meanwhile Rosalyn hunted the shadows for that sixth shape she had missed, when she spotted it sitting on top of the car, seeming to look straight at them, even though it made no move to approach.

"Not with Rayner on my back, and you two defenceless."

"Rayner's sword."

"You know how to use it?"

Rosalyn shook her head.

She wasn't really sure why she had even suggested it, but it was better than having nothing to defend herself with if they did come for them.

She had already used Niko's blade when she needed to inside the cabin. Surely Rayner's wouldn't be so different.

"To kill them, you must remove their heads. Are you ready for that?"

She may have used the sword to cut the creature's arm away to help Rayner break free, but she wasn't sure if she was prepared to take a life, even if it was the life of a monstrous creature like the Soulless. Niko's question alone enough to turn her stomach.

Niko sighed at her hesitation and slid Rayner from his shoulders, propping him up against a large tree before he retrieved his black bladed sword, thrusting it into her shaky hands.

"Just swing like you did before and call me if any of them get too close. It should buy you enough time for me to make it back to you and finish them off."

"I'll try," she whispered, taking a step toward Rayner's prone body. All those red marks appearing more black now she stared down at him, a lump in her throat. He must be in so much pain, and there wasn't anything she could do to stop it. Even if she had some form of painkiller on her, he'd told her before that their medicines didn't work on them in the same way.

"You," Niko began, turning his attention to Oliver as he held out one of his curved blades. "You need to come with me."

"I can't."

"We need to keep their attention away from her and Rayner. It's about time you made yourself useful."

"I don't know the first thing about fighting."

"Too late to worry about that now," Niko growled under his breath, pushing Oliver forward after he'd alerted the Soulless to their location. All six pairs of eyes landed on them before they rushed forward at once.

Rosalyn ducked down to keep herself and Rayner hidden, using his sword to keep her balance as she heard grunts and the clash of metal from just a few yards away.

She held her breath and looked over to Rayner noticing small beads of sweat cascade down his face, causing some of his hair to stick to his forehead while he groaned.

Rosalyn wanted to brush his hair aside and reassure him that he was going to be alright, that they were away from the Soulless and he would be better soon, but she couldn't. She wasn't able to touch him. He had suffered enough already, and her touch would only make it worse. Nor could she bring herself to lie to him when the Soulless were still so close.

They weren't out of the danger just yet.

"Little, *Rose.*"

A Soulless.

It had somehow slipped by Niko and managed to find their hiding spot, it's disjointed voice sending an uncontrollable shiver down her spine.

Using Rayner's sword to support her trembling body, Rosalyn pushed to her feet and lifted the blade, wobbling under its weight, barely able to lift the thing. Grateful to see that this particular Soulless wasn't carrying a weapon of its own, except for those claws, the cuts on her shoulder and arms still stinging.

If only she could lift the sword a little higher, she might have been able to swing it and keep the creature at bay long enough for Niko to reach them as he had suggested. Not too dissimilar from what she could see Oliver doing as he ducked and screamed, managing to defend himself in a clumsy, haphazard kind of way. There was no way she would be able to defend herself against another sword, blocking and dodging, especially with a blade as heavy as the one she carried. She had zero experience fighting, let alone protecting herself or anybody else. But damn it, she would try.

"All alone. Nobody to protect you."

Niko and Oliver were still busy with three more of them, Oliver actually able to catch one of them on the arm with his frantic swinging, forcing it back before he let out a cheer and Niko took its head off with a precise aim, silencing its piercing wail.

"Niko," she yelled, figuring it was pointless to try and remain quiet when the sounds of fighting and Soulless shrieks echoed all around them.

He may still be busy with the two remaining by them, and it was likely that she had drawn attention to herself and Rayner, but she knew better than to think she would be able to take the creature on by herself. She'd seen far too many movies for that, and she wasn't that stupid.

She saw Niko turn, ready to run in her direction when one of Soulless beat him to it, blocking his path with the other aiming his blade at Oliver.

She was alone for now at least, but now Niko knew she needed him when he was able to reach her. For now she would just have to do her best to keep Rayner and herself safe.

The Soulless approached, a combination of the low light and its disjointed way of moving through the shadows making it difficult to see exactly which direction it came from, until it lunged forward, grabbing her already stinging arms. The sword she held too long and heavy to slice its arm and loosen its grip.

"Easier if you give in."

"Never," she snapped, kicking out, knowing that she needed to keep as much distance between them as she possibly could, remembering that lethargic feeling that had washed over her when she'd been caught and fed on before.

"*Warriors* will never beat us all," it sneered, yanking roughly on her arm, its grip bruising. Long nails digging into her skin, causing her to shriek in pain as they sliced deeper with each pull.

Rosalyn wrestled to get free, pushing with all she had to break its hold on her and lift the sword between them, but its grip was too tight, and the sword too heavy.

Running out of options, but not willing to give in, she speared the blade downward into the creature's foot, making it howl and jump back. It's feral, menacing smile now vanished, A frightening rage now in its place.

"They demand you alive, but that doesn't mean intact," it snarled, darting forward once again. Its claws catching both her shoulders, slicing through her thin shirt and the flesh beneath before she had a chance to lift the sword any higher than her waist. The pointed tip piercing through the creature's abdomen. Black gunk spewed from its mouth where it snarled and gnashed its teeth at her, until its head began to fall. Niko standing there with his blade dripping more of that gunk before the Soulless fell to the ground with a thud.

"Sorry I took so long," he panted, several slices across his chest and arms, his red blood mixing with the black that sprayed from the Soulless as he bent down to retrieve Rayner, hauling him back up onto his shoulders.

"Let's get out of here before any more show up."

CHAPTER 18

This was the second time Rayner had passed out from the contact in a matter of weeks. The pain too much to bear, his entire body burning. Aches in his muscles, and from all that cuts that still healed.

He knew he should rest a little longer and give his body a chance to heal, but how could he lay around doing nothing when she had been there too. One of those bastards grabbing hold of her arm and cutting her creamy skin. Another clinging to her, absorbing her life force as he'd struggled to summon the energy to knock it back.

Rayner opened his eyes and cursed loudly.

The sun was bright against his face, the heat of it making the burn of his skin intensify.

He closed them again and turned away, trying to shield his eyes from the light when the scent of wild berries drifted to his nose.

"Is it too bright?" she asked, her soft voice, the knowledge that she was still alive and with him releasing some of the tension throughout his body.

"Yes," he grunted, his throat dry and hoarse.

Within moments the light had been dimmed, the heat receding with it and her face appearing by his side the next. His eyes instantly drawn to the bandages strapped across her shoulders and forearms.

He attempted to move to get a closer look, rage building inside of him upon seeing her injured, but he wasn't healed nearly as much as he should have been. The contact from the Soulless still excruciating across his stomach and side, the skin there far more sensitive than anywhere else, making him growl loudly and flop back down, noticing she stepped closer. Her hands hovering in mid air before they feel back to her sides.

For the first time since he'd met her, he was actually grateful that she didn't attempt to touch him.

Usually he longed for it, not giving a damn about the consequences if it meant he was able to feel her skin against his own, but right now, his body felt raw, the healing process far too slow compared to what it should be. He must have taken a lot more damage than he realised.

"They hurt you," he groaned, his gaze returning to her arms as she rubbed a hand up and down one of them, looking down at him with her big, deep blue eyes.

"Really? Have you seen the state of yourself?" she remarked, her eyes raking across his body. A whole new warmth burning him from head to toe. This one without the pain. One he didn't wish to end.

He liked her eyes on him, and the concern she had for him. A human, caring what happened to a mere demon. A Warrior. He never thought such a thing could be possible.

"Is there anything I can do?"

Her voice was so small and fragile, he barely heard her when the bed squeaked below him, the pain in his side making him groan when he turned and placed a hand on her shoulder, the bandages preventing any real risk of contact, his need to touch her outweighing the threat of more pain.

"No," she shrieked, jumping backward, "you'll hurt yourself even more."

"The bandage," he began, catching himself on the edge of the bed without her there to hold him upright in his awkward position, breathing heavily as he adjusted his position and attempted to sit and lean back against the pillows.

"And I told you before, Rosalyn. Your human medicines won't help me," he sighed, figuring she needed an answer to her question, even if she hadn't meant for him to hear it.

He could see the concern in her eyes all the while she tried to assess him, just like the doctor he knew she was training to be.

She wanted to ease his pain, and that alone was enough for him. Usually it was only his brothers who cared, in their own way. The rest of the Council and the Other didn't give a damn if they were hurt or killed on the job, figuring they could replace them sooner or later. Yet her, a human who knew nothing about this world, or them. A human who would normally fear a demon and flee from them, like she had to begin with, cared about him.

"What about inhuman medicines? I could ask Niko?"

Rayner shook his head and sighed. "Perhaps some water," he suggested, sensing that she needed to do something, and he really did need a drink. The cool liquid sliding down his throat soothing when he downed the contents of the glass she carefully held up for him. Some of his urges that she would touch him coming back when he spied yet another bandage further down her arm marked with fresh blood.

Those bastard Soulless really had gotten to her, and he'd been too out of it to protect her.

He'd failed her.

If Niko hadn't been there with them, she would likely have been taken, or killed, and there would have been nothing he could do to stop it.

"Won't stitches help you heal faster?"

"It's not the cuts that are the issue."

"But—"

"My cuts would have already healed, Rosalyn," he interrupted, lifting the corner of his t-shirt on the side closest to her so she could see for herself. The slashes and grazes on his skin already knitted together and barely visible thanks to his fast regeneration. It was the damn contact burns all over his body that needed to heal. The one thing that nobody could help him with. Something she seemed to realise the longer she stood over him, staring down at his stomach and the blackened marks that remained across it.

"Prolonged contact burns," he informed her, able to see the confusion in her expression. Her brows knitted together, studying the discolouration. Hers and the doctors' assumption that his reaction to contact was some skin condition was almost laughable, when it was nothing more than a barbaric curse the Council had inflicted upon him.

"It literally burns you?" she commented, taking an even closer look. "So, when Niko carried you out, it only made them worse."

Again Rayner nodded, knowing that Niko would have had to carry him for them to be where they were now. There was no way that her or the doctor could have managed it. His body would be far too heavy for a human to carry, though he seemed to remember her grabbing hold of his arm back there, pulling him toward the tunnel after he had tried to push the Soulless back, giving them enough time to get out.

Still, he should have been healed far more than he was now. Their prolonged contact would not have slowed his regeneration this badly.

A few hours of being unconscious should have been

more than sufficient to mend the majority of the damage, but his body still burnt all over, his muscles straining whenever he tried to move. Sweat clinging to him, causing the sheets to stick uncomfortably.

"You weren't exaggerating when you called it a curse, were you?"

"Each of us were punished for something we did. This was a part of mine."

"You went against your Council?"

Rayner raised a brow, unsure how she knew of the Council, watching her step forward and perch on the edge of the bed, her eyes still assessing him and the wounds she could see through his torn t-shirt. His earlier decision that he didn't want her to touch him fading more and more the longer she remained by his side. His body now aching with a different need.

She too seemed to struggle to keep her hands to herself, lifting them toward him every now and then, her gaze travelling across the expanse of his chest. Her long, raven hair tumbling over her shoulder when she leaned forward. His own eyes following the fall of the silken strands, down the curves of her body. Those bandages out of the corner of his eyes dousing the fire that built in the pit of his stomach, replacing it with rage.

How dare they touch her. She was his.

"Niko mentioned them before, when we were walking through the tunnel," she commented, distracting him from his thoughts.

None of them were supposed to tell her about the Council. She was a human after all, and the Council forbade such things, not that he paid much attention to what they dictated. He was surprised however that Niko had been the one to tell her. Out of them all, it was him who listened most.

"He said you were, Warriors?"

"Yes."

To begin with he had enjoyed the role and responsibilities. Taking care of the Other and making sure that they remained safe, not risking exposure, but over the last few decades, things had shifted. The Council had changed. The leaders gradually got worse and worse, demanding more and more tasks of them that they disagreed with.

"We were chosen a long time ago to protect the Other, and the Council," Rayner began slouching back on the bed, staring up at the blank ceiling as he spoke, needing the distraction to douse the fire that still threatened to consume him. A mixture of lust for her, the warmth of her skin seeping through the thin blanket somebody had draped over his lap, and the rage at the Soulless who had hurt her. But most importantly, to forget about the claim of her he had just made.

She couldn't be his, even if he longed for her unlike anybody else, both physically and mentally. Everything about her was captivating.

He couldn't have her.

But he didn't like the idea of anybody else having her either.

Every time he saw the doctor near her, all he could picture was that kiss from months ago, back at the hospital, making his blood boil. Yet, he couldn't deny her the affections of another knowing that he would never be the man she needed, no matter how much he wished otherwise.

"We made a pact that bound us to the Council so they could lead us. My brothers and I fight for them, and

155

the rest of the Other, keeping our existence hidden from the humans to keep us from war, and dealing with any rogues and creatures like the Soulless who pose a threat to all."

"Niko said something similar."

They'd started as nothing more than soldiers. The muscle the Council needed despite many of the members having enough power themselves. The role was a great privilege, meaning that others knew and respected their strength and skills. The Council working with the majority for the better. Everything had run smoothly, until the power play came into effect. The newer leaders craved more and more, treating them as nothing more than a pet that they could tame and bend to their will, or wash their hands of when it suited. Several of those prepared to do whatever it took to get to the top and stay there, rather than working alongside them. Henry being one of the more ruthless of them all, killing anybody who got in his way. All of them certain that he had been involved in their brother's death.

Lorkan had asked why he hadn't killed them too, the others wondering the same, but Rayner knew the answer. Henry wanted to break them, one by one, proving just how powerful he was. Using their brothers death as proof of what would happen if they pushed too hard. Unfortunately for him, he hadn't won yet.

"So, you're forced to do as they tell you?"

"They like to think so," Rayner scoffed, clenching his fists. "Our pact leaves us free to make our own decisions, much to the Council's disapproval. But we are still bound by some rules, as are all Other."

"And your curse, I assume you broke one of those rules?"

"We refused to uphold our pact after the death of our brother, and broke one of their biggest rules. Not to harm a

Council member. So they took our abilities and changed them, weakening us to some degree."

All of them had been furious with the changes within the Council, arguing with them and demanding action be taken against the hunters after they had recovered Xander from them, but they hadn't cared. They never did. They even claimed that they'd gone against orders in the first place, exposing themselves to the hunters and giving them further proof of their existence. It didn't matter that none of those hunters had made it out of the building alive to share their discovery. Nor did they care that Xander had been taken, or what the hunters had done to him.

Even now Xander was volatile and despised all humans. Most Other too.

But when Helmer was killed and taken from them, they had all gone on a rampage.

Not only did they prove that they didn't care about them, or anyone else, they had killed one of their own for personal gain.

The four of them that remained had stormed the Great hall in search of those members responsible, killing at least four high ranking Council members before the guards were able to overpower them with their vast numbers. None of them any the wiser that they had just helped Henry take his crown. All of it part of his conniving plan.

CHAPTER
19

Another day passed, and still Rayner remained in Oliver's spare room recovering.

Rosalyn hoped that he would be healed by now. She'd seen how fast their bodies regenerated for herself, watching as he'd sliced his hand to prove what he was. Able to see the skin close before her eyes. The stab wound he'd first come into the hospital with, and that cut across his chest when he'd come back for her at her apartment, both of them healed quicker than any human could possibly. But Niko had said just this morning that he still needed time before they moved somewhere more secure, unwilling to move him until he was able to walk by himself.

He'd done his best to convince her that she needn't worry before he left the house to find Lorkan to let him know where they were headed, but she had seen his own concern written on his face clear as day, only fueling her own fear.

This wasn't right. He should be up by now.

Rosalyn climbed from the bed she'd been resting on and slipped the jumper Oliver gave her over her shoulders, the evening chill cutting through to the bone when she removed the blankets and headed out of the room toward Rayner, needing to prove to herself that she was panicking for no reason.

Once there, she paused outside the door with a frown, an eerie feeling washing over her as her hand connected with the metal doorknob.

She shook it off and stepped inside, careful not to

make too much noise when she saw Rayner sleeping on the bed. That same eerie feeling from outside the door much stronger as she stepped further into the room, her eyes scanning the darkness for someone, or something out of place.

Satisfied that nothing lurked in the dark, Rosalyn made her way to Rayner's bedside, drawn to him in a way she seemed to have little control over, reaching her hand toward him before she got a hold of herself.

Touching him would only make his healing slower.

With a heavy sigh, she drew up a chair and sat down beside him, admiring his handsome face while he slept peacefully, his patterned body visible through the tears in his clothes now that some of his contact burns had faded.

She leaned a little closer in her seat to observe them more thoroughly, noticing a shiver work its way through him, making his body twitch and his hands clench. A sheen layer of sweat coating his neck and forehead as her eyes travelled the length of him.

"Why aren't you healing properly?" she asked the empty room, eyes narrowed with concern when he let out a small groan.

This didn't seem normal.

She may not know much about demons and all the other creatures that were out there, always trying her best in the past to ignore what she saw rather than learn about them, but she suspected there was something that they were all missing.

His injuries appeared closed from what she could see, but his contact burns were still there even if faded.

She'd never seen them this severe before, though Niko claimed he'd had worse.

She remembered those he had on his skin at the

hospital, how quickly he had gotten up and left even after being given a sedative.

His body jerked with another shiver, shaking the bed below him as she leaned in toward his face. It appeared more pale than usual, his cheeks tinted pink. A grimace on his face when he shivered again.

He appeared feverish, all the signs there even if she wasn't able to touch him and gauge his temperature.

She turned around ready to call for Oliver who was down the hall when she came face to face with a huge man. His pale eyes like ice as he stood scowling down at her, a sneer curling his lips.

"Going somewhere, *human*?"

Demon. He was a demon. Another of them perhaps.

What were the names Rayner mentioned before?

"X-Xander?"

It couldn't be the other one, Helmer, Rayner said he was dead. Nor did he sound the same as the man she had seen before who she believed to be him.

"What have you done?" he snarled, recovering from his obvious shock where she guessed his name correctly, his eyes leaving hers momentarily to glance at Rayner, a much softer expression on his face in that brief moment before he turned back to her.

"Nothing," she blurted, realising that just made her sound even more guilty.

She thought she was used to seeing demons now, and that none of them could possibly be as scary as the Soulless. She was wrong.

There was something off about this particular demon. His eyes weren't black like his brothers, but a crimson colour when they changed. He was something different from the rest. Not broken as Rayner had called

160

himself, but something else.

"I think he has a fever."

The other demon, Xander continued to look down at her, making her feel small.

He grabbed hold of her shoulder, his fingers pressing a little too firmly over her bandages making her wince as he leaned forward, coming face to face with her.

"Why is he here?"

"We didn't have a lot of choice in locations after the Soulless attacked your cabin. He needed somewhere nearby where he could heal."

She didn't expect him to listen, but to her surprise he loosened his hold on her and took a step back, his eyes still glued to her, frowning.

"I take it you know what he is, what I am if you know of them?"

Rosalyn nodded, returning her attention to Rayner who remained asleep on the bed.

It might have been a bad idea to turn her back on this particular demon, but if she was going to help Rayner like he had helped her so many times before, she needed this demon to trust her and allow her to call for Oliver. She wasn't sure she could do anything alone.

"To be honest, I don't really care what you are, but Rayner needs my friend down the hall to come look him over. If he is feverish, there might be something wrong with him," she answered, trying her best to sound confident and in control, turning back to him with new determination.

She would not let anything happen to Rayner now. Not when she had risked so much and tried so hard to get him out of that cabin. The wounds on her arms and shoulders proof of just how much she couldn't bear to see

161

him suffer, or die.

"Another human?" he scoffed, crossing his arms with another loud snarl, but this time he did nothing to stop her heading toward the door.

"Oliver!" she yelled, sticking her head out into the hallway, peering back over her shoulder at Xander, wary as his eyes darted between her and Rayner.

"Oliver!" she shouted even louder when he didn't appear, needing him to come to her, not wishing to leave Rayner alone, even if his brother was here with him and likely had been since before she entered the room. That eerie feeling she noticed outside, and when she stepped into the room, disappearing after he showed himself.

Oliver eventually emerged in the doorway, rubbing at his eyes as he stumbled into the room, halting his steps when he noticed she wasn't alone.

"Rose? Are you alright?"

"I'm fine, it's Rayner," she answered, trying to ignore the presence behind her in order to get back to Rayner's side, not bothering to wait to see if Oliver followed her. "He seems feverish. An infected wound perhaps?"

"Well, I don't really have the equipment on me to check, Rose."

"Would you just look," she groaned, yanking his arm toward the bed, drawing his attention from Xander who circled around them while she pointed out Rayner's reddened cheeks and the layer of sweat on his face and torso.

"Your attention to detail really is quite astounding," Oliver muttered, leaning over to look at his chest and the markings through the tears in his clothes, his brows knitted together as he searched for anything that could be infected.

162

"They look like burns," he muttered moving closer still, his tone light and quiet, almost in awe of what he was seeing. "I've never seen contact do this before."

"His curse," Xander growled, pulling Oliver a step back when he leaned in a little too close.

"They're demons, remember. Focus Oliver."

"I-I think you might be right. He is showing early signs of a fever, but from what I can see of his wounds, none of them look infected."

"No," Rosalyn sighed, clenching her fists in frustration, doing her best to ignore Xander's scowl when she stepped close to the bed, an idea popping into her head.

"Could you help me turn him?" she asked Xander with a glance back over her shoulder.

"No."

"I need to look at his back a moment," she said through gritted teeth, tugging the sheet below him.

"Stop it!" Xander growled, yanking her away from the bed with an arm held firm around her waist. Oliver fidgeted on the opposite side of the bed, eyes darting between them, likely too afraid to say or do anything to stop him.

Rosalyn guessed she should be afraid too, but right now she didn't care what he did to her. All she could think of was Rayner, and she needed them to stop being so damn stubborn and help her.

She may not know how demon bodies worked, or whether or not illnesses and infections affected them the same way they did in humans, but she wasn't willing to take the risk and do nothing. She would not risk him dying after everything. But she needed their help.

"You stop it," she snapped, punching and shoving at

163

his chest with all her might. Stamping down hard with her foot the moment his hold loosened slightly.

"Just help me, or get out," she demanded, clenching her fists as she stated back at Xander.

He released his hold on her but did not back away, just continued to glare down at her without a word.

"An infection could kill him, could it not?"

Rosalyn knew how heavy Rayner's body was after she had tried to pull him from the cabin so she knew she wouldn't be able to turn him alone, especially with the added complication of not being able to touch him. She needed Xander's strength, but she was prepared to do it herself if he still refused.

He continued to watch her, hesitant for far too long before he finally stepped forward, grumbling under his breath about her being a stubborn female, much like how Rayner had inside the cabin. The memory of his words causing an ache in her chest as she looked down at him.

Together they gathered the corners of the sheet and tugged. Xander made it look easy, while she struggled to maintain her grip.

Oliver rushed around the bed to help her, but even together, they couldn't lift the sheet as high as Xander. Their grip weak, the material sliding out of their hands, tugging them forward where they tried to hold on.

Rosalyn managed to catch herself on the headboard, knocking the wind from her, but Oliver lurched forward, his hand brushing against Rayner's arm, causing him to roar out in pain, his eyes snapping open and glowing brightly, focused on Oliver.

"I'm so sorry," Oliver blurted, taking several rushed steps back with Rayner's eyes still pinned to him. His breathing laboured as he attempted to reach for him before he gave up.

"Rayner?" Rosalyn called quietly, ignoring the other two as Xander grabbed Oliver by the scruff of his shirt and shoved him toward the door. Not that she could blame him. Oliver may have been trying to help, but he'd hurt Rayner who was already in so much pain. She could see it in his eyes when he turned to her. That roar clenching at her heart strings, making her blink back tears.

Xander was just looking out for his brother. No doubt scared to see him in this state.

"Rayner," she called again when his eyes flicked back to the others, trying to gain his attention despite the ferocious look that was on his face aimed at Oliver, and Xander's warning for her to keep back.

She believed that Rayner wouldn't hurt her, even if he was like this, and she proved herself right when he turned back to her, his expression softening. That fury seemed to ebb away the longer she held his gaze, before his eyes began to drift closed once more.

"No, no, Rayner. Not yet," she commanded, reaching forward before she was able to control herself, her hands coming into contact with his bare skin as she cupped his face. His skin hot and clammy against her palms.

His eyes shot open, staring at her before she dropped her hands away from him, kicking herself for what she had just done. Yet, he hadn't cried out in pain like he had when Oliver merely brushed against him.

"Rayner, please. I need you to try and roll over so I can look at your back."

He didn't answer, just continued to stare. Her own gaze was drawn to his cheeks to see if she had left any marks against his skin, like the tinged pink one she could see where Oliver had touched his arm.

165

"I need to see your wound."

He groaned loudly, sweat pouring down his face as he put more weight onto his back and attempted to push himself over. He needed help, a sure enough sign that something was wrong considering all she had seen him push through unphased, yet she hesitated.

Her hands may not have marked his face when she had grabbed him, but then the glyphs that covered his body did not reach his face. Those patterned markings danced beneath the surface when she glanced down at his neck and arms, where she hadn't noticed them move before. The two things she was almost certain had to be linked. A physical representation of his curse perhaps?

She shouldn't risk helping him by giving him an extra push. His thin, torn t-shirt wouldn't protect him enough from the contact, but she really did need to see his back. Surely a short burst of pain from her lending him a hand would be better than the suffering he endured right now, right?

Decision made, Rosalyn stretched over the bed and placed her hands on his side, careful of the wound she could now partially see below his ribs, close to his back. A wound that appeared red and sore. Something she knew couldn't be normal for him with his fast regeneration. Yet, with her hands on him, he still didn't roar out in pain.

His body grew heavier and heavier as she continued to help him push, until at last he was laying on his side. His breathing rapid and his skin burning against her hands.

"That's not right," Xander growled from just behind her ear.

"That most certainly looks infected," Oliver muttered, taking a step closer to have a look, keeping half his attention on Xander as he crouched down and pointed at

166

the wound on Rayner's back.

A long narrow slit surrounded by a large area of skin that was red and inflamed. A yellowish tinge in the centre, weeping a clear fluid that crept down his skin toward the bed.

"That needs to be cleaned and drained," Oliver commented, already headed toward the door, his tone loud and clear, just like she remembered from the hospital. Nothing like it had been over the last few days.

His sudden change filled her with confidence. Oliver knew that he was doing. Rayner would be fine.

The ache in her chest eased when after a short while Oliver returned to the room carrying a bowl of warm water, several pieces of cloth, and a small knife.

"No," Xander barked, stepping in front of Oliver as he placed the bowl on the small table beside the bed. "Not you. Her."

"But, he's the doctor. I'm just a–"

"Let's not anger the demon, shall we, Rose," Oliver said in a rush, shoving the knife and a damp cloth into her hands. "He's right anyway. You saw how he was a moment ago when I touched him. He didn't react the same with you. It has to be you."

Rosalyn gulped and took a deep breath, looking from Oliver, to Xander who both stood watching her, waiting.

She knew what Oliver said made sense. For whatever reason, Rayner didn't react the same to her touch as he did with everyone else, but she wasn't sure she could do this. Training and learning about all the different techniques and procedures was one thing, performing them on a living person that was clearly in a lot of pain was another thing entirely.

"I'm sure you remember your training, but I'll be

167

here to guide you nonetheless. Just start with a quick swipe of the cloth to clean the wound," Oliver instructed, resting a firm hand on her shoulder when she hesitated.

With a shaky hand, Rosalyn tugged on his t-shirt, wincing when it stuck to the wound and made him moan, gently lifting it higher until she could see the full extent of the wound.

She pressed the damp cloth against his back and wiped slowly across it.

"Good. Now make a small incision over the inflamed skin near that discoloured area to help drain it."

Clenching her trembling hands, Rosalyn leaned closer, glancing over at Xander who now stood at the foot of the bed, watching as she pressed the knife into his brothers skin, flinching and slicing a little wider than she planned when Rayner growled and his body jerked. Xander's hands gripping tightly around the bed frame, his eyes a lot darker than they had been before. No longer an icy, pale blue, but almost grey in colour before they flashed red.

"That's ok, just take a clean cloth and press a little harder on the wound, just above your incision to help push out the fluid. You're doing great, Rose."

Rosalyn continued to follow Oliver's instructions despite her shaking hands and Xander's intense glare, unaware how long she had been at it before Oliver squeezed her shoulder and told her to stop, taking the cloth and bowl away before he headed out of the room, leaving her alone with Xander and Rayner.

Rayner's breathing seemed to have slowed at some point during the process, which she hoped was a good sign.

"Is that it?"

Rosalyn nodded, unable to move or speak as she continued to stare at the wound on Rayner's back.

They would just have to wait and see how successful she had been over the next few days.

Rosalyn crossed her fingers that he would heal quickly, like he should have done to begin with. Hoping that she had rid him of as much of the infection as she could, leaving his body to take care of the rest. They couldn't rely on any antibiotics to make sure the infection cleared, not after he had told her that their medicines didn't work as intended on him and his kind.

"I guess you're alright. For a human."

CHAPTER 20

Rayner groaned, stretching out his aching body, wishing he could have slept a little longer and enjoyed the dream he'd been interrupted from, before he caught the scent of Rosalyn nearby, making his body ache for a whole other reason.

He scanned the unfamiliar room for her with a frown, unable to see her anywhere, until he heard her soft breathing from beside him, spying the top of her head rested on the side of the bed he lay in. Her back rose and fell slowly telling him she was asleep.

How long had she been there? He couldn't remember her being in the room with him when he'd fallen asleep after Niko came to talk to him, but perhaps her presence would explain his wild dream.

It wasn't the first time that he'd imagined her touching him, only this time it had felt almost real. His body responding accordingly to her teasing, his hands greedy to explore her skin as their lips met in a passionate kiss.

Even now he felt stiff and struggled to move, but for the first time since the Soulless attack, his body didn't feel like an inferno.

He pushed himself into a seated position, careful not to knock and wake her, noticing that the movement seemed a little easier than it had before. The blackened marks on his skin faded to a deep red.

"I thought it would work, but I didn't think you'd be

moving this quickly," he heard the doctor mutter from the doorway before Rayner pinned him with a glare and he stumbled, taking a step back.

He still wasn't used to the silence when humans were around, not knowing where the doc was when he couldn't hear his thoughts thanks to Rosalyn beside him. Of course, he could still attempt to read his mind if he chose to, much like he used to before the choice was taken from him, but why would he want to. The human mind was incredibly boring, and surprisingly dark.

"I'm sorry I came to the cabin before, but surely you can understand that I was worried for her. I didn't think they would follow me. I hadn't seen any sign of them."

"What worked?" Rayner asked, trying to ignore the doctors ramblings.

Yes he knew why he had done it, and even though he understood his reasoning, knowing he likely would have done the same if he were the doctor, it still bothered him that he had put her in so much danger. His actions had destroyed one of their safe houses because of it.

"The wound on your back became infected. Rose cleaned it up under my instruction, but we weren't convinced it would work that well without any antibiotics."

Rayner glanced down at Rosalyn still sleeping soundly beside him, before he reached around and felt a slight indent where a cut had been made, never realising he was caught across his back. His slow healing and the burning pain that continued throughout his body suddenly making a lot more sense.

His wounds would not heal at their normal rate if he fought off an infection.

"Thanks."

"Never expected that," Oliver muttered, stepping into the room, making his way to the bed on the opposite side to Rosalyn, keeping his distance as he leaned over and looked at Rayner's back.

"Remarkable. It's almost completely healed."

"Perhaps you're not as bad as I thought, doc."

"I could say the same."

Both of them remained silent while Oliver continued to stare at his back in awe, Rayner's attention focused solely on Rosalyn beside him. Her hand twitched in her sleep, before she let out a slight moan making him prick up his ears and lean forward to make sure she was alright.

"You're lucky you know," Oliver sighed, crossing his arms in front of him before he stepped back and glanced down at Rosalyn. The way he looked at her made Rayner clench his fists and teeth, wishing he could take his previous statement back.

"The rate at which your symptoms appeared, you could have gone down hill real quick. Do demons always react so severely?"

Rayner huffed out an amused snort.

He knew the doc still struggled to accept what he was, and what Rosalyn could see, but he seemed to be coming around to the idea, actually noticing some of the differences between them. Still, Rayner wasn't sure he liked being stared at like some lab rat the doctor couldn't wait to dissect and discover all the secrets of.

The Council would have a meltdown if they found out that not one, but two humans knew what they were and they were still breathing, let alone him telling them the ins and outs of how they worked, and what their bodies could withstand.

He wasn't wrong though.

Just like they healed fast, infections and poisons made their way through their bodies at an accelerated rate, an attempt to speed up their recovery, often having the opposite effect.

"I just hope you're able to repay her kindness and keep her safe from whatever those things are."

"I plan to."

"You actually care about her, don't you?" he asked, letting out another sigh, his eyes glancing his way before they returned to her. A sadness in his expression that confirmed Rayner's suspicion that he had feelings for her. His nails digging into his palms in order to restrain himself. That kiss they'd shared back at the hospital a flash before his eyes, making his chest vibrate where he tried to contain his growl.

"It's pretty obvious she cares about you too."

Rayner had to agree. Even back at the hospital, she was the one to notice the pain and put an end to it.

She may have feared him after that first Soulless encounter, something he couldn't blame her for, especially when she had no idea what they were, but even then, she had come back for him, unable to allow him to fight alone against a male with a weapon. Unable to remain angry at them when she realised they had been helping her, figuring out quickly that the Soulless were not creatures to be trifled with. The relief on her face when she had seen him rather than a Soulless back at her apartment jarring. All her fear seemed to have vanished more recently, replaced by concern for him after she had that vision. Pulling him to safety when his consciousness faded. Being the first one there when he woke, and doing her best to take care of him. Just like now.

He wasn't used to this. None of them were. Never

having anyone but each other to care for, unsure how to handle it from anyone else.

"Oh yeah," the doctor began, already headed toward the door, pausing to look back over his shoulder at her, then him. "She was able to touch you last night, twice, and you didn't react the same as I've seen with anybody else. I just thought you'd want to know."

Before Rayner had a chance for his words to sink in and ask any questions in return, like how and where she had touched him. Whether or not there were clothes or bed sheets between them as they had already discovered prevented the pain, Oliver was gone, leaving him alone with Rosalyn once more.

Her back continued to rise and fall with each breath whilst she slept by his side. His hands itching to touch her and find out how much truth was in the docs words. Only, they weren't alone like Rayner had first thought, her nearness seeming to dull his senses, not just his inability to hear others thoughts.

"Xander?" he growled, knowing his brother's presence the moment he allowed himself to concentrate.

"Imagine my surprise when I returned home to find my brothers missing and the cabin ransacked, only to track them here, to a human's house," he grumbled, stepping forward, his pale blue eyes the first thing Rayner saw as he approached.

"Don't fret. I'm not going to touch your female," he huffed below his breath when Rayner jumped from the bed, stumbling as he tried to block his brother's path to her, waking her in the process.

"You're awake?" she gasped, her eyes scanning him, leaving burning hot trails over his body everywhere her eyes lingered, his longing to touch her becoming more and

174

more overwhelming whenever she was near him. The dream he'd woken from fueling his desires.

"She's alright, for a human," Xander remarked, a slight curve to his lips before he nodded his head in her direction, much to Rayner's disbelief.

Xander loathed all humans, for good reason after all he had suffered at the hands of the human hunters. All those experiments they performed on him and the rest of the Other they'd captured. The torture he had to endure day and night. Finding his mate in that hell hole, only to have them take her away, never to be seen again.

"Yes, we've met," Rosalyn muttered, stepping slowly around the side of him, showing little sign of fear for his brother.

"Met me?" Xander scoffed, crossing his arms as he raised a brow at her, "she punched at me and stomped on my foot."

Rayner laughed aloud at the thought, wishing he could have seen it, turning to smile down at her, his chest filled with warmth and pride.

She was incredible. Fearless when she set her mind to things, and a hell of a lot more courageous than she gave herself credit for.

He would be proud to belong to someone like her. To have her as his mate, even if he knew such a thing could and would never happen.

"You wouldn't listen," she mumbled, her cheeks tinged pink as she lowered her gaze to the floor, doing her best not to look at him.

"Seems you met your match, Xander," Rayner sighed, sitting back on the edge of the bed. His tense body relaxing now he knew that Xander wasn't a threat to her.

He cared deeply for each of his brothers, but if

Xander made any move to hurt her, he wouldn't have held himself back from defending her. He would protect her from anybody, even though he knew he had his work cut out for him if the Council found out about her and their connection. Or if the Soulless managed to find them in their restless pursuit of her.

"Apparently so."

CHAPTER 21

Rosalyn paced from one side of the room to the other, heart pounding painfully against her ribs, making her head feel light. Hands trembling despite her efforts to control it.

She couldn't sleep.

Nightmare after nightmare plagued her, until finally she had given up trying.

That was hours ago now, and ever since then, she'd had the unnerving feeling that she wasn't alone in the room. That someone was there with her, watching. Similar to how she had felt when Xander had been in the room with her and Rayner before, only this time, it felt stronger and more intense.

The feeling was still there even after she turned on the lights and checked all the corners of the room. Under the bed, and even in the small wardrobe. Everywhere somebody could possibly hide.

Nothing.

"Trouble sleeping?" Xander asked, leaning back against the doorframe as he took a swig from the bottle of beer in his hands. His icy blue eyes watching her roam around the room.

"I haven't had nightmares like this in a while."

"To be expected. It's not everyday you find yourself running from Soulless, or surrounded by demons."

She supposed he had a point. The past few months had been eventful to say the least.

Deep down she had always believed in the things she

saw, but with so many others telling her she was wrong, it was hard to accept.

She had no clue about this world she had been thrust into. How it worked. What other creatures were out there. Even what the Soulless wanted from her.

Perhaps the nightmares were just playing on all her fears, her brain needing to unload all of her thoughts and concerns, but none of that could explain the unnerving feeling that had come with the dreams, even if it had vanished after Xander entered the room.

Could it be something to do with him? He was different from his brothers after all.

"Fancy one?" he asked, tipping the bottle toward her, motioning out the door with his head. "The doc has a surprisingly good supply that I plan to make use of."

Normally Rosalyn wasn't much of a drinker, only having the odd one of two when Sara forced her to go out, or when it was Christmas and New years, allowing herself to unwind a little. She'd always found that she saw more unusual things after she'd had a little too much to drink so she tended to steer clear of the stuff. But there was little to worry about right now. She knew she had demons around her, and she doubted there would be anything else to see in Oliver's house that could scare her. There was little reason for her not to try and relax. It might even help her sleep.

"Alright."

Rosalyn followed Xander down the dark hallway in silence as he led her to the kitchen, hugging herself tightly.

The room she was staying in was fairly warm, especially under all the blankets, but out here, in her freshly washed vest top and jeans, it was cold, sending a shiver through her body.

"He's not got very good taste when it comes to drink,

178

but it's better than nothing," Xander commented as he opened the fridge and pulled out two more glass bottles, flicking the caps off with his thumb before he held one out to her.

"Thanks," she muttered, taking a long sip of the cool drink, shivering again at the bitter taste sliding down her throat. "I'm surprised you asked me to join you though. I get the impression you don't like humans much."

"Don't like? I despise humans," he sneered, downing the remains of his drink before he slammed the bottle against the table, making her flinch, "but, I find myself interested in you, and why my brothers risked so much to keep you safe."

Rosalyn stared down at the bottle in her hands to avoid his watchful gaze, trying her best to act normal and not intimidated.

She didn't fear him lunging for her like she had before, but he was still a lot more frightening than his brothers. A darkness in him that she could feel, making her wary. His behaviour was a lot more volatile and aggressive compared to his brothers.

"You're different from other humans. More accepting."

There goes that word again. Different. But she was beginning to think that perhaps it wasn't such a bad thing.

"It's a little difficult to deny when you've always believed it deep down. Seeing creatures isn't exactly a new thing for me, just everybody always told me I was wrong."

"Everyone, even your parents? They couldn't see us too?"

"I don't know. They died before I turned three, so I didn't get a chance to learn about them."

"I see," he sighed, studying her. Looking at her as

179

though she were a puzzle he couldn't figure out. Trying his best to put all the pieces together but struggling to find the connection.

She'd tried her whole life to work out why she was different from everyone else, but if anybody stood a chance, it was them. If they managed to work out why, or even had a theory, she would be only too happy to listen. Her mind was currently coming up blank, unable to find any explanation.

There wasn't much she remembered about her parents. A vague image of what they looked like, but even then she wasn't sure how real that was. All she knew was that they had loved her. The memory of their smiles and affection was something she held dear. But they had been taken from her far too soon.

People claimed that it was a miracle she had gotten out of the car wreck in one piece, until the visions and talk of monsters began. Then she became the child who needed help. Her brain had clearly been damaged in the accident. The rejection from them all still painful, even more so now she knew she had been right all along.

"You're different too," she commented, gulping a large mouthful of her drink to settle her nerves and give her more courage as she sat across from Xander.

All of them appeared to have their differences, and not just in appearance. None of them looked alike so far as she could tell, aside from their sizing, still unsure whether they were brothers by blood, or by some other bond.

"Niko and Lorkan's eyes change black like other demons I've seen before. Rayner's are unable to switch. And yours. Well, yours are red."

Xander stood abruptly, causing her to do the same, fearing that she had said something she wasn't supposed to, clinging tightly onto the neck of her bottle, prepared to use it as a weapon if she needed to, but he didn't say a word, nor did he crowd over her threateningly like she expected. He just made his way to the fridge with his hands clenched, and grabbed several more bottles of beer, dumping the armfull on top of the table they'd been sitting at.

"Hunters," he growled at last, plonking back down in his seat before he started on his next drink, seeming to think that was all the explanation she needed. Though if she was honest, she hadn't expected any answer at all. "Human hunters."

"They did it to you? That's why you dislike humans so much?"

"Partly," he groaned, swishing the contents of his drink as he continued to stare down at the bottle. The shadows around him seemed to grow denser as she watched in fascination, and horror. Her heart beat faster as they spread toward her. Long tendril slivers reaching for her like fingers, forcing her to lean back before Xander looked up, those shadows receding just as quickly as they had appeared.

"My loathing, and that of my brothers came a long time before the hunters got their hands on me. My experience with them just intensified those feelings," he sneered, emptying yet another bottle. The third since she'd accompanied him. "Humans are quick to judge and kill anything they deem a threat."

Rosalyn couldn't really disagree. She had been on the other side of their judgement too. She knew what it was like to feel that she didn't belong, and had found herself disgusted by those around her. For a demon, those feelings had to be stronger.

In stories and films it was always the demons who

181

were portrayed as the bad guys, possessing people and forcing them to do terrible things. Killing and torturing. But she knew differently. She had seen just how kind and gentle they could be, despite their intimidating size and demeanour, unlike most humans she had come across in her life. Blaming others for their wrong doings.

She understood Xander's reaction to finding her in Rayner's room the other night. Likely believing her to be one of the hunters he mentioned come to kill him. Not that she could ever do that. She couldn't hurt any of them, but Rayner especially.

Out of them all, she felt the most connected to him. Scared just how much she did care.

She shook her head and took another long gulp of drink, scrunching her nose at the foul taste that hit the back of her throat.

She needed to stop thinking of Rayner and her feelings for him. She was fooling herself to think there could ever be something more between them.

He was a demon, and a Warrior. She wasn't. Not to mention the issue with his inability to touch, which would surely mean he had no desire to get close to anybody, much less her.

She couldn't keep thinking of him that way and risk Xander, or any one of them detecting her feelings.

"You know what that's like though, don't you? The judging. Being treated differently because of what you see?"

Rosalyn downed the rest of her beer and let out a long sigh, unsure whether she should tell him the things she hadn't told anybody else in her life, or try to change the subject.

Part of her longed to get everything off her chest and

see if he accepted her unlike everybody else, but part of her was afraid. Afraid of the ridicule and rejection she had always received when she had tried to be honest any open before.

She hadn't spoken about the past with anybody since she left Greenbryer, and the words were difficult to summon. Her throat already tightening at the thought, like a lump was lodged in place, still unsure whether she could trust him when she barely knew him. Only, when she looked at him, there was a kindness in his eyes that she hadn't noticed before, too afraid to really look before now. A gentleness that was hidden deep beneath his brash front. A man who had been through a lot and was used to guarding himself well. Just like her.

Perhaps if she opened up a little, he might even do the same.

Those dark shadows around him began to thicken the longer she hesitated.

He was doing it, controlling them somehow, something she had never seen or heard of before.

In truth she knew very little about these demons and what they were capable of, but she wished to learn, and this time with him, when he appeared quite talkative seemed like a good time to start.

"Yes," Rosalyn answered, reaching for another bottle of beer from the table, chugging half the contents with a shudder and cringe before she closed her eyes and took a deep breath.

"After my parents died, I was moved around a lot. None of them wanted to keep me for any length of time because they '*couldn't handle me*', before I ended up staying with my Aunt and Uncle," she mumbled, tightening the grip on the bottle as she looked across the table at him.

The shadows around gaining mass, but not moving toward her as they had before. A good sign she hoped.

"I've seen *things*, for as long as I can remember. Black eyes on strangers when they passed me by. Ghost-like shapes that resembled animals across the faces of others. Even the faint glittering outline of wings on some, but nobody ever believed me."

At first they had all told her what an incredible imagination she had, talking of fantasy creatures and just being a playful child, but the more she said, the quicker those smiles changed into disgust, fear, or pity. All of them believed she needed help, passing her along to the next family so they no longer had to deal with it, or her.

Eventually she had stopped telling others what she saw. Stopping talking altogether for some time, but the result had been the same. Those looking after her getting fed up of having to deal with a child that wouldn't talk, passing her along just as the others had.

She'd thought all of that would change when her Aunt and Uncle requested that she come live with them, but they had turned out to be the worst of them all.

Neither of them had wanted her because she was family and they cared, like she had mistakenly believed. They just wanted her because it made them look like good, charitable people, and the money they received to keep her in their care. But like the rest, there came a day when they could no longer handle her.

She'd been about eight at the time, playing alone in the front garden, before a man had approached her with red eyes and long fangs. She'd screamed out in terror, drawing the attention of the whole street.

A vampire. His face still haunted her dreams. Vampires being the one creature she hated the most ever since that day.

"When I was eight, my Aunt and Uncle sent me to the Greenbryer psychiatric unit."

"Eight?" Xander growled, his hand clenched tightly around the neck of his bottle before he slammed it down in an instant and took hold of her trembling hand, his brows knitted together between his eyes as he stared at her, a throbbing pain pounding at the front of her head, his grip growing a little tighter on her hand, before eventually he let go and sat back with a frown.

"Your mind is blocked," he muttered, still scowling. "I can only see a glimpse of your fears when I try to look inside."

"Y-you can do that?"

"We each have our strengths," he sighed, slouching back in his seat, still watching her with that perplexed expression. "All demons have psychic powers, stronger than the majority of Other. Able to manipulate memories and read others thoughts."

"Possession?"

"No, we don't possess people. That's a spirit thing your horror movies love to get wrong," he scoffed, wrinkling his nose in disgust. "We use our abilities to make others forget they've seen us, or to read minds in order to gain information."

"But, for some reason you can't do that with me?"

Rosalyn recalled Rayner saying something similar when she had first been brought to the cabin and Niko had attempted to do something then. The pain she'd felt just now similar to what she'd felt before.

Rayner had known it wouldn't work and claimed that Niko's attempt to make her forget them had failed, which was true. But all those in the hospital, even Oliver, had

185

forgotten all about Rayner and the night he was brought in, until more recently. She however remembered everything. From the sounds of Rayner's pain, to the look of fury on his face as he'd tried to free himself from their touch. All of them had looked at her as thought she were mad for intervening. A look she was accustomed to.

"As I said. Glimpses. Like, I know you can see my shadows, and that you're frightened, but curious, right?"

Rosalyn nodded, watching them gather and move around him. Focused on his crimson eyes whilst he stared at her, reminding her of the man who had come toward her all those years ago.

"I was an experiment, like the rest they caught. Now, along with my other abilities, I can manipulate the shadows and fears of others. Though, thanks to the blood Council's interference, my control isn't as it should be."

"Your punishment?"

"So, they told you about them too?"

Rosalyn nodded once more.

Rayner had told her that his inability to touch was a curse. His punishment for breaking the rules. Telling her how cruel and selfish their Council could be, making her wary of what they would make of her should they find out. Something that both Rayner and Niko seemed afraid of.

"Interesting," Xander remarked, leaning toward her when she drank a little more. "The more you're afraid, the less I can see. Usually it's the opposite way around."

Rosalyn wasn't sure how to respond.

It seemed that the more she got involved in this world, the more she discovered about herself. Still, none of it helped her. She was still no closer to discovering why she could see and do these things.

She thought talking to Xander might help her figure

something out, but aside from learning a little more about him, and what she could do, she was left with even more questions.

"You've somehow learnt to shield your mind at an expert level."

CHAPTER 22

Rayner knew she was in the room before he even opened his eyes.

A shiver worked its way through his body when he felt her eyes roam across him like a caress. Her alluring scent filled his lungs as he took in a deep breath and sat up. Another more bitter odour hitting him the closer she stumbled, bracing her hands on the base of the bed to keep herself upright.

"You've been drinking?" he growled, not liking the idea of her being vulnerable among so many males, especially when he noticed her flushed cheeks, mused hair, and skimpy top that showed far too much of her creamy skin, despite the bandages still in place over her shoulders and down her left arm.

"A little," she chuckled, sitting on the edge of the bed, her eyes wandering across his clothed body again, making his heart thump a little quicker. Even more so when he spied the top of her tongue moisten her top lip, turning his body to stone before she slipped and nearly fell to the floor.

"I couldn't sleep," she muttered, scooting back a little further until her legs swung back and forth in the air, her hands caressing the sheets either side of her before she flopped backward and stared up at the ceiling. Her hair fanned out beneath her as she tugged the sheets closer. Her breasts almost spilled out the top of her vest.

A growl rumbled deep in his chest at the sight of her

this way in front of him.

"I had a drink with Xander."

"Xander?" he grumbled, clenching his jaw. Torn whether he should confront his brother for whatever he'd done to her, furious at him for allowing her to get in this state when the Soulless still hunted her, or to stay and watch her while she made herself more comfortable at the foot of his bed. Her chest rising and falling quickly as she looked up at him.

"I thought I'd learn something, but I'm still confused," she pouted, propping herself up on her elbows when he climbed from the bed and began to pace beside her. His muscles tense, fighting his desires to crush his lips against her and run his fingers through her long, silken, black hair. A longing deep down that he hadn't been able to ignore since the day he'd woken in that hospital bed.

He craved her contact, not giving a damn about his curse. He just wanted to touch her.

"Rayner?" she spoke softly, reaching a hand toward him before he paused and held his breath.

If he allowed her to grab him now as he had before, he wasn't sure he would be strong enough to stop himself from pulling her closer. The pain he knew would come was nothing compared to the agony of his want. But if he gave in and cried out unable to hide it, he knew she would back away unwilling to hurt him.

He didn't want her to leave.

Once again he found himself furious at the Council, wishing Deyanira rotted somewhere for what she had done to him.

"Why am I different?"

He didn't know what to say. The look in her eyes pleaded with him to give an answer, but he hadn't one to

189

give her. He didn't know why she was able to see the things she did, or how it was possible for her to stop her thoughts from leaking to him, let alone all those around her. She was unique, but he had a feeling that wasn't what she wanted to hear.

"Why can't I be like everyone else?"

"You want to be like them?" Rayner asked, his voice coming out a little strained.

"Sometimes," she whispered, her eyes returning to his before she scooted forward, perching back on the edge of the bed, closer to him, "but then you wouldn't have come back if I were."

That wasn't entirely true.

Though he had certainly been intrigued by her ability to silence the chatter inside his head, that hadn't been the reason he couldn't get her from his mind. Nor did he know of her sight and inability to have her memories altered, or any of that. There was something more to her and his desires. Not just one thing about her that he could pinpoint, but everything she was.

"I would," he whispered back, knowing for certain that he told the truth.

She was his, and he belonged to her. Whether she accepted him or not, he already knew his fate.

Rosalyn slowly and carefully lifted herself from the bed, taking a few hesitant steps, closing the distance between them whilst he remained motionless in front of her, too afraid to move and scare her away, watching and longing for her to just touch him.

Painfully slowly, she lifted her hand and placed it against his clothed chest, pulling it back suddenly when he sucked in a deep breath.

The jolt of electricity that passed through him

sparked his body to life, and yet he forced himself to keep still, letting her come to him, knowing that she would flee if he pushed too hard. His body tense not only from anticipation and longing, but bracing against the pain he knew would come. The docs words from the night before ringing through his head.

She touched you last night, twice.

"It doesn't hurt," he muttered, taking a small step forward so her hands brushed against him again. His eyes closing in ecstasy when he felt her press a little firmer against his chest.

Her other hand joined the first, sending shivers through his body, wishing his shirt wasn't between them, knowing it was likely the only thing that protected him.

"The markings aren't on your face," she commented, her voice quiet and close when he opened his eyes and saw her looking up at him. A small gap between them, and yet it was the closest he had allowed anybody to stand near him in such a long time.

"Do it," he demanded, noticing how her hand hovered by his shoulder, his voice hoarse and laced with desire. All thoughts of pain pushed to the back of his mind if it meant he could feel her skin against his, even if only for a brief moment.

He watched her throat work, her hand creeping closer and closer to his face. His heart pounding as he braced himself.

She closed her eyes and gasped, her hand finally meeting his skin. His whole body sparked to life with energy flowing through him as though it was charged. Her soft, silky skin warming his face, but not with the burning pain he expected.

Slowly she opened her eyes and gaped up at him.

The reflection of his green eye glowed brightly in hers.

"Doesn't it hurt?" she asked, stroking her thumb so delicately over the ridges of his jaw, her head tilted to the side, looking at the markings he knew she could see on the top of his neck, her hands hesitant to explore lower.

Rayner shook his head, not trusting his voice to work as he stared down at her in wonder.

Aside from Deyanira, nobody had touched him in years without it causing him pain, yet here she was, with her hand against his bare skin, something he never believed possible.

The doc was right after all.

Except, it wasn't enough. He hungered for more, needing to feel her skin below his fingers.

He reached up his hand and wrapped it around hers, his chest painfully tight as he held his breath and guided her hand lower down his neck.

"No," she shrieked, attempting to pull her hand away, stumbling and falling closer to him instead. "The marks aren't on your face," she whispered, staring wide eyed as he continued to hold her hands against him, letting out a shuddering breath.

Though she was right that the glyphs were linked to his curse, he knew he would have felt the pain on his face just the same as anywhere else on his body.

In the beginning he had pushed to see the true extent of his curse, learning quickly there wasn't a sliver of his skin that could be touched by another without the pain and burning that came with it. The markings only visible over his torso to begin with, slowly spreading up his neck and down his arms, his face, legs and hands still free from them, for now. Yet the pain remained the same, like a concentrated flame held against his flesh. The only person

192

able to touch him before now, Deyanira, taking joy in having so much power over him, her touch causing his skin to crawl.

With Rosalyn, it was different. The sensation, indescribable.

He wanted more. Her lips beckoning him closer, needing to taste her.

"It really doesn't hurt you?" she asked again when he lifted his hand from hers, and raised it to her head, running his fingers through her thick locks like he'd wanted to for so long, holding her still as he leant forward and brushed his lips against hers in a fleeting kiss.

The surge of energy that coursed through him made his body shiver as he held on to her, bringing their lips together once more, lingering this time and deepening the kiss. Her hands reached up to cup his cheeks when she gave in and accepted the truth.

Her touch didn't hurt him.

He wasn't sure how it was possible, or even if this was just a dream, but he planned to savour it while he could, allowing his hands to explore her curves as he brought them closer together, crushing her against him. The moan that escaped her lips spurring him on. His need to keep his hands on her overwhelming.

Reluctant he broke away, breathing heavily, groaning at the sight of her kiss swollen lips, his hands clenched by his sides when she licked them.

He wanted to continue their kiss. To allow himself to feel her skin beneath his fingertips and enjoy her touch in return, but he sensed something nearby. Something almost familiar but too faint to make out.

"You should get some rest," he ground out, his voice deep and guttural when he turned away and clenched his fists.

She'd been drinking earlier so he needed to control himself and not get too carried away, possibly taking advantage of her state. He had to distract himself. An impossible task when she placed her hands against his back, stroking them across his shoulders. Her scent surrounding him.

He turned, grabbed hold of her wrists in one hand, and circled the other around her waist, crushing her lips beneath his when the shrill sounds of an alarm triggered.

Part of him was relieved for the distraction he needed to move away from her before he did something she may regret when sober, the other part was furious at having to leave her to see what was happening. The sound of footsteps in the hall and the banging of doors making him growl.

He turned and snatched up his sword, holding it tightly in one hand, grabbing hold of her with the other before he left the room, headed toward the voices he could hear down the hall.

CHAPTER 23

"What's with all the noise?" Rayner shouted over the commotion, his hand warm around hers where he continued to hold it tight.

She still couldn't believe it. She was touching him. Touching him without him howling in pain. No marks visible on his skin when she'd looked across at his neck. Nothing, but those glyphs swirling beneath the surface in a mesmerising pattern.

"Something triggered the alarm and the human can't remember the code to switch it off," Xander growled, shoving Oliver aside to punch the console, only for it to make an even higher pitched noise, making all of them flinch and cover their ears.

"Turn that damn thing off," Xander commanded, turning to face them with a raised brow when he stepped closer, peering close at her face. "Don't think I didn't see that."

Her cheeks were aflame, and all she could do to try and hide it was turn away, unable to remove her hands from her ears with that deafening sound still ringing.

"Move," Rayner snapped, lifting his sword the moment Oliver stepped aside, spearing the panel until the blade hit the wall behind. The alarm letting out one last high pitched screech before it faded and died out completely.

"Anyone want to tell me why the alarm was going off?"

"Perimeter search didn't show anything," Xander

commented, crossing his arms over his chest, a smile curving the corner of his lips when he looked across at her again, only adding to the fire in her cheeks.

"Niko called. They've emptied out the old safe house which should be more secure than here."

The colour seemed to drain from Rayner's face, his sword now held loosely by his side. His jaw set hard.

"Rayner?" she whispered, stepping a little closer, glancing over at Oliver who still frowned and fiddled with the alarm console, and Xander who still watched her.

"I know we–" Xander began.

"It's fine," Rayner interrupted, holding a hand out to Xander in order to silence him, "it's safer there."

He looked down at her and took her hand in his once again. The colour returning to her cheeks. Her heart fluttering inside her chest when he smiled. He really was handsome, especially when he gave her that look, revealing those deep hollows in his cheeks that made her knees feel weak.

It really wasn't some drink induced hallucination. Rayner really was touching her. No redness on his skin. No cries of agony. Just his hand wrapped around hers.

She squeezed a little tighter, her legs wobbling beneath her when she heard him stuck in a breath, momentarily believing she had hurt him until she spied his green eye glow, both of them filled with lust, for her.

He wasn't in pain at all. He was enjoying her touch.

"So, she really can touch you, huh?" Oliver commented on a breathy whisper, his eyes glued to their entwined hands. "How is that possible?"

"Details don't matter," Xander growled, gripping Oliver's shoulder roughly, steering him down the hall. "This place is no longer safe."

"But you said you didn't see anything."

"Exactly."

"A person, or even an animal could have triggered the alarm, but Xander saw nothing, which means whatever caused it was either extremely fast, or able to hide, even from us," Rayner explained, tugging Rosalyn by the hand back to the room he'd been using to recover in.

"I have a camera system that records the front and back door. You could check that to see if you spot anything?" Oliver commented from the open doorway, watching Rayner place his sword on the bedside cabinet, before he lifted his torn t-shirt over his head.

"Bring the recording. The sooner we leave the better," he commented, turning back around to face her and Oliver. "You got a top with less holes, doc? Preferably with long sleeves."

"Debatable," Oliver scoffed, heading out of the room, leaving her alone with Rayner, very aware of his half naked body as he strolled across the room and glanced out the window, before he turned back to her.

"Don't worry. You'll be safe where we're going."

Rosalyn didn't doubt his words, but it wasn't fear that had her staring. Her eyes were drawn to his powerful body, licking her suddenly parched lips before she stepped a little closer and placed her hands against the hard ridges of his stomach, pulling them back when he took in a shuddering breath.

It was still so difficult to believe that her touch didn't hurt him. Every time he made a noise she thought the worse, but just as before, there were no red marks on his skin, only proving she could.

She pressed forward again, a smile curving her lips this time when his eyes closed and he groaned. His chest rising and falling quickly when her hands began to explore him. Watching the pattern under his skin that seemed to leave a shimmering trail behind her caress.

Gorgeous, even if they were the source of his pain.

With his eyes still closed, she moved in even closer, reaching up on her tiptoes to kiss his cheek, gasping when his arm snaked around her waist and his eyes flew open. The green dazzlingly bright, and the black, breathtaking this close. Those star-like specks seemed to glitter the longer as she stared, the faint white cracks still reminding her of how he had called himself *broken*.

"Beautiful," she whispered under her breath.

"Funny, I was thinking the same thing."

He pressed his lips against hers in a fierce, yet gentle and possessive kiss, his tongue stroking across her bottom lip making her legs tremble as she pressed her body against his, wrapping her arms around his neck to keep herself upright, afraid that if she let go she would fall to the floor. Her own tongue tasted his mouth, her teeth scraping against his lip causing him to growl and squeeze even tighter. His hardened length pressed into her hip.

A rumble built in his chest before he pulled back and stared over her shoulder.

Heart thumping, Rosalyn glanced to where he was looking just as Xander appeared in the doorway clearing his throat.

"We're all set," he commented, tossing Rayner a t-shirt that he instantly pulled over his head. The material tight across his broad frame, clinging to his muscled chest, doing little to douse the desire burning inside of her.

She knew now wasn't the time to lose herself in his embrace, still wary of what had triggered Oliver's alarms, but after fantasising about him for so long, she couldn't help herself. Those first dreams she'd had seemed more and more like a possibility. Her mind was still in shock how it was even possible.

"Here," Xander grunted, tossing a jumper in her direction, "it's cold out."

Rosalyn couldn't help but smile, appreciating his concern for her, something she never thought would happen, not with his hatred for her kind.

"Let's go. The doctor had the tapes and is starting the car."

"Stop," Rayner blurted, "go back a bit."

Oliver did as instructed, rewinding the footage from his security cameras for Rayner to watch while Xander drove them to their new location. Clearly he had seen something that caught his eye, but Rosalyn hadn't noticed anything among the dark frames. Her eyes still a little blurred from the drink she had consumed earlier. A constant throb in her head telling her she needed some water, and most likely sleep.

"There. Can it play back slower?"

"If it was still connected to the computer it could, but not here."

The video played as normal, Rayner sliding forward in his seat to get a better look, his brows furrowed in concentration.

"There," he growled, pointing a finger at the small screen on the portable player.

Rosalyn scooted forward next to him, squinting her eyes to see what he pointed at. A shadow that appeared to move unnaturally at the side of the building. There one moment and gone the next.

"Soulless?" she asked, gripping tightly at her knees.

How had they found them at Oliver's? Unless they had followed him from the hospital in hopes of finding her before. And how was it possible that Rayner and Xander hadn't noticed them?

When they were at the cabin, Rayner had silenced them, sure he could either hear or sense something a long while before they had seen anything outside. She supposed he could have been distracted, they had been a little preoccupied at the time. A blush coloured her cheeks as she moved back in her seat, remembering the feel and taste of his mouth against hers. His warm powerful body beneath her hands.

"I don't know," Rayner grumbled, still frowning at the small screen Oliver held in his hands. The picture paused on the very scene with the odd looking shadow. No real distinct shape to it. Just a mass of darkness.

"If it was them, why didn't they attack like they did before?" Oliver asked quietly, looking from Xander beside him, back to Rayner who sat behind, next to her.

It was possible they didn't have the numbers this time like they did back at the cabin, but even so, when they had been at the hospital, one of them had still approached when it was alone. They didn't seem to really care about themselves, just their goal, whatever that was.

"We'll have Lorkan look over the footage when we arrive. He's better with all the tech stuff."

Oliver continued to play through the tapes, Rayner still leaning forward in his seat to see the screen more clearly, the white noise lulling Rosalyn to sleep. Her exhaustion finally got the better of her, eyes already closed to half mast.

She took one last look at the screen before adjusting her position, scooting a little closer to Rayner before she leaned back against the headrest.

She reached out her hand and placed it on his thigh, a smile on her lips when he covered it with his own and squeezed tight, taking some comfort in having him close, hoping it was enough to rid her of the nightmares that had already robbed her of her sleep once this evening.

CHAPTER 24

It felt like only seconds had passed before Rosalyn's eyes flew open. The sound of tires squealed and the loud curses of those around her snapping her awake with a start.

The car was out of control, veering toward a ditch at high speed while Xander fought to control it.. The ground came toward the windscreen fast as the car flipped onto the roof. A large pole crumpling the bonnet, causing smoke to billow from the engine.

Her head slammed back against the headrest she'd been leaning on, making her vision blur.

Rosalyn looked across at Rayner beside her, her heart in her throat when she spied dark blood running down his face. His eyes closed tight even when she reached over and brushed her hand against his cheek.

Xander groaned in front of her, pushing hard against the steering wheel in an attempt to gain some leverage with no avail. Oliver was unconscious beside him, blood pooling beneath his clothes from the shattered glass all over him. The portable player no longer ran the footage they'd been watching, but filled the car with the sound of static.

"You alright?" Xander groaned, looking back over his shoulder.

Rosalyn opened her mouth to respond when she spotted a shadow in the broken mirrors, making her heart race, her ears ringing loudly as she tried to turn around.

More shadows joined the first. The sound of footsteps crunching over the gravel and glass sent a shiver through her body.

Xander cursed loudly, pushing with all his might against the wheel, causing the car to groan in protest.

"Maybe someone saw the car crash and came to help?" Rosalyn whispered, though she didn't really believe her own words.

She looked back over to Rayner and nudged him again, panic making her hands unsteady as scanned his body for wounds, releasing her belt so she could get a better look. She yelped in pain when she landed on the car ceiling and twisted her leg in an uncomfortable position.

"Rayner?" she called again, shuffling a little closer, tears in her eyes, making them sting with the smoke.

He'd only just healed from his infection. Perhaps his body wasn't as strong as it should be yet.

She nudged him again, looking for the source of his bleeding, pleased to see that the flow had already begun to slow. The deep gash by his jaw already knitting itself together.

"W-what happened?" Oliver stirred, his seat squeaking when he attempted to move and brush some of the glass from his clothes. Lots of tiny scratches over his face when he turned to the side. Blood was still oozing from his chest, but at least he was conscious and speaking now, unlike Rayner.

Rosalyn squeezed her eyes and held her breath, moving herself over even further until she sat in front of Rayner. His head in her lap.

She couldn't see any more wounds, aside from that gash that appeared to be healing, so why was he still not waking like the rest of them?

She leant forward with a wince, ready to place a kiss against his lips in an attempt to rouse him from sleep when someone grabbed hold of her arm.

"What–?"

Her sentence died on her tongue seeing a face mere inches from her own.

Bright blue eyes surrounded by red. A wide open mouth revealing sharp teeth, and a red tongue that reached toward her face. Its nails dug deep into her wrist before it yanked at her arm, a scream escaping her lips at the scraping of claws behind her.

"Soulless," Xander growled, grabbing onto some of the shards of glass to defend himself, ready to slash at any arms that reached in, but none attempted to grab him. Just those two in the back, holding onto her. One pulling at her arm, trying to bring her closer. Its rancid breath overpowering the smoking car, making her cough and gag. The other one climbed through the broken window snatching hold of her leg, pulling hard in the opposite direction.

"Rayner's sword!" Xander yelled, pushing again at the wheel to move it and get free, growling loudly when the metal squealed and buckled beneath the force. Still his legs were pinned, unable to help in her struggle.

Rosalyn searched around her. "It isn't here!" she yelled.

Had it been flung from the car when it spun out of control?

Another Soulless joined the other two, its nails scraping on the metal ceiling as if crawled through the back window, making its way toward her, its face moving closer and closer. The smile on its lips grew wider as it clawed its way up her legs and torso, stopping with its face almost nose to nose with hers.

She couldn't get away, pinned there by the weight of the thing on top of her and the other two holding her in place. Xander and Oliver trapped in the front, both rocking the car as they fought to get free, and Rayner still unconscious beside her.

"Rayner!" she shrieked, needing him to wake up and help her, but still he didn't move. Tears cascaded down her face as the Soulless wrapped around her began to pull hard, dragging her along the roof of the car.

With her free arm, Rosalyn grabbed the seatbelt she'd been using and wrapped it around her arm, yelping loudly when it tightened and rubbed against her skin, digging into her flesh. The Soulless fought to pull her further, only causing the belt to wrap tighter.

Rosalyn kicked out with her feet, trying to free herself from their grasp enough to move further into the car where Xander might be able to reach her. The shadows around him were already thick and menacing while he rattled the wheel and roared, pulling at his own legs to get free. The damage he must be doing to himself, excruciating.

Rosalyn kicked out again with her free leg and heard the crunch of bone when her foot collided with one of the Soulless's face, giving her enough leeway to scurry away and cling to the back of Oliver's seat when a piercing roar filled the air, making her blood run cold.

Rayner. He was awake at last, but the Soulless that had been pulling on her arm was now clawing at his chest, tearing through his shirt and skin, leaving black burns everywhere it touched.

His eyes closed as he thrashed and wrapped his bare hands around its throat, squeezing tight.

"Rayner?" she gasped, kicking out with her legs again in an attempt to reach him and help fight the creature off, but he beat her to it, snapping the Soulless's neck. His chest rose and fell rapidly as he panted for breath, eyes focused on her, yelping in pain when her hand touched his stomach.

Quickly she pulled her hand away, her own heart missing a beat when she looked down at the blackened mark across his skin. Had she caused that? No, it had to be there already. She couldn't accept never being able to touch him again after only just discovering she could.

She shook her head, her hand hovering above his body, afraid to touch him again in case it was true, when the Soulless she'd kicked grabbed her ankles, yanking hard and pulling her across the ceiling of the car, until Rayner's arm circled around her chest, holding her body to his. His free hand struggled to unlock his own belt to release him.

Part of her sighed in relief knowing that at least she hadn't hurt him with her touch, but how could she relax when there were still at least two more Soulless grabbing for her?

Rosalyn didn't know what they wanted with her, but she suspected her ability to touch Rayner may have something to do with it. Nobody else could touch him without the pain, so whatever allowed her to do so must be why the Soulless were so set on getting to her.

"He wants you," the Soulless wrapped around her ankles sneered, climbing its way up her legs despite her struggles, trying to gain more leverage and pry her from Rayner's arms.

"He can go to hell," Rayner spat, giving up with the buckle to yank hard on the belt, ripping it free from the seat, causing him to crash to the ceiling with her still clung to his side. A grunt from both of them when they hit the solid surface. Rayner still held firmly around her while the Soulless snarled and let out a piercing shriek. Three more of them appeared at the windows reaching in to grab at him. The roar he let out made her ears ring whilst he continued to hold on as tightly as he could, not willing to let her go despite the pain he suffered.

Rosalyn's eyes filled with tears, her nightmares from earlier this evening coming back to her. Rayner's cries of pain. The Soulless faces close to hers.

She'd seen this coming. Not the crash, but the struggle that was happening right now.

She didn't want them to take her, unsure what this man the Soulless mentioned wanted with her, but she couldn't allow them to hurt Rayner again because of her either.

He'd been lucky to survive the last attack, especially with that infected wound. What if they did something like that again?

Rosalyn squeezed her eyes closed, tears falling, leaving burning hot trails across her cheeks, and released herself from his grip while he struggled to free himself from their greedy hands, allowing the creature at her feet to pull her the rest of the way out of the car.

Rayner's deafening roar made her tears fall faster and her heart clench tight.

The Soulless's face approached hers, its mouth opened wide the last thing she saw before everything faded black.

CHAPTER 25

Her head throbbed when she woke. The lights above her blinding, forcing her to squeeze them closed. Her body felt heavy and sluggish, nausea churning in her stomach as she attempted to lift her head.

The Soulless. It must have fed on her again. The sensation felt the same as before, like she was in quicksand. Every movement was slow, her limbs too numb to move, fueling her panic. But why hadn't it killed her?

He wants you, the creature had said in its oddly disjointed voice. But who was *he?*

Rosalyn turned her head to one side, a sharp pain shooting through her neck, and cracked an eye open, wincing once more at the bright lights above her. Nothing but bleached white walls surrounded her.

Heart in her throat, she turned to the other side, a whimper escaping her when she saw the tinted glass wall she'd expected, knowing exactly where she was.

Greenbryer.

She'd spent days at a time locked in a room just like this during her stay. But why was she here now? She wasn't crazy. She knew that demons were real now.

It couldn't have all been a dream, could it?

No, that wasn't possible.

Tears stung her eyes. A new bout of nausea turned her stomach as her entire body shook, sweat trickling down her face.

"No," she gasped, her airways closing, making it difficult to swallow.

She thrashed on top of the bed, her hands bound either side of her, impeding her movements. The material rubbing against her skin with each pull and twist she made. All the noises muffled, as though she were in deep water. A cool touch against her ankle making her freeze to the spot, her heart thumping wildly in her chest.

"Good evening, Miss Manar," came a familiar voice that made her heart skip a beat.

"D-doctor Holter?"

No. No. It couldn't be him. If he was here, it meant she was locked up again. That everything was a fabrication of her mind, just like he'd told her so long ago.

Tears streamed anew down her cheeks, a sob escaping her throat before she was able to stop it.

She couldn't have imagined all of them.

Niko. Lorkan. Xander, and especially Rayner.

She refused to believe that she could create them all in her mind, no matter how crazy people had told her she was. No matter how much he had told her that she couldn't be seeing what she claimed. The Soulless too haunting and unlike anything she had ever seen before. Her connection to the demons who she had grown to care about.

"No!" she screamed, unwilling to believe it.

"Calm down, Rosalyn. You're safe here. There are no more monsters to frighten you."

"I can't be here. I was in the car. They took me."

"Who took you, Rosalyn? Was it the demons? Or perhaps that man you thought was a vampire?" Dr Holter asked, studying her with that same condescending look he had always given her. The one that made her think she was insane. The one she had always hated.

"There is no car, Rosalyn."

He was lying. He had to be.

There had to be something she was missing, something that was out of place meaning this wasn't real.

He was human, she knew that much. He'd never appeared anything but to her, even now, but he had to be linked with the Soulless somehow. He just had to be. She refused to believe that none of them were real. That Rayner was not real.

Perhaps there would be a weapon nearby in case she needed it, or something on her that told her she wasn't making it up. Only, there was nothing. Even her clothes were different from what she was wearing when she had been in that car, her body too numb to feel whether she still had the bandages on her arms and shoulders, or any cuts or bruises from the wreck.

But she wouldn't give in. There needed to be something.

The way he watched her was just the same as before. An expression filled with pity, and something she couldn't place, making her clench her hands and bite down on the insides of her cheeks.

"You're lying!"

"You came to us a few weeks ago, Rosalyn. You've been in and out of sleep for days now, talking of demons, and strange creatures I don't remember you mentioning until more recently," Dr holter sighed, approaching her bedside. The sound of a chair squealing against the tiles making her grit her teeth and wince. "You seem to have had a major relapse, which is such a shame. You were doing so well. You had even made it into your medical school, learning at Green Oaks. Do you remember Green Oaks, Rosalyn?"

"Yes."

"There was an incident outside the hospital. You

claimed to the policemen that you saw a man be killed, but there was no evidence to suggest what you were saying was true. No camera footage. No body to be found."

"Oliver was there."

"We haven't had a chance to speak with him yet, but a lot of nurses and doctors claimed you asked them of a man who nobody could remember. Who was he?"

Rosalyn opened her mouth to respond, but quickly closed it again.

There was something off about what he was asking, as though he were fishing for information.

She could be wrong, that all of this was just a dream like he seemed to be claiming, but she wasn't prepared to take the risk. If Rayner was real, like she was certain he was, she couldn't give his name over to Dr Holter. She didn't trust him. She never had.

"No name?"

"I never knew their names, Dr Holter, you should know that."

He turned away from her, glancing toward the door, but not before she saw his lips curl back with a sneer. A shadow-like figure moving on the other side of the glass behind him. Something she shouldn't have been able to see through.

Something was off.

The room may have been one she was used to from her time here, but there was something different about it. A lack of equipment that made her suspicious. The fact she could see something behind the two way glass off putting.

Who was there?

She doubted it was another doctor, or even a nurse, but she hoped it wasn't the Soulless. She'd had enough of seeing those for a lifetime.

211

Dr Holter appeared to pick up on her stare, looking behind him to see what she looked at, frowning when he turned back to her.

"Can you see a monster now, Rosalyn?"

She wanted to say he was the monster here, but thought it best not to antagonize him when she was tied up and had no idea what he wanted. That shadow seemed to grow darker when she peeked back toward the glass, wondering who or what could be behind it.

"You're not going to talk to me today? I've been waiting so long to speak with you."

"Where are the other doctors and nurses?"

She hadn't remembered until now, but whenever she was seen by a doctor or nurse, there was always more than one present, especially when in rooms such as this one.

Again an almost angered expression crossed his face before he gained control of himself, replacing it with a fake smile that only made her feel more nervous.

"But of course."

Dr Holter held up his hand and flicked his fingers back and forth, calling someone into the room with them. Her heart pounded when she saw the shadow behind the glass move, and heard the doorknob to the room turn.

Trying her best not to show her fear, she peeked down toward her toes, unable to see anybody until she felt the bed dip on her other side, making her turn slowly around.

Rosalyn gasped aloud, coming face to face with two bright green eyes that stared down at her. Pale, shimmering glyphs stretching up the man's neck and across his jaw and cheeks, so similar to Rayner's it made her heart ache.

"H-Helmer?" she whispered, tears pooling in her eyes as he watched her. His lips curved up into a crooked smile before he placed his cold hand on her stomach and sucked in a deep breath, turning her body to ice as he caressed her skin, lowering his eyes to follow his own movements with a look of wonder on his face.

"Perhaps I was a little hasty before," he chuckled, his hand stroking higher and higher up her stomach, before he paused and squeezed tightly over her ribs. "I now understand what my brother sees in you."

His eyes flashed black when he turned back to her, his smile now vanished, even though his hand remained on her stomach, continuing with his exploration of her body, making it difficult for her to concentrate on her thoughts, trying in vain to escape his touch.

Why was he here, with Dr Holter?

Dr. Holter had been one of those to claim she was mad, yet here he was with a demon. A Warrior demon at that. Did he not know what he was? Impossible. He had to know. But what did they want with her?

"It's been such a long time since I was able to touch anybody," he spoke in a deep, guttural voice before he leaned toward her neck and inhaled, his body shuddering before he finally removed his hand, only to bring it up to her head, running his fingers through her hair. His face alarmingly close to hers.

She choked down the sob in her throat, not wishing to give him the satisfaction of her fear, fighting her body to remain still when his hands caressed her cheek, and down her neck, making her shiver uncontrollably.

Helmer may be their brother, but he was nothing like the rest of them. Her fear when she had met each of them was different from what she felt now. A cold, bitterness about him that outweighed even that of Xander.

"What do you want from me?"

213

"Everything," he snarled, shoving her head painfully to the side before he stepped away from her and began to pace back and forth. His footsteps deafening in the near empty room. Dr Holter sitting beside her in silence, watching Helmer.

"He can't have you."

Rosalyn wasn't sure if she was doing the right thing or not, but anything was better than lying here in silence, with his hands roaming over her body, making her skin crawl.

She needed answers, and Helmer seemed to know a lot more about her than she would have expected, unless he had been watching her for some time.

"Why?"

"So many questions," he growled, stomping back over to her, glancing across at the doctor before he leaned in close to her face again. "But I have one for you. Does he love you? Does he know what you are to him, what he is to you?"

Rosalyn just stared at him blankly unsure how to answer his questions.

She had no idea about Rayner's feelings, let alone her own.

She cared for him deeply, unwilling to see him hurt or suffer. The thought of losing him too much to bear, but did that mean she loved him? She had no idea what love meant. What it really was, never having experienced such things growing up. Never being on the receiving end of them either.

What she felt for him was incredible, and painful all at the same time, but she had no idea what that meant, and she had no idea whether he loved her.

He had risked his life for her on more than one

occasion, but that was him just doing his job, wasn't it?

She'd thought so at first, but then he'd shown he cared for her too, allowing her and nobody else close to him before he knew that her touch would not cause him pain, risking the agony when he had demanded she touch him when she hesitated, forcing her hands against his skin, throwing himself to the Soulless in the cabin even though he knew he wouldn't be able to escape.

Was that love?

"Your silence is all the answer I need," Helmer sneered, still smirking when he looked at the doctor, nodding to him, and passing along some kind of message before he stood and left them alone. His eyes back on her the moment the door clicked shut behind him.

"I doubt you ever mentioned this place to him, or your history here."

She hadn't told anybody about this place for years, unwilling to admit what had happened in her past, ashamed of what she was, until more recently, when she had decided to trust and confide in Xander.

Rayner didn't know of this place, but he did.

But after she had given herself over to the Soulless, would they bother looking for her?

"Don't worry. No matter how long it takes him, he will come for you."

CHAPTER 26

Rayner panted for breath, his hands pulsing from the burns that spread up his arms as he grappled another Soulless by the neck and twisted it hard at an angle, until he heard the bones snap. He stomped down with his boot on the creature's skull when it slumped to the group in a heap. His body was almost numb to the pain as he ran forward to intercept the next one that let out a piercing shriek, alerting more and more of them to their location. He slammed his elbow into its nose.

None of the contact was as agonising as seeing Rosalyn dragged from the car after she had let go of him, knowing she had done it to spare him.

He pushed himself onward, across the field, his sword discarded on the ground only a few more yards ahead of them, flung from the car when it flipped over onto its roof. Xander limped behind him after he'd yanked his legs free from the crumpled wreckage, trying to get to Rosalyn whilst Rayner fought off the Soulless that clung to him.

"Isn't that hurting him?" he heard the doc ask Xander, his own legs injured in the crash, but thankfully unbroken, leaning on Xander for a bit of support.

"Yes, but he's just lost his mate. Nothing hurts more than that."

"She is not lost," Rayner snarled, roaring loudly when another Soulless dove at him from the long grass around them. The creature wrapped itself around him, clawing at his face. "I will find her."

Xander pulled the creature away and impaled it through the side of its head with a long shard of glass he'd been clutching, shaking his head when Oliver went to speak, silencing him.

Neither of them said another word when Rayner reclaimed his sword and swung at yet another oncoming Soulless, it's head crashing to the ground. More and more sweat ran down his back as held on to his consciousness.

He couldn't fail her again. He needed her just as much as she needed him. The voices in his head came back to him in a rush the more distance there was between them. The Soulless's dark desires flooding into his mind like a torrent of sound he couldn't break through, almost bringing him to his knees. The clash of noise gradually got quieter the more of them he killed, but it was still deafening.

He'd gotten used to having Rosalyn nearby. The voices that plagued him daily were almost forgotten about, but he didn't care about that. If it meant she was back with him and safe, he would gladly suffer the noise for the rest of eternity. Willing to accept anything the Council threw at him so long as she remained unharmed. Not caring if even her touch caused him pain after this. He would endure it all.

"I'm sorry I didn't make it sooner," Niko sighed, glancing across at Rayner while he drove them to their old home. The secure building they'd been headed toward when Xander had lost control of the car and his whole world that crashed down around him again.

Losing their brother had been painful and difficult for them all, especially after almost losing Xander a few years before. But having Rosalyn give up and allow them to take her away was the worst kind of agony he had ever

217

felt.

He didn't know how Xander did it. His cold and bitter attitude since finding and rescuing him from the hunters was even more understandable now. But Rayner wasn't ready to give up just yet.

He didn't know where to start looking for her, but he would find her, or die trying.

"What happened?"

"I saw someone," Xander began, his eyes glued to Rayner, burning a hole in the back of his head. "Or something."

"What?"

"You're not going to believe me, but it looked like Helmer."

"Impossible," Niko exclaimed, glaring into the rear view mirror at him.

"I know what I saw."

"W-who is Helmer?" Oliver asked, his voice quiet, eyes darting between them as Rayner spun in his seat to look at Xander.

Xander may be rash at times, and a bit of a troublemaker, but Rayner trusted his brother and knew he would not make something like this up. But Helmer? Helmer was dead.

"He was our brother," Niko answered with a drawn out breath, clenching his hands around the steering wheel when the car rolled to a stop. His knuckles white from the pressure of his hold. "He died over twenty years ago."

"Oh."

Twenty years was a long time for somebody to be gone and not hear anything from them if they were still alive.

Why wouldn't he have come back to them sooner if

it was him? Why didn't he help them if he saw their car wreck like that?

Helmer was their eldest brother, taking care of them all when he was alive. He wouldn't have abandoned them like that. He wouldn't have stayed hidden all these years without finding a way of getting word to them.

Xander had to be mistaken.

"I know it sounds crazy, alright. Why the hell do you think I lost control? Seeing him standing in the middle of the road was the last thing I expected to see."

Rayner closed his eyes and massaged his temples while the others continued to bicker and moan, his head throbbed with the constant chatter of Oliver's thoughts inside his head all jumbled together into a mishmash of words that made little sense.

Take. Control. Rosalyn. Vision. Brother. Dead. Rosalyn.

Rayner needed to get away from him to make sense of his own thoughts. His words just repeated themselves over and over again.

Rosalyn. Dead. Brother. Many.

Rayner pinched the bridge of his nose and climbed from the car, slamming the door behind him.

Still he could hear Oliver's thoughts, only a little quieter now.

He stumbled toward the house and paused, leaning back on the stone wall to support his aching body.

How many brothers do you have?

I thought I saw him before you came in.

Rayner's hands dropped down by his sides before he slowly turned back to the car.

When Rosalyn's visions had come back to her, stealing her sight, she had asked him about his brothers,

219

claiming she saw him when he said his name.

He'd thought nothing of it at the time, figuring that she had just seen a vision from the past that made her curious and confused about what she was seeing when there was nothing in the room, even though she had clearly been afraid before he walked in.

She'd been panting for breath, her wrist twisted from her awkward landing. Cowering away from him when he had stood over her. Reaching her hand out to him in that first touch they shared.

I wanted to be sure it was really you, she'd said. Now, with what Xander claimed to have seen earlier, he wasn't so sure that his brother hadn't been in the room with her.

"Rayner?" Niko asked, stepping out of the car to approach him.

"I think it was Helmer," he muttered, clenching his hands tightly as bile filled his throat at the thought of his own brother abandoning them, and allowing one of their mates to be taken away. The shadow on the recording Oliver had been playing for them looking less and less likely to have been just another Soulless after all.

"Why would you think that?"

"Rosalyn."

Though part of him was glad to know that his brother was still alive, the other half was filled with dread.

What if he had played a hand in the Soulless attacking the car? What if he was the one the Soulless claimed wanted her?

"She saw him, didn't she?"

Rayner nodded, certain that whatever she had seen in the cabin that day had not been just a vision.

The thud he had heard from down the hall that

alerted him to her fall, and the odd smell in the room when he entered. A spicy odour that was out of place in her room when she smelled like sweet wild berries.

He had been in that room with her somehow, for some reason. Unwilling to show himself to any of them. Neither he nor Niko were able to detect his presence from just a short distance away, something he never would have thought possible.

CHAPTER 27

Rosalyn had never liked this room. The bright lights and bleached walls. That large glass wall where she could feel people's eyes on her constantly observing and judging. Only now she knew she wasn't crazy.

Still, this room and this place had a way of making her doubt herself.

All the doctors and psychiatrists told her she was wrong, that it was all in her head and that she needed their help to get better. Refusing to release her even when she had pleaded with them over and over again. Telling her that she was unwell, and had no place else to go. That her only remaining family had abandoned her.

Helmer may have released her from the restraints before he left. His fingers lingered on her skin far longer than she would have liked, but that didn't help her much. She was still trapped in here.

This room was designed with no way out aside from that big heavy door she knew to be locked.

Even the glass wall was enforced, unable to be broken by anything she had around her, even if she wasn't feeling so sluggish.

All she could do was sit and wait, either for one of them to come back for her, hoping she was fast enough to slip by them and escape, an impossible task when she had seen how the other demons moved. But if Dr Holter came in, she might have a little more luck. Or she would have to wait until Rayner, or one of the others to found her, walking into whatever trap they had set up for them.

Movement on the other side of the glass caught her attention. A shadow much smaller than the one she had seen last time pacing back and forth in the other room. Another similar sized shadow joining the first. And another, before a hand slammed against it, squealing as it slid downward. A face moving in closer.

Soulless.

More and more hands joined the first pair, scraping and sliding against the glass. The noise cutting through her, making her cringe and cover her ears, thankful that at least she couldn't see their terrifying faces.

Rosalyn covered her ears and hid her face behind her knees, trying to quieten the horrid sound, rocking back and forth as she hummed, gradually getting louder and louder, but nothing was working. That noise too much to bear, the bright lighting above her robbing her of sleep. Her mouth dry and sore from the screams and shrieks the day before. All of it reminding her of her stay here, causing her to yet again second guess herself, to wonder whether she truly belonged here.

"Rosalyn?" a quiet voice called, a gentle touch on her leg shocking her from her sleep. Her hands strapped down on either side of her waist.

"It's Dr. Holter. I think I can help you get out of this ward if you're willing to talk to me?"

Rosalyn remained silent, staring up at the man who hovered over her. His grey tinted glasses concealing his eyes from her. She didn't trust this man, or the fake smile he gave her.

"I hear you see monsters. Can you tell me when that started?"

Rosalyn shook her head.

The last time she had mentioned monsters, she had been brought to this room and tied up. She didn't want to speak of them again. She wanted it all to go away. Him. This place. The things she saw. She wanted to be normal.

"Your parents died when you were very young, correct?"

"Three," she answered, choking on the lump in her throat, tears streaming from her eyes, matting her long hair beneath her, even though she couldn't feel any emotions as she spoke. She felt numb.

"A car wreck I'm told. You were lucky to have survived."

Again Rosalyn chose to remain silent, unsure why he was asking about the car crash or stating facts.

Clearly he thought she was mad too. Brain damaged in the accident perhaps.

She didn't remember much about it. Everybody she had stayed with had spoken about it, but never to her. They would always go quiet when she walked in the room, but not before she would hear a few snippets of information. Each family saying something a little different, leaving her unsure of what was real, and what was just their speculation. She did remember them calling her crazy though. Damaged another family had said. Hard work, and too much trouble, another.

Still, it was Aunt and Uncle who had hurt her the most. Unlike the first few families who had taken her in with good intentions, unable to handle her after just a short amount of time, they had only taken her for their own gain. They were the ones who had sent her to this place rather than putting her back into the system, greedy and still wanting their money.

They were the reason she was stuck here now, tied to

this bed.

"Do you remember the day you were sent here, Rosalyn?"

How could she forget.

She'd chosen to remain silent after her Aunt had chastised her when she told another child on the street about what she saw. She hadn't spoken to anyone for weeks, not that either of them seemed to mind. They liked the fact that she didn't bother them. It was easier for them to forget she was there.

But that day, when she had been playing in the garden alone, a man had come to the fence and called out to her. When she had looked up, the man's crimson eyes bored into her with each step he made toward her. A cold, sinister smile on his lips, exposing his abnormally large canines that appeared to grow longer and longer. The scream she'd let out piercing.

She'd still been screaming when the ambulance had come for her. None of the nurses were able to console her, resorting to injecting her with something to calm her down.

"You saw a monster that day, didn't you? What do you think he was?"

"V-vampire."

"Very good."

Rosalyn opened up her eyes, tears falling down her cheeks, leaving burning hot trails against her skin, dripping red onto her hands, making her gasp.

She still wasn't used to that yet, fearing she never would be, the sight even more alarming than seeing Dr. Holter at the foot of her bed with a surprisingly genuine smile on his face.

"You knew. You knew that what I saw was real, and you kept me in here?" she accused, swallowing the sob that threatened to choke her words. "Why?"

"Isn't it obvious, Rosalyn?" he commented with a chuckle. "I wanted to use you and your marvelous gift. I mean, it's not everyday that you find someone who can spot a supernatural creature without them choosing to reveal themselves first."

"What about Helmer?"

"Him?" Dr. Holter sneered, wrinkling his nose in disgust. "I can't stand the guy, but I do as I'm told and leave him be. He does the same."

"So, you're not in charge?"

"So many questions, Rosalyn," he chuckled, standing from his seat to approach the exit. "All in good time."

The moment he opened the door, three Soulless pushed their way into the room, making her sit up straight, heart hammering in her chest, but they didn't approach her. They just stood across the room snarling. Their long teeth exposed by their menacing grins, before Helmer stepped in, the Soulless moving aside to make way for him. The way they avoided him, odd.

How did he do that?

She had seen them try and feed on his brothers. Had seen the damage they were capable of with their nasty claws and teeth, but with Helmer, it was almost as though they couldn't stand to be close to him.

He must be the one controlling them somehow, but why?

Dr. Holter was a hunter, she was certain of that by his admission right now and what Xander had told her before, but Helmer was once a Warrior. He couldn't work with the hunters now, could he? Why would they need her if he was? He would be able to see through their glamour just as well if not better than her.

He said he wanted everything. But she had no idea what he meant, and why he seemed to hate his brothers so much.

He continued to approach her, those three Soulless remaining by the door, before he plonked down in the seat Dr. Holter had been using only moments before. A stoic expression on his face whilst he watched her.

"Why am I here?" she asked, figuring there was little point in sitting in silence.

If they planned to kill her, they would have done so already. Helmer's only interest seemed to lay in getting back at his brothers, but for what reason? They all thought he was dead.

"I already told you."

"You want Rayner?"

"I want them all," he snapped, his hands clenching around the metal frame of the bed she sat on, making it shake beneath her.

"Why?"

"They abandoned me. Left me for dead. Now look at me," he snarled, gesturing with his arms wide open. But she didn't understand. He appeared fine to her.

He had the same markings as Rayner on his body, from what she could see, and his mention of not being able to touch another, but he was alive which is much more than his brothers believed.

"They think you're dead."

"Of course they do. But did they bother to check for themselves?"

He stood abruptly, causing the chair to crash to the

ground loudly, making her wince before he began to pace by her feet, his hands and jaw clenched.

"They weren't there. They weren't the ones who helped me out and fixed me."

"They went to the Council–"

"They did nothing!" he snapped, pinning her with a glare.

The look of fury on his face made her swallow her words.

Truly she had no idea what had happened to him, but it was clearly a sore subject and something she should avoid if she wished him to keep away from her.

He may not have the intention of killing her yet, still needing her to lure his brothers here, but if she pushed him too far, he might not hold back.

His eyes were filled with hatred. For his brothers. A hatred she couldn't possibly understand.

CHAPTER 28

Oliver looked at each of them in turn. "So your brother is still alive?"

Rayner paced on the far side of the room trying to control his temper.

This was all taking too long.

Lorkan still struggled to salvage the evidence from the security footage after the crash, able to finally get the damn thing to play back after what felt like hours. Niko was quiet, as he usually was, trying to figure everything out before he decided to share anything with them. And Xander, he was just as loud and restless as always.

None of them helped.

Rayner had no idea where Helmer could have taken Rosalyn, if he was even responsible. It made no sense. What did he want from her? Why hide from them all these years?

Rayner swung out his fist and punched the wall, the pain dull as he continued to pace.

This was pointless.

They should be out there hunting the Soulless as they had done for months, searching for any of those that could talk and demand answers from them, not sit around here, waiting.

So many questions fired around in his head, none of which he had answers for. All he did know was that he needed to find Rosalyn, and fast. The longer she was away from them, from him, the more danger she was in. The hunters. The Council. Both of them would want her if they knew what she was capable of, just like the Soulless did. The memory of how they had fed on her made his blood boil.

"Rayner?" Niko called, gaining his attention. "You need to calm yourself and think."

"Calm?" Rayner snapped and approached his brother, pausing a breath away from him, their chests almost touching.

"You're no good to her, or us, like this," Niko continued.

Rayner clenched his teeth and fists, fighting the urge to punch his brother, snarling in his face before he turned away from him.

He knew deep down that what Niko said was true, but he was losing the battle for his control, and he needed answers. He needed her.

Rayner was the one who had failed her. His damn curse the reason she had given herself over to them in the first place. His inability to control his desires around her, allowing her to get close to him when he knew it would only put her in greater danger. Everything led him down the same path, left with more questions and zero answers.

Why? Why did the Soulless want her? Who did they work for, and how had they changed? Why was she able to see the things she did? Maybe if he could work out an answer to one of those questions, he might be able to work out where she was, but his mind was in chaos, and the damn doctor's continual thoughts inside his head were not helping.

Rosalyn. Helmer. Brother. Soulless.

Rayner held onto his head and tried in vain to push the thoughts away, to focus on his own, but nothing worked. The constant noise only made his control slip further away from him.

Rosalyn. Vision. Hospital.

"You had a vision," Rayner commented, freezing in his steps to turn to Niko. "You warned us to stay away from the hospital. Why?"

Niko never shared with them what he had seen and why he warned them away, but Rayner was certain from his expression when he'd first met Rosalyn that he had seen her before, in a vision. Perhaps whatever he had seen would help them find her now.

"No."

Rayner finally snapped.

"No?" he growled as he pinned Niko to the wall behind him by his throat. The burn across his hand ignored as he glared into his brother's golden eyes. Oliver's gasp and rushed thoughts making him shudder and cringe.

Danger. Death. Vision. Pain.

"What I saw will not help you, Rayner."

"I will be the judge of that," he said through gritted teeth, his grip tight despite the burning pain that made his legs wobble.

"Niko, just tell him," Xander groaned.

Niko closed his eyes and sighed, his expression filled with remorse before he opened them and stared at Rayner. The sorrow he saw more of an answer than the words that followed. "I saw her die."

Rayner released his brother in an instant. His body numb before he fell to his knees.

She couldn't die.

He had to be wrong.

He must have seen something else, or came out of the vision too soon.

"Why warn us away if she was going to die? Our job

231

is to stop that happening," Lorkan asked over his shoulder. His voice muffled as Rayner struggled to breathe and control his anger.

"I saw us with her when it happened. I thought that if we stayed away she would remain safe."

That had to mean that she wasn't dead already. That they somehow found her before it happened. That there was a chance that he could prevent it somehow.

He would not allow them to take her from him.

"Where?" Rayner asked, bringing his eyes back up to his brothers. His jaw set hard knowing what had to be done.

"I don't know. I didn't recognise the place. It was clinical, but not in the same way as Green Oaks."

He would find Rosalyn and he would destroy those who had taken her. He would give his life in order to keep her safe, demanding his brothers take her from there while he stayed and fought them off.

There was no way he would allow Niko's vision to come true.

"Greenbryer," Xander muttered, causing all eyes to turn to him.

"The psychiatric unit?" Oliver asked skeptically. "Why would they take her there? That place has been abandoned for years."

"She told me about it before. She was sent there when she was a child."

A child? She had seen them for that long? No wonder she accepted the truth so much sooner than any human could. She had seen them almost all her life.

"Let's go."

Rayner had seen this place in passing a few times and had never thought much of it.

To him it was a place of little importance. A building that was abandoned and dilapidated, crumbling at the edges.

It had been a hotbed for Soulless activity, but they tended to like the dark and quiet areas where they could easily hide, like the woods and old factories the other side of town. He never would have thought that something else could link them here. That she would have links here.

The thought of her being here as a child, alone and scared only made him clench his hands tighter.

All those people who had made her feel mad and unloved. A liar. The way she repressed her sight leaving her blinded.

Why can't I be like everyone else?

Rayner clenched his fists.

Her words made more sense to him now.

They had made her feel that way. Made her feel like she was different, and not in a good way. That she was a freak. An attention seeker perhaps, when in fact she had seen them all along. The only one of them who knew that they weren't alone in the world. That there were creatures among them.

He still didn't know why she saw the things she did, or how she silenced his mind. Or even how she was able to touch him, but he knew that somehow she was at the centre of all of this. An important piece in this puzzle that none of them had been able to figure out.

"Do you know this place, doc?" Xander asked, adjusting his long sleeves as the rest of them pulled out their weapons. Xander much preferred to use his hands and the shadows around him while he fought.

"Not very well. I only heard of the place. They were forced to close several years ago when a few patients went to the papers about some of the treatments they practiced here."

Lorkan glanced from one side to the other, all of them wary of how quiet and empty the place appeared. Rayner sure this had to be the right place.

"So, we spread out then?" Lorkan asked.

"We stick in groups," Niko commanded, looking to Rayner first, before he turned to Oliver and the other two. "I'll go with Rayner. Xander, Lorkan, take the doctor with you."

Rayner didn't wait around for the others, he headed toward the front door that hung from its hinges. The floral scent of the Soulless still lingered by the entrance when he stepped inside, the stench so strong he thought they would pop out on him at any moment, but it was just as empty inside as it had appeared outside.

"We go up," Niko whispered, already headed toward the stairs he had spotted not far away, Rayner close behind him.

Neither of them spoke of what happened back home, they didn't need to. Niko knew he had pushed Rayner too far, and Rayner knew that Niko was only trying to protect him. They had both seen what happened to Xander after he lost his mate, and Niko likely knew who she was, and what she would mean to Rayner the moment he met her.

He was still angry at his brother for not telling him sooner, and for trying to keep them apart, but he understood his motives, likely to have done a similar thing if he was in his shoes.

Niko paused and held a finger to his lips as they climbed the second flight of stairs. A shuffling noise sounded from close by. The clash of dark, horrid thoughts entered Rayner's mind the closer they got to the Soulless. Not words like it was with humans, or the Other, but just a bombardment of noise that made his skin crawl. The depravity manipulating his own thoughts.

Niko held up three fingers, indicating how many he could see and shook his head before he pointed up the next flight of stairs.

Rayner wanted to engage them. To kill them all and watch them bleed, but he knew the thoughts were not his own, that he needed to remain in control. Rosalyn needed him, and three Soulless were not going to ruin his chances of finding her. He could deal with them later, when he knew she was safe.

He followed along behind Niko for what felt like a lifetime, before he noticed the sounds around him grew quieter. He paused, looking one way, then the other. Niko raised a brow before he saw him point down a hallway he had already passed.

Only Rosalyn could be responsible for the lack of noise in his head.

The further down the corridor they went, the less he could hear. She was close, but where?

They went from door to door and listened for any movement inside.

Despite some shuffling sounds the first room appeared empty, but there was an unusual odour that

Rayner couldn't quite put his finger on. Something familiar, and yet strange at the same time.

Niko opened up the next room revealing two Soulless.

Good.

Rayner was itching for a fight and needed to kill something, or someone, his mind clouded in darkness. He burst into the room and speared the first creature with his sword, ramming him into the wall. He grabbed its head and twisted to one side with a grunt, before he turned to the next.

Niko beat him to it, his curved blade already halfway through the Soulless's neck before Rayner was able to make it across the room.

Rayner clenched his fists.

He knew Niko was doing his job, that they needed to stop the Soulless before they made too much noise and alerted more to their whereabouts, but he needed this. He needed a way to let out the darkness that was clouding his mind.

Rayner left the room without a word and made his way further down the hall. He moved quickly, cutting his way through any Soulless that emerged, but it wasn't working. Every creature he took down only made him hunger for more, and still they were no closer to Rosalyn. The sound around him was eerily quiet now, but they were running out of doors.

Where was she?

Together they rounded the next corner, coming face to face with three more Soulless.

Rayner engaged first with a swing of his blade and took off one of their heads before it let out so much as a murmur, Niko grappled the next, snapping its neck with ease, but not before the creature was able to slice deep through his thigh with its long claws, causing him to let out a loud roar of pain, his blood like a beacon to any others around them.

The last of them ran, something Rayner had never seen before. The Soulless did not think or try to preserve themselves, all they knew was food. This Soulless was different. It carried no weapon that Rayner could see, but it had to be one of the newer breeds.

Together they gave chase, sure it would lead them somewhere, but what they hadn't expected was a trap.

Waiting for them a little further down the hall was seven more Soulless, two carried their blades, the rest snarled and cackled, waiting.

Another two appeared from behind, both carrying weapons.

They were surrounded, all the Soulless hissing, snarling, gnashing their teeth.

"Shit," Niko muttered, a curved blade grasped in each hand, Rayner close behind him, their backs only inches apart as they waited.

They'd been in tougher odds, like back at the cabin, but they needed to make this quick. Neither of them knew how many more lurked inside the building, who was in charge, or even if they were here. They needed to get to Rosalyn, before it was too late.

CHAPTER 30

Rosalyn wasn't sure when she had fallen asleep, but the squealing on the glass had finally stopped. She could still see their shadows still on the other side, but they no longer attempted to get into the room, which was a good thing really. Not only was the noise driving her mad, she had heard one or two cracks as they'd pounded, fearing that eventually their tireless efforts would see the glass shatter.

She yawned wide and glanced around the room, thankful to see that she was alone.

Her encounters with Dr. Holter and Helmer had been somewhat forthcoming with information, but she needed some time to try and figure things out.

She still wasn't sure what had happened to Helmer, but she knew he was furious with his brothers, and Dr. Holter, he was a hunter of some sort. He wanted to use her to find the Other. Neither of them were particularly keen on one another, but they worked together whether they liked it or not. Someone in control of them both. Their Council perhaps? But that didn't make much sense. Why would they work with hunters if they were trying to kill them? She still didn't have enough information to work it out. There was still so much she didn't know.

She might be important to Dr. Holter for his own purposes, and Helmer as a means to lure his brothers here. He seemed to believe that Rayner's feelings for her alone would be enough motivation, but she didn't understand how, or why.

She was still as confused as ever.

238

Rosalyn bought her knees up to her chest and hugged herself tight, squeezing her eyes as she tried not to think of either of them and concentrate on when she had first seen the creatures she had.

She knew she was young the first time, but she couldn't think what it was that she saw, or even her exact age, though she was pretty certain it was after her parents had died. Trauma perhaps?

In her studies she had learnt that trauma of any kind could force the body to do all manner of different things, fragmenting the mind in some cases. Perhaps the crash had caused her to be different. Not damaged in the way others believed, but able to see things that she perhaps wouldn't have otherwise. A near death experience maybe?

So much information swirled around inside her head, forcing her to grip tightly onto her skull and press against her temples, the pain more intense than the visions that came to her, making her to grit her teeth and groan, before she heard a loud noise from the room beside her.

Rosalyn looked up, her heart racing, afraid the Soulless had found a way through when she saw their shadows all rush to one side. A piercing shriek, muffled only slightly by the glass making her shudder, when one of those shadows smashed against the wall. Her body froze as she watched on in horror, unsure what was happening, the sounds in the room difficult to discern over the shrieks, wails, and the roars.

She didn't have to wait much longer to find out what caused the noise when one of the Soulless was pelted toward the glass, causing one of the windows to shatter and reveal Niko, and Rayner on the other side, both of them covered in thick black gunk from head to toe.

When her eyes met Rayner's she almost sagged in

relief.

He will come for you.

Helmer had known he would.

She had hoped he would. But now he was here, headed toward her, she was torn. Relieved and happy to see him, especially when he stepped through the glass wall and crushed her against him, but scared at the same time. This is what Helmer wanted. Rayner would be in trouble all over again, because of her.

Rosalyn pushed him away with tears in her eyes, unsure what to say and do, before he crushed her lips against his and held on tight.

She melted in his arms, all her fears forgotten by his gentle touch, wishing she could hold onto this moment forever, when she felt a sharp sensation in her back that took her breath away.

"No!" Niko roared, limping into the room with them as she swayed. Rayner's eyes opened wide while he held onto her.

She nearly slipped from his grasp as a warmth spread across her back, her body growing heavy, and cool, even with Rayner pressed against her.

"No!" he snarled. His fingers into her sides, his other hand stroking through her hair as she struggled to keep her eyes open.

"You came for me," she whispered, a smile on her lips before she spied tears in his eyes.

She reached her hand up and cupped his face, wiping her thumb beneath his eye, frowning when it came away wet.

Niko turned away to look at the floor behind him, his hands clenched tightly around each of his blades.

"I will always come for you," Rayner whispered as

he pressed his forehead against hers.

Her eyes fluttered. The ability to stay awake became far too difficult.

She couldn't still be tired. She had been asleep not too long ago, still unsure how she had managed it. But the desire to close her eyes still grew. An urge to lean into Rayner and sleep in his arms.

More tears cascaded down his cheeks when he lay her down gently.

The coolness of the bed below took her breath away.

The pain in her back spread further.

Then she saw the wet blood against Rayner's chest and stomach. Blood she hadn't noticed there before. His hands were covered and dripped onto the bed, turning the sheets red below her.

It wasn't his blood she could see, it was hers. That sharp pain in her back almost completely numb now. Cold.

Rayner stroked her cheek once more before he pressed his lips gently against her forehead and looked up, his expression frightful. His eyes darker than she had ever seen them before. Filled with hatred.

Rosalyn turned her head to the side and saw Helmer stood behind her with one of those long, needle like blades in his hand. The metal gleamed in the light, coated in her blood.

The last thing she heard before her eyes drifted closed was the agonising roar of Rayner as he leapt across the bed toward his brother. A sound so heartbreaking, her own tears tumbled from her eyes.

CHAPTER 31

"I said get her out of here!" Rayner snapped, pinning Helmer to the floor. Both their skin burning from the contact. "Take her to the Doc."

Niko nodded, reluctantly scooping Rosalyn's prone body in his arms before he stepped back through the glass wall and rushed from the room.

Oliver would be able to save her. He had to.

"Why?" Rayner roared, slamming Helmer's head against the tiled floor. "You know what she is to me, and you took her away anyway."

"Yes, I knew," he chuckled, seeming not to care about the pain he endured, or the pain he had put his own brother through. Blood coated his teeth as he smiled up at him.

Rayner released him and jumped back to his feet, holding his sword toward his brother's chest, his hand wobbling in rage, sorrow, and unacceptance.

His own brother.

"Do it then."

Part of him wanted to. A big part of him that he was struggling to keep in check. But Helmer was still his brother.

What had caused him to change like this? The Helmer he knew was nothing like the man in front of him. He had always been the one to look after them. To teach them.

This Helmer was a monster.

"I killed your mate, Rayner. Aren't you going to kill me?"

"You want me to kill you? Is that why?"

An unreadable expression passed across his features while he stood waiting, his eyes never leaving Rayner's as he gripped tighter to the blade in his hands.

"I already died, brother, a long time ago."

Rayner didn't understand.

They all told them that he was dead, that there was nothing that could be done to save him. Never allowing them to see his body. They had lied. All these years, keeping him hidden from them.

"You never came for me."

"We tried."

"You failed."

His words were like a punch to Rayner's gut. He was right, they had failed him.

If any of them had known he was still alive, they would have kept fighting, but they hadn't. They'd given up. Their punishments didn't seem like enough now he knew they should have kept going. The burns on his skin did not seem like enough for leaving his brother alone all these years.

"And now you failed to save your mate."

"She'll make it."

"I wouldn't be so sure."

Rayner lunged forward, the tip of his sword pressing into Helmer's throat. Several droplets of blood trickled across the blade when he pushed a little harder.

"Why?" Rayner roared, his knuckles white from his tight grip.

"I was trapped for nearly two decades and none of you come for me. Not one of you."

243

"We took on the Council for you. We demanded answers and never got any."

"You gave up!"

Rayner winced.

There was some truth to his words, even if they believed them false.

They never gave up on their quest for information about what had happened, and who had been involved, but they had stopped looking for him, all of them believing that he was gone. None of them were able to sense him any longer. Even now, he couldn't pick up his energy, just like he hadn't before he had appeared and stabbed Rosalyn in the back with that needle-like blade. The same weapon the Soulless carried.

"You're too late," Helmer chuckled, pushing himself even closer. More blood oozing from the wound he was inflicting upon himself. "She's slipping away even now, I can feel her energy waning."

Rayner's hand shook, gritting his teeth against the strain of holding his blade extended for so long, unsure what to do.

"You have a choice, brother. You can stay here and get the answers you want, or you return to your mate before she is lost forever."

Rayner roared, tossing his blade to the floor, torn in two.

He wanted answers. Needing to know where he had been and how he had survived, but most importantly, why he had done it? Everything. But what he longed for more than anything was to be with Rosalyn.

He needed to see her. To be sure she would pull through, and that the doctor was able to save her even though he could feel it too, her energy slipping away from him. All the noise around him came back fast and deafeningly loud.

"She will die. If not today. Soon. She won't let her live."

"Who?" Rayner asked, clenching his fists, his eyes drifting to the door. His feet itching to run after Rosalyn.

"Your mate was already dead, just like me. She saved us. She fixed us. Now we belong to her. She won't let you have her."

"Whoever she is can rot in hell!" Rayner snapped, finally having heard enough.

He didn't care any longer.

His brother was not the same man anymore. He was changed. Ruthless and unfeeling.

The answers he possessed would likely prove to be of importance later, like who this woman he spoke of was and what she wanted from them, but all he could think of was Rosalyn.

He needed to be there with her.

He needed to make sure she was going to make it.

Rayner would find Helmer again. Or he would find them.

CHAPTER 32

Rayner fled the building, his chest heaving up and down as he searched frantically for her. His body almost collapsed on the ground when he spied them by the car. Oliver's head pressed against her chest, holding up her wrist while he checked for a pulse.

No.

He couldn't be too late.

She couldn't give up.

Rayner rushed toward them, shoving Oliver aside the moment he shook his head and sighed, crushing her against his chest.

She was not gone yet. He wouldn't allow it.

"Look out," Lorkan groaned, a dagger flying through the air above Rayner's head as Soulless poured from the building behind him, having followed him out.

He didn't care. He scooped Rosalyn into his arms, squeezing her tightly, numb to everything, even the pain when someone rested a hand on his shoulder.

There had to be something he could do. Somewhere he could take her.

"She's gone, brother," Niko whispered, kneeling in front of him. "There is nothing more we can do."

"Like hell there isn't!" Rayner roared, his face wet with tears that ran down his face as he pushed to his feet. "There has to be something."

Niko sighed, frowning down at Rosalyn limp in Rayner's arms, his own eyes glassy and black.

"You won't like the idea, but what if we ask the

Council?"

"Why would they help us? They've never helped us before."

No, Henry wouldn't help them, he would take enjoyment in their suffering, as he always did.

Rayner had feared him discovering Rosalyn since the beginning. Taking her to him now would only seal her fate. The bastard would condemn her for what she saw and likely punish them for trying to keep her safe.

"Then not the Council, but the resistance?"

Rayner raised a brow at his brother, unsure why and how they could possibly help.

"Lothaire is ancient, his blood powerful, he might be able to save her, if he turns her."

Would Rosalyn want that? Rayner wasn't so sure. She was accepting of who they were, but she had claimed to want to be normal on more than one occasion since he'd known her.

He would be taking the choice from her, but he couldn't allow her to die.

What other choice did he have?

"Stand down," Lotharire demanded when the three of them stormed into the room, Rayner clutching Rosalyn to his chest when the vampires surrounded them, snarling, hungering for her blood. Lothaire's two guards ready with weapons held in front of them, aimed in their direction.

"What brings you here, Warriors?" Lothaire asked, his eyes flashing crimson when he looked down at Rosalyn in his arms.

Her body felt frightfully cold next to his, her energy hanging on by the tiniest sliver.

"Save her," Rayner pleaded, falling to his knees in

front of the ancient vampire, not a care about how weak he may look in that moment.

He would do anything to save his mate, even if it meant risking his own life. He would fight for her with all he had.

"A human?" Lothaire sneered, wrinkling his nose in disgust, which only fueled Rayner's anger.

Gently he placed her on the floor, tucking a strand of her hair behind her ear before he stood and faced the vampire.

"Save her, or I will kill everyone in this room," he roared, clenching his fists, eyes trained on the two guards situated either side of Lothaire. Both of them gulping visually when they looked to their master, their thoughts crashing into his mind the further Rosalyn slipped from him.

"Why should I save a human? A creature that prosecutes our kind and wages war."

"She's not like them."

"You may be ancient, Lothaire, but you think your clan can take on all three of us?" Xander snarled behind Rayner, Niko ready with his blades in his hands in case he needed to fight.

Lothaire was silent for a moment, his eyes drifting down to Rosalyn on the floor before he approached them, an unreadable expression on his face.

"She barely has anything left."

"Then make it quick."

"She could hate you for this?"

"But she would be alive."

He already knew all of this.

He knew what choice he was making, and what he may be taking away from her, but he couldn't sit back and watch her die. He couldn't let his brother get away with this.

Lothaire nodded, crouching down to the ground, his expression changing when he peered into her face. A look of recognition passing his features.

Rayner was curious how the vampire could possibly recognise her, intrigued to discover the answer, but right now all he could think of was helping her. Any questions he had would have to wait.

"Will you save her, or not?" Rayner asked through gritted teeth, taking a step toward Lothaire before he was able to control himself, the vampires around him all gnashing their teeth in warning.

"She may already be too far gone, are you prepared for that, Warrior?"

"Yes," Rayner sighed, knowing that he lied. He would never be prepared to let her go, but he knew that her life was hanging on by the tiniest of threads. The longer they spoke and debated this, the more likely she wouldn't make it. "Just do it."

Lothaire's fangs sprung from his mouth. Long and deadly, before he tore into his own wrist, holding it to her mouth. His blood dripped onto her face and lips, matting in her hair.

Still, she did not swallow. Too weak to even move.

Drink, Rayner pleaded in his mind, squeezing his eyes closed as he rested his hand across her heart.

He couldn't be too late. She had to have some fight left in her.

"Come back to me," he spoke softly by her ear when he leaned toward her. A slight tingle against his skin when he rested his head against hers. But the voices continued to grow stronger, the vampires around him not bothering to hide their thoughts. Her ability to silence them faded with every second she lay still.

She couldn't be gone. She just couldn't.

"I'm sorry, brother," Niko whispered behind him, his presence moving closer before he crouched down beside him and rested his hand on her forehead.

"No!" Rayner roared, shoving his brother away.

He wasn't ready to give up yet. Lothaire's blood was still dripping into her mouth. Some of it had to make its way down her throat. She would make it. She had to.

"She was too far gone. We were too late."

"Give her a moment," Lothaire declared, clenching and unclenching his fist to make his blood flow faster. His eyes matched the stream of liquid that poured into her mouth, and spilled over her face. "Her energy grows, even if only slightly."

Niko remained crouched by his side in silence, Xander joining them on his other side.

"Master?" a female vampire spoke, stepping toward them all. "You must stop."

"I know my own limits, child," Lothaire snapped, snarling at the woman before she nodded her head and stepped back, eyes fixed upon the floor.

She was right though. Lothaire couldn't go on forever. He would have to stop soon. His blood was not infinite and he could not spare it all.

He might not be able to save her.

CHAPTER 33

Rayner clutched his head as he sat by Rosalyn's side, still unsure whether she was going to live, or die.

Her body was so weak. Her skin sickeningly pale and cold to the touch.

Lothaire had declared there was nothing more he could do before he signaled his guards to take her to one of the nearby rooms to see if she would come round. The same room that Rayner sat in now, holding onto her hand.

Niko and Xander returned to the car to let Lorkan and Oliver know what happened, neither of them had returned since. Lothaire was the only one who remained in the room with him after Rayner demanded that his Guards leave. Their voices were too much for him to bear, still there but muffled the other side of the door, making his head pound and his heart race. If he could still hear their thoughts, he wasn't sure what that meant for Rosalyn. Her ability to silence the chatter in his mind no longer worked, making him fear the worst.

"Did you know she had died once before?" Lothaire asked from his seat across the room, watching Rayner brush her hair from her face.

Rayner nodded, before he let out a long sigh and squeezed her hand tightly.

"Helmer said the same," he commented, lifting his eyes to the vampire. "He's alive, and I'm not really sure what I believe anymore."

His brother's words came back to him, making him shudder.

Your mate was already dead, just like me. She saved us. She fixed us. Now we belong to her.

"Who has the ability to bring someone back from the dead?"

"I wondered that myself for a long time," Lothaire sighed, tapping his long fingers on the table beside him.

Vampires were able to extend a life if the person still lived when they fed from their blood, but they didn't have the ability to bring someone back from the dead. So far as Rayner believed, no creature lived that could do such a thing. Then again, he never believed that a human would be able to see and do the things Rosalyn could, yet here she was, proof that he didn't know everything.

"I'm afraid I still don't have the answer to that question," Lothair sighed, "all I know is that she isn't technically human either. I can smell it in her blood. Something else. Something magical."

Could that be what drew the Soulless to her? A scent that he was unable to detect, his nose nowhere near as powerful as a vampire's, especially when it came to blood. Or was there more to it than that? Was Helmer the one that controlled them somehow, or this woman that he claimed owned him?

He still had so many questions, he suspected that only Helmer would be able to answer, but he did not regret leaving when he had.

He needed to get to Rosalyn.

Even now he was unsure whether they had done enough to save her, but if he had stayed and waited for answers that might never come, she would have definitely been lost to him. That thought alone made his body tense and his hands itch with the need to kill.

Lothaire may have tried to save her, but Rayner

252

wasn't sure whether that would save him should she not pull through. His mind was already filled with dark thoughts. The desires of those around him that penetrated his head. He wasn't sure if he would be able to hold back his fury if she slipped away from him altogether.

"The fact you can touch her surprised me however, what with those glyphs."

"I was quite surprised myself," Rayner huffed, squeezing his eyes closed, trying not to remember how she had held on to him and kissed him. Or how she had run her hands across his body in a greedy caress. He couldn't allow himself to think of that. Not yet. Not when he wasn't sure whether he would ever be able to feel her touch again.

"I'm afraid that if she does survive, she will be a vampire, that magic in her gone. She might not be able to touch you anymore."

Rayner lifted his eyes back to the vampire, his jaw clenched, before he glanced down at her.

"I'm prepared for that," he sighed, cupping her cheek in his hand. Her skin still alarmingly cool against his, tingling from the contact.

Was that the beginning, as she slowly turned? Would he be able to touch her less and less, before the agony became too much?

He shook his head.

It didn't matter.

All that mattered was that she was alive. If he could no longer touch her without the pain, he would manage. It would hurt to see her and never be able to get close, but he didn't care. Her life was more important. He would have to either put up with the pain, or let her go. A life of not being able to touch your mate would not be fair to her.

"Then I shall leave you alone. I do not know how long it

will take for her to wake, if she does at all."

"Thank you, Lothaire," Rayner rushed to say when the vampire's hand closed around the doorknob. "And I'm sorry we burst into your home."

"Do not worry yourself, Warrior. I know what a mate's bond is like, what it can make us do." He opened up the door and paused, looking from Rosalyn back to him. "I do hope it works. I have some questions for the child, if she wakes, if you would allow me?"

Rayner nodded his head and let out a long, shuddering breath when the door clicked shut behind him. The guards' voices receded as they followed their master away. Still, there was too much noise around him that made his head pound.

He may have been able to express his gratitude to Lothaire in a moment of clarity, but the more those voices persisted, the more his anger grabbed hold of him. He needed to take her away from here. Someplace safe. Quiet. Where he could think and rest by her side awaiting the time she finally woke.

Rayner scooped her into his arms and shivered as another jolt buzzed through his body. His arms and chest prickled slightly, but not yet painful where he held her tight against him.

He would take her back home. Where she should have been all along. With him.

CHAPTER 34

Rosalyn gasped for breath when she woke. Her lungs burnt, her eyes sore, but not as sore as her back. Memories from earlier swam through her mind.

Helmer. He had stabbed her in the back with one of those long, needle like blades. The pain still radiated throughout her torso.

Tentatively she reached around behind her and felt her back.

Nothing.

The skin was smooth. Tender, but smooth, and surprisingly cool to the touch.

She looked around the room, unsure where she was, but able to see quite clearly considering the lack of light around her.

Where was Rayner? He'd been holding her when she fell unconscious.

A lump formed in her throat when she remembered his tears before she had brushed them from his face, sure she was going to die.

Had he left her behind, figuring she was gone? No he wouldn't, would he?

"You gave us quite the scare," Xander spoke as his face appeared from the shadows in the furthest most corner away from her.

"Rayner?" she asked, some relief flooding into her knowing they hadn't left her in that place.

"He went for the doctor the moment you began to stir. He won't be long."

No sooner had the words left his mouth, Rayner burst through the doors, Oliver panting behind him.

Her body all but sagged.

He was here, and all she wanted to do was fall into his arms and hold him close, but Oliver was there, blocking her path with a stern and worried expression upon his face, and Rayner let him.

What was happening? Rayner would never have allowed Oliver to stop her before.

"I need to check your vitals, Rose."

"Can't that wait?" she asked, her voice quiet and slurred. Her throat felt dry and scratchy. Something sharp prickled at her lips, making it difficult to speak.

She lifted her hand to her mouth and gasped.

Fangs? She had fangs? What had they done?

"We will explain everything in a moment, but I need to check you over first, starting with the wound on your back," Oliver spoke softly.

"It's gone," she attempted to say around those fangs, tears prickling in her eyes as she spun and lifted the back of her shirt. "I'm gone," she whispered to herself. A tear escaped down her cheek before she could stop it, lifting her hand to discreetly wipe it away before she turned back to them. To Rayner.

His eyes were glued to her, but he made no attempt to approach.

Did she repulse him now, now she was whatever this was?

"Remarkable," Oliver breathed, stepping closer, his head tilted to one side, staring at her mouth.

"Get out!" Rosalyn shouted, her voice much louder than she had intended, scratching painfully at her dry throat.

Oliver froze and stood upright, looking from her to Rayner and Xander. None of them spoke to one another, but they filed out of the room. All except Rayner that was. And yet, he remained halfway across the room, his expression unreadable.

"W-what am I?" she asked quietly.

She suspected she knew the answer, but she couldn't be sure. There were still so many creatures and things out there that she knew nothing about.

"A vampire," he answered, lowering his eyes to the floor.

Rosalyn's chest tightened, her heart pumping far too quickly making her head feel light. The room seemed to close in around her, her whole body trembling when she looked down at her hands. The tears she had been attempting to hold back in front of them all falling where she lost control of her body.

She couldn't breathe.

She gripped onto the bed and stared in Rayner's direction, unsure what to think or do when he looked at her with horror in his eyes.

"We had no choice," he said in a rush, taking a tentative step toward her. His hand lifting to reach out to her before he lowered it again.

Her body felt hot, burning as the room continued to press inward, despite the coolness of her skin.

"I had no choice," he said a little more confidently. "I would not allow you to die."

Rosalyn remained silent, unable to speak past the choking feeling in her throat.

Why bother saving her when he couldn't even bear to look at her now, let alone come closer?

She needed him. His touch. His comfort. Anything.

257

But he looked afraid, and that hurt more than knowing that she was different now. A creature she feared more than any other. Even the Soulless that hunted her. More than Helmer who made her this.

It was that vampire's fault all those years ago that she had been locked away, and now she was one of them.

The thought of blood repulsed her. Her stomach churned at the very thought of having to feed from someone else to keep going. She wouldn't do it. She couldn't.

More tears fell, leaving hot, scorching trails down her face.

"I'm sorry Rosalyn, but I couldn't let you go."

He stepped a little closer, his own eyes glistening when he finally looked up. And yet, he still remained at a safe distance from her. "I understand if you hate me for the choice I made for you, but a life as a vampire was better than watching you slip away. I couldn't do it."

"H-hate you?" she whispered, trying to control her breathing for fear of passing out. Some of the pain in her head receded when she began to count backward, squeezing her eyes tight, and wrapping her fingers around the bed sheets beneath her.

"Lothaire will look after you, teach you, if you wish."

"You're sending me away?" she gasped, snapping her eyes open. All her work of trying to calm herself undone.

"Never," he stated, closing the distance between them, his hand lifting toward her face, before he paused and clenched his fists, looking away from her.

"Do I repulse you now?" she whispered, her heart breaking in two.

She hadn't truly known whether she loved Rayner before when Helmer asked her, but now she knew she did.

His inability to look at her, to touch her, was more painful than the blade through her back.

She loved this man, this demon, and he could no longer bear to look at her.

Rayner looked up, his jaw clenched. Eyes locked onto hers before he gripped her face between his hands and inhaled deeply. His tense body seemed to sag a little, the longer he held onto her, before he brought his lips to hers and rested his forehead against hers.

"Of course not," he whispered, his body shaking.

Rosalyn pushed up onto her knees and kissed him back, tears streaming from her eyes as she wrapped her arms around his neck and pulled him toward her, needing him closer.

Her body felt drained. Weak. Thankful she was on a bed and had Rayner in front of her to lean upon when she broke away from their kiss.

"You wouldn't come near me," she mumbled, stroking a hand over his cheek, resting it on his shoulder when he scowled down at her. "I thought–"

"You thought wrong," he declared, crushing her body against his. His hand rubbing up and down her back, soothing her. "You're different now, Rosalyn."

She knew that much. She could feel the differences in her body, and not just from her cool skin.

Her vision was more crisp, even in the darkness. Her hearing was incredible, yet terrifying, able to hear her own heart beat, slowing with every moment longer she remained in his arms. Able to hear his heart beating too, and the blood that rushed through his veins. The fangs in her mouth throbbing and itchy.

"We weren't sure–" he paused, taking one of her hands in his, lacing their fingers together before he brought it to his lips.

"You thought I'd hurt you?" Rosalyn asked.

Rayner nodded and sighed. "Your touch is different too."

"It hurts?" she asked, attempting to pull her hands away from him.

"Not exactly," he said with a frown, gripping tighter to stop her from pulling away.

Realization dawned on her. The horror on his face. The sadness in his eyes when he'd come back into the room and saw her for how different she was. He thought the contact would be the same as with everyone else. Of course he would be afraid to come too close, and how she had pulled away from him just now, when she thought that she had hurt him was exactly what he thought would happen.

"It's not painful, but different. Like a pulse of electricity," he explained, splaying out her hand with his, before running his fingers down her wrist and arm, making her shiver. "I don't know how long it will last."

Rosalyn's eyes lowered to his hand exploring her skin, his touch leaving goosebumps in its wake from his gentle caress. His green eye brightened the more his hand travelled, his heart thumping quicker, louder to her ears.

"The more you change, the less of you will remain. The magic Lothaire said was inside of you is vanishing."

Magic? Rosalyn wasn't sure she understood what he meant, but she wasn't sure she was ready for the answer right now. All she wanted was to feel his touch. To be close to him and make the most of this situation should what he was saying come true.

Does he know what you are to him, what he is to you?

"What am I to you?" she asked quietly, closing her eyes and breathing deeply when he caressed her side, tickling over her ribs.

"You're my mate, Rosalyn," he whispered back, his voice laced with desire, velvety smooth, "I belong to you."

She didn't know what being a mate meant, but she understood his other words perfectly. He was hers. He cared just as deeply for her as she did for him.

Without a second thought, she took his face between her hands and brought her lips back to his, pressing her body against his when he moved a little closer, allowing her to direct him.

His sharp intake of breath made her freeze, a sound mixed with pleasure and pain.

Rosalyn opened her eyes and saw the tiniest droplet of blood on his lip.

"I'm so sorry," she gasped, attempting to move away, horrified by what she had just done.

Her chest tightening all over again as panic began to grip hold of her.

Rayner didn't speak, just wrapped his big arm around her waist, pinning her body to him despite her fights against him. His strength even now far superior to her own.

He brought his lips back toward hers, her heart pounding with every inch, every centimetre he came closer.

"I'm a monster," she gasped, before he sealed her lips beneath his, his own teeth nibbling at her lip.

"Never," he whispered, stroking his tongue against one of her elongated fangs, the sensation making her body tense and quiver. Heat pooling between her thighs.

Goodness. She hadn't felt anything like that before. Her teeth were so sensitive. It was as though he caressed her core with such a simple flick of his tongue.

She wanted him to do it again, and he did, forcing a moan from her lips before she could stop herself.

He pulled back with a sly grin on his face, his hand cupping her neck. His green eye dazzling. The black, mesmerizing.

She'd felt so weak only moments ago, but now, her body felt alive. Hungry. Her eyes lowered to his neck.

A shudder worked through her.

No. She couldn't do that. That was disgusting. She couldn't feed on his blood. The thought alone repulsed her. It had to be him licking her fangs that made her even consider such a thing.

"Do it," he growled. His deep, guttural and desire filled voice sending a shiver through her body, his words the same as before, when she had first touched his skin. But could she? Should she?

If stories and movies were correct, she would need to feed in order to stay alive, but to drink from a living person or creature, she wasn't sure she could do it. The thought nauseated her, and yet she was curious. The sound of his blood called to her. An ache deep in her stomach, like a growling hunger.

It wasn't so bad if it was Rayner.

He appeared quite content with her nicking his lip with her teeth, eager to show her how sensitive they were. Perhaps he would enjoy this too?

Rosalyn leaned her mouth in closer toward his neck and opened up ready to bite him when he tipped his head to the side, granting her access, before she froze. The horror of what she was about to do making her body shudder.

"I-I can't."

"You must," he answered, stroking his thumb by the side of her mouth. "You need blood to fully heal, and to energise you."

"But then there will be no going back," she spoke quietly, lowering her eyes. "What if I fully turn and can no longer touch you?"

Rayner tipped her chin up so she faced him, and rested his head against hers. His breath tickling her face when he sighed.

"We'll find a way, no matter what it takes."

It wasn't that she doubted his words, but Rosalyn wasn't sure they would be able to figure it out. He'd been living with his punishment for so long already. He would have found a way before now if there was one. But she knew he would not give up, and neither would she.

CHAPTER
35

Rosalyn closed her eyes and leaned into Rayner, kissing him softly against his neck.

His groans of pleasure made her disgust somewhat easier to manage as she pressed a little harder into him, grazing the tips of her fangs along his throat. A shiver coursed through her body when she felt his chest rumble against hers, the sensation indescribable when she did it again. That same warmth from where he had stroked her fangs with his tongue sending another shockwave of pleasure between her legs. A deep ache within her belly making her press her body against the hardness of his. A loud moan escaping her lips when his hands travelled down her back and cupped her rear. His fingers brushing against the inside of her thigh.

Before she was aware what she was doing, her head snapped forward, her fangs plunging into his throat. His fingers dug deeper, caressing her skin and urging her on. Her body quivered when she drew in a mouthful of his blood.

Rosalyn expected a metallic, coppery taste like she was used to whenever she cut her finger and sucked the droplets away, or when she had bitten her lip, but his blood tasted different. She wasn't sure if it was because of what she now was, or whether it was because of what he was, his blood perhaps different from that of a human. But it tasted good. A sweetness she hadn't been expecting, like a fine champagne slid across her tongue and down her throat making her hunger for more.

It was like someone had taken her lifeless body and injected her with pure energy, every nerve in her body sparking to life. The warmth she'd felt before nothing compared to this sensual feeling that had her moaning against his neck, before she came up gasping for air. Her chest heaved as she panted, eyes glued to his. He looked back at her with a smile, those hollows in his cheeks making her knees tremble.

"Beautiful," he whispered, tucking a loose strand of her hair behind her ear with one hand. His other still rested against her rear, his fingers caressing her as he lowered his eyes back to her lips.

Rosalyn had felt tired and weak before, she now felt energized, and ready for anything. The buzz that coffee had given her in the past was mediocre compared to how she felt now. Her body tingled, needing to feel more of him, especially when his hand brushed the inside of her thigh once more.

Rosalyn grabbed hold of Rayner's shoulders and pulled him closer, pressing her lips firmly against his.

She ran her fingers through his hair and tugged him forward so their bodies met all the way down, letting out another groan when his other hand joined the first, pressing her hips flush against his own. His hard ridge rubbing so temptingly against her with their every movement.

All conscious thought abandoned Rosalyn in that moment. Her body a slave to the sensations she was feeling when she tugged on the bottom of his t-shirt in an attempt to lift it from his body.

She heard him chuckle, before he gripped the material and pulled it up over his head. His muscles flexed and moved deliciously with each movement. She watched on hungrily. Her eyes raked over him, drinking in the sight of him. Those shimmering glyphs dancing below his skin, drawing her gaze.

Rosalyn placed her hand against the hard ridges of his body, smiling to herself when he sucked in a breath, before she let her fingers trace those lines, following the patterns over his chest and stomach, before they disappeared below his dark jeans.

Rayner's eyes were already closed, enjoying her touch and allowing her to explore him however she pleased.

She wasn't used to this. To being in control. But she quite enjoyed it.

She leaned up and took his mouth again, wrapping her arms around his shoulders, pulling him toward her. His eyes opened when his thighs hit the side of the bed. Still she tugged him closer, until he gave in and climbed up next to her, allowing her to push him onto his back.

He was magnificent to look at as she sat above him, staring down at his sculpted body.

Her improved sight allowed her to see him clearly. From those patterns that swirled and moved, to the paler scars she could see all across him. Most she had no idea how they'd gotten there, others she recognized, like the one by his heart, and the other below his ribs. With a leg either side of one of his, Rosalyn bent forward and pressed her lips to each of them. A smirk on her lips when he shuddered and gripped tightly at her waist. A deep, throaty rumble vibrating his chest.

Each kiss brought her lower down his body. Her fangs itching to taste him again, only this time she gave in without holding back. Pressing her mouth to his hip, and biting down gently.

Another full body shiver ran through her when he

groaned and tensed below her. His erection strained to be freed from his jeans as she drank in another mouthful of his blood.

Drinking from him, like this was perhaps something she might be able to get used to.

"You're not allowed to feed from anyone else if this is your reaction," he growled when her hands stroked slowly up his thighs, playing with jeans clasp.

Rosalyn didn't respond when she broke away from him, she didn't need to, she just continued to unfasten his jeans and tug them down his legs, following the patterns lower, where they stopped just above his knees.

Rosalyn bit down on her lip, flinching at the sharpness of her fangs before she looked up into his face, noticing he watched her.

"It still doesn't hurt?" she asked, resting her palm on his thigh, tilting her head to the side while she stroked along the pattern which seemed paler across his legs.

"No," he responded, his voice more of a drawn out growl as her hand continued to travel upward, rubbing across the hardness of his cock through his boxers, his body tensing from the contact.

She expected him to grab her wrist and pull it away, or to tug her up his body claiming control, but he did neither. He lay there watching, allowing her to take her time and explore his body how she wished, just like he had in her dreams. Dreams that felt like a lifetime ago now, still unsure whether they were in fact visions. Only in them, she hadn't had fangs, unlike now, torn whether she should taste him through fear of catching his sensitive flesh with her teeth, or whether she should climb above him and finally release the tension she could feel building between her own thighs.

She wanted to saviour this moment and enjoy it, afraid of what could happen later. Whether her touch would soon cause him pain, or whether those who had taken her would come back again.

Rosalyn bent over him, pressing her lips to his inner thigh, running her tongue along the pale markings she could see. A smile tugging the corners of her mouth when his body flinched at that first contact. His throaty growl of pleasure spurring her forward, her mouth landing on his throbbing cock the moment she managed to slide his boxers far enough down his legs.

She licked her way up his shaft, chuckling to herself when he cursed loudly, his hands clenched tightly into the sheets below them.

Never before had Rosalyn felt so powerful. To have this Warrior below her, allowing her to do as she wished. Restraining himself even when she continued to tease. Her hand slid up and down his length while she flicked her tongue across the head of his penis, before she took him in her mouth and slowly drew back. His curse even louder. One of his hands gripping hold of her hair, tugging gently with her every movement, moaning.

Rosalyn wanted more. His sounds of pleasure drove her mad.

She knelt between his legs and pulled on her own jeans, sliding them down her legs, biting on her lip while he watched her. His eyes half closed, breathing rapidly.

He reached a hand toward her, to tug on her shirt, before she pushed it away and climbed up his body. Her lips found his as she made herself comfortable above his hips, his hard length prodding at her wet folds causing her to shudder and pause.

She lowered herself over his lap, her groan mixing

with his as she slid herself back and forth over his cock, her body quivering, needing more of him.

"Rosalyn," he growled, his hands gripped tightly at her waist. His fingers digging in deep.

Rosalyn thought that her dreams had been hot, often waking up on edge and in need of release, but the friction against her now was something different altogether. Her body tightening like a coil.

"Enough," Rayner roared below her, lifting her from his lap to flip her over. A smile on her lips at how long he had lasted before he seized control.

She had enjoyed her exploration of his body, and the control he had allowed her, but seeing him above her, his eyes hungry as he raked them over her and ripped her shirt from her body had her gasping in anticipation.

She much preferred this, especially when he took her hands in one of his and pinned them above her head in an unbreakable hold. His other hand softly cupping one of her breasts before he flicked his tongue across her nipple, circling before he moved to the other. Her eyes closed in delight.

Then she felt his hand cup between her thighs, his fingers stroking slowly through her wet folds, stealing a gasp from her lips, before he sealed them with his own, her sounds of pleasure muffled by his mouth.

His tongue slid across her sharpened fang once more, a single, large finger pressing against her clit, rolling it back and forth, making her head fall back as she lifted her hips to meet his touch.

Her gasps of joy filled the air, her blood racing through her veins as he pet her, sliding another finger inside.

She came apart beneath him, his growl of satisfaction blended with her cries of release. Her body quivering as he continued to stroke and rub at her, drawing out her orgasm.

CHAPTER  36

This was the last thing Rayner expected when Rosalyn began to stir late this evening.

He'd been sat by her side for almost two days waiting for her to wake, fearing that she would be lost to him forever.

When he'd seen her sitting upright in the bed with her eyes open, the faintest tint of red within them, he'd wanted to fall to his knees in relief. She was alive. They'd gotten to Lothaire in time. Then he had noticed the panicked look in her eyes. Her chest rising and falling quickly when she'd looked his way.

He'd thought she was angry at him for the choice he had made on her behalf, a new kind of sorrow weighing heavy on his mind when the others had left them alone.

He'd been wrong.

She feared what she was he could tell that, but what she feared most was his rejection and he was to stupid to realise it.

The way she had melted and relaxed when he touched made his chest squeeze tight.

She was his, and he was hers.

He should never have kept his distance. That curse had held him back for far too long. Pain be damned. He should have gone to her right away and seen for himself whether her touch was different now.

He was a coward, and he had hurt her.

Well, no longer.

Whether this was their last night together without the agony or not, Rayner planned on making her feel cherished.

He'd intended to show her that he accepted what she was, embraced it even when he kissed her and touched her fangs with his tongue, especially when she had called herself a monster. He hadn't expected the action to fill her with lust. The look in her eyes begging him to do it again. He'd been happy to oblige, quite enjoying the sensation himself, and her moans of pleasure.

He had never allowed anyone to feed from him before. He doubted he would have even without his curse holding him back, but with her, seeing her reactions to a simple touch of her fangs, he'd been curious, the sensation unlike anything he had ever felt before.

Her hands against his skin only fueled the fire that built within him.

For so long he had dreamt of touching her in this way. To bring her pleasure with his touch, never realising such a thing was possible until recently. Then Helmer had nearly taken her from him.

He'd thought he would never touch her again.

"Rayner?" Rosalyn panted beneath him, her chest heaving up and down, eyes closed to half mast as she looked up at him. "I want you."

Those words nearly undone him then and there.

Now he would take her properly, like he'd wanted for so long.

"Then you shall have me."

Rayner leaned forward and took her lips with his mouth, kissing her deeply as he settled himself between her legs, caressing her body with his hands. Her hips lifted to meet him, needy for more.

272

Rayner could deny her no longer. He had to be inside of her, to feel her warmth around him, but he wasn't sure how gentle he could be. His own need was strong.

He eased himself closer, his tongue sliding against hers when he took her mouth again. His heart thumping hard, before he pressed between her folds and delved in deep.

She cried out as he took her and began to move back and forth slowly. Her leg hooked around his hips encouraging him forward. Deeper.

Rayner ignored her urgings and gritted his teeth, trying to keep in control of his need to be sure he didn't hurt her.

Rosalyn wrapped her arms around his neck and brought him toward her, kissing him passionately, her hands stroking down his back, the tips of her nails digging in when she brought them back up again, making him growl.

"Bite me," he demanded, tilting his head to the side to give her access while he continued to glide in and out of her. His blood pounding through his body as she did as she was told and sunk her fangs into his neck.

The sensation alone nearly had him bursting inside of her, groaning loudly as she gasped and looked up at him with a fine coat of his blood across her lips and fangs, her eyes matching the shade.

Her body tightened and throbbed around him as she found her own release.

He lost control.

He thrust deeper into her. Harder. Her every moan spurring him on, making it more and more difficult to keep himself from pounding into her. Her nails in his shoulders were the last push he could bear.

He drove into her, burying himself deep. Her cries mingled with his own when she lifted her hips from the bed, meeting him with her own thrusts and making his head spin.

He growled her name and gripped hold of her waist, his fingers digging into her flesh.

Her head rolled back in ecstasy, a shuddering gasp filled the air as she clenched around him one last time, taking him along with her.

He collapsed on top of her, his breath mingling with hers as she relaxed and drooped back against the bed, looking down at him against her chest.

"Give me a moment," he groaned, knowing he crushed her beneath his weight, but too exhausted to move. The events of the last few days finally caught up with him.

"Stay," she whispered, nuzzling into his neck before she wrapped her arms around him, kissing at his neck.

He wanted nothing more than to stay with her like this, but not on top of her.

Summoning up the remnants of his energy, Rayner rolled to one side and pulled her along with him, holding her close to his side, letting out a contented sigh when she snuggled against him and rested her head on his chest, circling her fingers over his skin.

"I love you," she whispered, glancing up at him, still unsure of herself.

He tugged on her chin and brought his lips to hers, kissing her briefly before repeating her words against her lips.

"I love you."

"Even if I can't touch you soon, don't leave," she said quietly, tears pooling in her eyes.

"You deserve better."

"I don't want anyone else," she said with conviction, leaning up on her elbow to frown down at him. "Even before I knew I could touch you Rayner, when I knew I shouldn't, I wanted nobody else."

The side of his lips curved before he reached up and kissed her lips, falling back against the bed and pulling her down with him, knowing that she had wanted him as much as he had wanted her.

Whatever happened in the morning, or later when she completed her transition, he would stay by her side. He would keep on protecting her, no matter what.

CHAPTER 37

"Morning," Xander said, clearing his throat when Rosalyn entered the room. "Good night?"

Normally Rosalyn would have become embarrassed and looked away, hiding her rosy cheeks, but not today.

"Great, thanks," she answered with a smirk when he raised a brow and smiled back at her.

"Feeling better now then?" he asked with a more serious tone. His face lost all signs of humour.

She hadn't been thinking clearly last night, too afraid of what had happened. What she was, and Rayner's reaction. She hadn't stopped to think that Xander was a vampire too. The choice not one he would have perhaps made for himself.

She wasn't angry with Rayner for the choice he had made for her. She suspected that if she were in his shoes, she would have done the same. She'd already risked herself to save him and knew she couldn't allow him to die as much as he couldn't her. But perhaps Xander would help her understand what it was like. Help her to come to terms with what she was without having to speak with any vampires.

"It was a bit of a shock."

"Yeah, tell me about it," he huffed, his eyes glinting red for a brief moment before he gestured to the seat opposite him.

"Do my eyes do that too?" she asked when she took a seat, biting on her lip before she lifted her eyes to his.

"What? Change?"

Rosalyn nodded, digging her fingers into her knees whilst she awaited his answer.

She wasn't sure what the information would do for her exactly, but she was curious. Frightened by the ascept, but needing to know more about herself.

"Yeah, they will. You'll get hungrier now too, but not just for blood. Vampires have an insatiable appetite. Food will replenish you and some of your own blood, allowing you to heal, but blood is what gives you your energy."

Rosalyn couldn't imagine drinking anyone but Rayner's blood. After last night, and how her body responded to the sensation, she didn't want to think about biting anybody else. But what if she couldn't touch him for much longer? Food would have to be enough. Unless she could drink it by another means. She wasn't sure what was worse. All those test tubes of blood she had seen at the hospital. How the blood congealed.

"It'll take time to get used to."

"Do you need to drink blood?" Rosalyn asked, unsure whether he was the same. Xander was only part vampire after all, and a demon for the other half. His needs would surely be different from her own.

"On occasion, though not that often."

Rosalyn had only fed from Rayner last night, and already she was beginning to feel famished, but she wasn't sure whether that was for something as simple as food, or more blood. Either thought was enough to make her feel queasy. She couldn't feed off Rayner that frequently even if he did heal and regenerate his own blood and body quickly.

"Your wound may be gone, but your body is still healing and adjusting to the change. Give yourself time," Xander told her.

Rosalyn smiled across at him even though she didn't

feel much joy at his words, or her situation.

She was happy to be alive, and to be with Rayner and the rest of them again, but she was different now. Everything was different. She was no longer a human who could see supernatural creatures, or had visions of the past and future. She was a vampire. A monster. She wasn't sure whether she would ever get used to a life like this, even with Rayner by her side.

Then there was the possibility that she would never get to touch Rayner again. The more she changed, the more her touch could hurt him.

Everything was just so messed up.

She'd been happy with how things were. Discovering that she could touch him when nobody else could. Finally coming to terms with what she could see and do after nearly twenty years of denial.

How long would it take her to get her head around this she wondered.

Rosalyn looked back across the table, noticing that Xander hadn't taken his eyes from her. His mouth opened a few times, but he remained silent, an apprehensive expression on his face.

"What is it?" she asked, knowing there was something on his mind. "You look like you want to ask me something?"

"Rayner and Niko said it was Helmer who stabbed you and took you there."

Rosalyn nodded, gripping hold of her knees beneath the table.

She still didn't fully understand what was happening, and what Helmer wanted from her. His words hadn't made a lot of sense. All she kept thinking was how he claimed Rayner would come for her, sure that she meant something important to him, which as it turned out, she did.

He can't have you.

"Dr. Holter was there too," she told him, looking down to her legs while she fiddled with her thumbs. "I'm not sure who gave the order to take me, but they both had different motives. Dr. Holter wanted to use my sight for his own gain, and Helmer, he said he wanted all of you. He's angry."

"No surprise there," Xander sighed, slouching back in his chair, staring up at the ceiling. "We were told he was dead. We believed them."

"The Council?"

Xander closed his eyes and nodded. His arms hung by his sides, hands clenched before he spoke again. "We demanded answers from them. Demanded they give us his body, but they refused. Some told us of an accident. A car wreck that killed several humans as well."

Though Rosalyn's heart rate was much slower than normal since the change had begun, she could feel it pounding now. The car wreck that had supposedly killed their brother couldn't possibly be the one she was in as a child, could it?

"They said he was a mess, that none of us would want to see what he'd become. We didn't back down."

"That's when you got punished?"

Again Xander nodded, glancing briefly toward the door before looking back at her.

"We lashed out and killed several members within the Council. Each of us having our abilities turned against us when they finally managed to stop us."

Rosalyn gulped and wrung her hands tighter, unsure what this Council would make of her. Whether they would still wish to kill her for the things she had seen and heard.

279

Surely they wouldn't kill without a reason, would they? She was one of them now after all. She was a vampire.

"I guess he thought we didn't try hard enough."

"I don't think he is the brother you once knew."

"No, he's not," Rayner spoke from the doorway, his deep, gravelly voice sending a shiver down Rosalyn's spine before she turned to him, her mouth agape.

The glyphs on his skin. The ones that had always been bright and shimmering now appeared faded. A whisper of what they once were.

Without thinking, Rosalyn approached him and pressed her hand against his shoulder.

"You're glyphs," she commented, breathless, "they've faded."

She continued to touch his arm, stroking lower over his exposed skin, amazed to see that the patterns no longer writhed beneath the surface like they did every other time she had touched him or stood close. The shimmering light vanished.

Rayner looked down at his arm, clearly not having noticed a difference himself as he frowned and rubbed at his skin, before his eyes rose to his brothers.

"That's not possible," Xander muttered, approaching from behind her, hesitant to approach his brother. "The magic in the glyphs is dying."

"What does that mean?" Rosalyn asked.

"It means that somehow the curse he was put under has been broken. That he should be able to touch anyone without the pain that comes with it."

To test his own theory, Xander reached forward and grabbed hold of Rayner's other arm.

At first Rayner growled and shrugged from his hold,

before he paused and looked down at where his brother had touched him, the skin there the same as it had been before. No red marks. No burning skin. Nothing.

"Do it again," Rayner demanded.

Xander did as he was told and held onto his arm, both of them huffing out a laugh before Xander wrapped his arms around his brother and crushed him tight.

Tears filled in Rosalyn's eyes at the expressions on both their faces.

"It's still there, but dull," Rayner commented, his eyes drifting to her over Xander's shoulder. "Like a pressure rather than pain."

"It will take some time to get used to, I'm sure," Rosalyn commented as the two of them broke apart. A smile on her lips when he approached her and sealed her lips with his own. His hand snaking around her waist and holding her to him.

If his glyphs were fading, the curse broken somehow, she no longer needed to fear him slipping away from her.

She was still unsure how being a vampire would change her and whether she was ready for it, but she would have Rayner by her side, and he would make everything more bearable. Enjoyable even.

CHAPTER ~38~

"So, what's next?" Lorkan asked when Niko finally joined them in the sitting room, taking a seat beside Xander who quickly passed him a bottle of beer.

"We hunt for Helmer, of course," Rayner growled, his hands clenched tight on his lap, before Rosalyn took them in hers and squeezed tight, releasing some of the tension.

He still didn't have the answers he was looking for, and nor did Rosalyn.

Helmer seemed to know a lot more of her past than even she remembered. Somehow knowing that she had died when she had no idea.

Rayner wanted to find out more, and he wanted to confront his brother.

She wont let her live.

Who was she? And why was she so determined to take Rosalyn from him?

Rayner glanced across at Rosalyn and squeezed her hands back. A tightness gripped at chest at the thought of them trying to take her from him again.

He would have to do better at keeping her safe.

Contact wouldn't be an issue any longer, but there was still the problem of the voices in his head.

Rosalyn's gift of silence vanished the moment she slipped away and the magic in her faded, but perhaps he could make use of them, if he just managed to filter through the noise and pick up on the information he needed.

"I have a feeling Helmer will find us before we find him," Niko sighed, taking a long swig of beer. "He appeared to Rosalyn in the cabin, and Xander said he saw him in the road."

"Pretty sure he was at the doc's too," Xander groaned.

"What do you plan once you find him?" Oliver asked, looking at each of them.

Rayner was still unsure what to make of the doc, but he had proven to be helpful on more than one occasion recently, and he was beginning to show a little more promise in his abilities having sparred with Lorkan a few times in the past week, wishing to learn how to defend himself properly. But was he willing to let go of his past life like Rosalyn?

Rosalyn had little choice with what she was now.

A hospital was no place for a new vampire.

Besides, she had them to nurse back to health now, and Niko had told her of some acquaintances she could learn more medicine from. Medicines that would work on them and the Other, something she had seemed quite eager to learn. Whether she would still be pleased once her training began, Rayner wasn't so sure. Some of those witches and vampires she would learn from were a little on the odd side, and Rosalyn still hadn't overcome her fear of vampires, despite now being one, something he would have to help her overcome with time.

But Oliver, he was a renowned doctor at the hospital. A well-off one with a good career.

He couldn't stay with them and travel back and forth to the hospital, it would draw too much attention, and he'd already been followed once. It wouldn't take the Council long to discover him.

But he was already very much a part of their world after all the things he had seen and done. Trying to get his life back the way it was would be almost impossible. Always second guessing who and what he was treating. Whether he was being watched.

It wasn't something you could easily walk away from.

Oliver had a choice to make, one Rayner wasn't sure he was ready for.

"Simple," Xander grumbled, banging his empty bottle down on the table, "we capture him and demand our answers, starting with where he has been all these years."

THE END

 Afterword

I would like to thank all of my beta readers, and my ARC's for all of their comments and taking the time to read this book and make it what it is.

And, of course, I would like to thank all of my readers. I hope that you enjoyed this book, and that you are just as excited to read the next in this series.

BOOKS BY THIS AUTHOR

THE OTHERWORLD GUARDIANS

Reluctant Guardian

Hunter Guardian – Coming Soon

DEMON WARRIORS

Touch

Sight – Coming Soon

STAND ALONE BOOKS

The Wolves of Wulfric Manor

ABOUT THE AUTHOR

ELISHA BUGG

Elisha comes from a small town in the east of England where she lives with her husband and her two daughters.

Elisha has always enjoyed reading, writing and creating art, but it was only when she attended University that she rekindled her love for books, falling in love with the romance genre, Paranormal Romance in particular. It was then that she decided to get back into writing and try and write her first book.

Several years later, after a long process of drafts and editing, Elisha was ready to debut book, Reluctant Guardian, the first in her Otherworld Guardians series.

Since then, she has released other books and plans on releasing many more, expanding on the worlds she has already created.

Follow her on social media, or her website to keep up to date with all the latest news and releases -

@ElishabWrites

www.facebook.com/ElishaBuggauthor/

www.elishabugg.com

Printed in Great Britain
by Amazon

84051537R00169